THE ROAD TO SAN JACINTO

Why were Dain Galway and Cleo hunted like animals? Dain was prepared to meet trouble and protect them both with his gun. Why were the two fugitives constantly forced to hide? Only Cleo could answer, for the secret was hidden in her birth—and she dared not reveal her dangerous heritage to the man she loved!

L(eonard) L(ondon) Foreman was born in London, England in 1901. He served in the British army during the Great War, prior to his emigration to the United States. He became an itinerant, holding a series of odd jobs in the western States as he traveled. He began his writing career by introducing his most widely known and best-loved character, Preacher Devlin, in "Noose Fodder" in *Western Aces* (12/34), a pulp magazine. Throughout the mid thirties, this character, a combination gunfighter, gambler, and philosopher, appeared regularly in Western Aces. Near the end of the decade, Foreman's Western stories began appearing in Street & Smith's *Western Story Magazine*, where the pay was better. Foreman's first Western novels began appearing in the 1940s, largely historical Westerns such as *Don Desperado* (1941) and *The Renegade* (1942). The New York Herald Tribune reviewer commented on *Don Desperado* that "admirers of the late beloved Dane Coolidge better take a look at this. It has that same all-wool-and-a-yard-wide quality." Foreman continued to write prolifically for the magazine market as long as it lasted, before specializing exclusively for the book trade with one of his finest novels, *Arrow in the Dust* (1954) which was filmed under this title the same year. Two years earlier *The Renegade* was filmed as *The Savage* (Paramount, 1952), the two are among several films based on his work. Foreman's last years were spent living in the state of Oregon. Perhaps his most popular character after Preacher Devlin was Rogue Bishop, appearing in a series of novels published by Doubleday in the 1960s. George Walsh, writing in *Twentieth Century Western Writers*, said of Foreman: "His novels have a sense of authority because he does not deal in simple characters or simple answers." In fact, most of his fiction is not centered on a confrontation between good and evil, but rather on his characters and the changes they undergo. His female characters, above all, are memorably drawn and central to his stories.

THE ROAD TO
SAN JACINTO

L. L. Foreman

GUNSMOKE

This hardback edition 2004
by BBC Audiobooks Ltd
by arrangement with
Golden West Literary Agency

Copyright ® 1943 by L.L. Foreman.
Copyright © renewed 1971 by the estate
of L.L. Foreman.

ISBN 0 7540 6298 8

British Library Cataloguing in Publication Data available.

Printed and bound in Great Britain by
Antony Rowe Ltd., Chippenham, Wiltshire

CHAPTER ONE

Hatless, his heavy greatcoat flaring open, the man striding down the muddy plantation pathway stopped at the curve and swung around to stare back at the lighted windows of the house on the hill. Contempt for bad weather had brought him splashing through the boggy puddles. Anger caused him to stand there under the dripping trees, splashed with rain and spattered with mud, disregardful of everything but the house that he had left. The lighted windows, suspended squares of yellow light in a black nothingness, stared dispassionately back at him.

He had a heavy riding whip in his right hand, and he raised that arm to shake it up at the windows; but it was a futile kind of gesture that was foreign to him, and he did not finish it. But while his arm was half upraised, the storm burst from its brief respite as if acting upon that signal.

They attacked together, the mad trio of wind, rain and lightning. The wind roared through the trees, hurling the rain in lashing sheets before it. Lightning sliced the sky, and the house on the hill emerged from darkness, looming arrogantly high, the angles and planes of its roof glistening wet. Beyond and below that high roof, other and smaller roofs crouched humbly; these were the hand-hewn shingles of the slave quarters. No lawn greened the hill's wide slope, but only a bleak expanse of bald clay. This was a great plantation, and there stood the master's house, but without grace or elegance, showing to the outside world only an oppressive grimness.

The glaring flashes of lightning showed up the man, too,

as tall and big, and arrogant in his anger; but his grimness was of the kind that bannered lusty masculine traits of temper, untamed capacity for strong feeling, and a readiness to violence. The wind blew his tawny hair to a wet and shaggy mane, and when his eyes caught reflections from the lightning they glittered green-grey. A broad forehead and wide mouth gave a massiveness to his face, but it was inherently a face of lean strength, darkened by many kinds of weather. There was about him a close-grained quality and a supple ranginess. He was like the hard shaft of a lance; not old, but seasoned, the roughness worn to an unpolished smoothness by use, the straight timber capable of taking scars without weakening, and of bending without breaking.

He became aware of the whip in his hand. In his anger he had been gripping it tightly while striding down the path, as if it were a saber. He flung it away from him, and closed his greatcoat against the gusting rain.

"I should've used a club!" he growled, and after a final look at the house on the hill, he stalked on down toward the river landing.

A black willow, old and forked, grew on the river bank at the end of the path. At some high flood time the river had clawed at this jut of the shore line and undermined the bank, causing a section of it to cave in and lay bare some of the willow's roots. The old tree leaned at an angle, one thick limb of its forked trunk stretching out toward the water, where it had long served as a mooring post for such small boats as came to the plantation landing. Its drunken position and low-growing branches made it grotesque, and the bared roots made a gutted behemoth of it, wounded and crouching, dumbly refusing to fall and die.

The three silent men, waiting behind the forked trunk, watched the pathway.

One of the watchers kept grinding the palms of his hands together, and locking and unlocking his fingers. They were enormous hands, but not out of proportion to the rest of his body. He was as black as the night around him. Only his eyes and a silver earring caught any reflected shine from the lightning, for he was a giant Negro. He shivered constantly, not only because he was drenched and cold, but because a doglike eagerness was in him, an eagerness to obey a bidding and please a master. His eyes, too, were dog-like, mirroring a mind that verged on the swamp of idiocy.

The strangely repulsive working of the slave's great hands got on the nerves of the man nearest him. This was a white man, thick-bodied and bearded. He cursed softly and struck the Negro a backhand blow in the face, and the Negro pouted and let his arms dangle.

Behind them both, the third man stood aloof, draped to the ankles in a weather cloak, the wide brim of his planters' hat pulled down to shed the rain. He was tall, with a face as colorless as candle wax. He reached an arm out from beneath his cloak and tapped a finger on the back of the bearded man. The bearded man turned his head and almost cringed, meeting the cold stare of two eyes that had the look of tarnished silver. The waxen-faced man said nothing, letting his silver-pale eyes convey rebuke and contempt. He gestured briefly then, as the lightning flashed again. It was a command that needed no repetition and no spoken word. The bearded man and the black giant turned their faces toward the path.

Down toward the landing came the tawny lance of a man, striding rapidly through the mud, his shaggy hair flying, as heedless of the storm's wind and rain as a ship's gilded figurehead.

He saw nothing of the three watchers. His thoughts ran in a channel from the big house behind him to the thing that he had yet to do ahead. Although he had a certain habit of wariness, he looked for no danger between those two points. The three men were well covered by the black willow and the night, and their faint noises were taken up by the storm, so he neither saw the bearded man creep up fast behind him, nor heard the swish of the heavy stick.

The blow knocked him forward, but failed to stun him completely. He reeled around, throwing open his greatcoat and automatically groping for the long pistol slung at his belt. The next blow drove him to his knees, and he swayed there, trying desperately to hang on to consciousness and raise his pistol. The bearded man struck him again, full across the forehead, with such force that the wet stick slipped from his fingers, and the victim toppled over and lay in the mud.

The pale-eyed man in the long weather cloak had not moved. He had merely stood there under the black willow, looking on. Now he spoke for the first time. "Quaw!"

The black giant plunged forward at the sound of his name, grunting, vastly pleased to become so important in the eyes of the master. He stood himself astride of the senseless man, worked his crushing hands, and stooped to do the one thing at which he was adept. The next second he jerked upright, his magnificent black body rigid, his eyes two glaring dots ringed with shining white. The bearded man, too, stood motionless, and even the impassive master raised his head to listen.

A long, howling scream pierced through the racket of the storm, rising, coming rapidly closer. The river caught the tone of it, and magnified it until it seemed to be coming from all directions and closing in on this spot. It rose higher, tearing at the nerves, shocking in its stark voicing of wild rage. A white shape flitted for an instant against a black tree trunk, and vanished, and appeared again.

The half idiot Quaw leaped blindly off the path, gibbering unintelligibly. The bearded man caught him by his tattered shirt to hold him from fleeing. One sweep of a huge arm sent him sprawling, and when he scrambled up he ran to the black willow, himself made unreasoning by the contagion of Quaw's panic, the ghastly scream, and the flitting white figure among the trees.

The waxen-faced master cursed him in low, controlled tones. "You damned yellow scum! Go back there and finish the . . . Look!" The white screamer had reached the clubbed victim on the path, was hovering over him. Swiftly it bent and rose again. The next flash of lightning drew a bright gleam from the barrel of a long pistol, tugged from the senseless man's belt.

The bearded man dodged and turned to bolt, but the master stepped into his way, blocking him. They came together, forming one shape in the darkness. Quaw had vanished. The long pistol roared its abrupt discharge. Then the master was slipping off alone, along the river bank, and the bearded man lay rolling and beating his arms on the ground under the black willow.

The screamer bent again over the clubbed man, searching him for the extra weapon that a gentleman of his kind would be likely to carry in reserve. Finding it—an ugly little pocket pistol—but finding no immediate use for it, she gave herself to the task of dragging the man down onto the landing.

She was a girl, but she had strength, and no undue daintiness about using it. A flat-bottomed rowboat rocked and bumped at the landing's edge, with soaked seats and an inch of rain water in the bottom. She hauled and tugged in a fever of haste, getting her burden onto and across the planks of the landing, at the same time keeping watch for any return of the waylayers. At last she managed to ease the body into the boat. Breathing hard, she got in after it and cast off.

The boat swung slowly into the swollen current while she found the oars and fitted them into the rowlocks. She looked down at the face of the unconscious man in the bottom of the boat, and the glow that came over her eyes was almost a holy one.

"I'll look after you," she whispered. "I'm going with you. You can't stop me now!" She thought of the bearded man, rolling on the ground with her bullet in him. "I hope he dies! I hope he dies slow and hard, for what he's done to you!"

Faint and far away a voice called sharply and commandingly, and other voices began replying to it. There would be a hunt, a long and persistent hunt. From what she knew, the girl vaguely realized that she and this injured man were living on a thin margin of chance. She rowed steadily downstream with the current. Her strong young body moved rhythmically. She didn't feel the cold wind and the chilling discomfort of her wet clothes. She kept looking at the bloodied face of the tawny-haired man. After a while she began softly singing in time with the pull of the oars.

The storm brawled past, its thunder trundling ponderously after it and rumbling into the distance. Trees shed their gathering of rain, dripping monotonously. The moon at last broke out and threw light on the scudding rear flanks of the passing clouds, and now that the wind was gone the land went back to calm silence.

The man and the girl lay hiding on a strip of brushy bank, the river on one side, furrowed fields on the other. Two boats had already passed, rowed fast downstream by straining men whose eyes shone like white flecks in their black faces. In the bow of the first had sat a cloaked figure, motionless except for the slow, constant turning of his head from side to side, a rifle across his knees.

Fear of that quiet and impassive figure had caused the girl to hold her breath until it passed, and only when the sound of the oars came back as a whisper did she stir from her stillness. She had pulled in to this bank, sensing pursuit behind her and knowing that she could not keep ahead of it. After dragging the injured man ashore, she hid the boat in thick marsh grass and rejoined him.

She crouched beside him, listening for the return of the two longboats. He had partly regained consciousness, but he lay without moving or speaking. He was badly hurt, and she wanted desperately to nurse and help him, but there was little that she could do. His hair was blotched darkly with blood, and across his broad forehead was a gash that made her shudder for him when she looked at it. The blood from it had spread and dried on his face, horribly marring his features. He gave no groan as consciousness gradually returned to him. When the moonlight fell upon him he was frowning, his brows bunched puzzledly.

She moved a little on her knees, cramped by her position, and he became aware of her beside him. His right hand slid shakily over the ground and touched her, and he turned his face in her direction, but she felt that he was not seeing her.

"Who are you?" he muttered.

"Cleo," she said. "I'm Cleo, Mr. Dain."

He seemed to grapple with that for a long time. "Is that my name—Dain?" He put his hand to his head. "I'm hurt. Why am I hurt? What place is this? It's wet. Why don't we have a light? I can't see anything."

His eyes were open, but they had a fixedness and no focus. She bent over him, so that her head shaded the moonlight from his face. "Can't you see me now?"

His troubled frown deepened. "Of course not. Where are you? I hear water somewhere. Dain, you called me? Queer, I don't remember that name." He closed his eyes and sighed tiredly. "I can't seem to remember at all. Can't remember—anything. . . ."

He was unconscious again when the girl, Cleo, gently lifted his battered head and cradled it in her lap. She tore strips from her cotton dress and covered his hurts, and when there was nothing more that she could do for him she stroked his matted hair and cried soundlessly.

In an hour the two longboats returned up the river. The moon now being up, the girl did not dare to watch them for fear of being seen. She lay trembling, and they passed northward without seeing the little rowboat hidden in the marsh grass. This night's hunt, she divined, would be only the beginning of it. Things would get worse, much worse. Yet she began making simple plans for herself and the man she called Dain; plans that had to do with simple necessities. She knew little of the broad geography of the country, and she thought of escape only in terms of distance. Somewhere—somewhere far away from here—there was surely a land where fugitives could walk upright and break free from the past. It was just a matter of getting there, of keeping alive and on the move until it was reached. But to leave the river did not even occur to her, and would not have done so even had the man been able to walk. To her, the river was a road. When you started out to go anywhere, you always took to the river.

It worried her to leave Dain lying alone, but the need of food for tomorrow drove her to do it. Food they would have to have, and the getting of it could not be left until daylight. She crept off toward the farm buildings on the other side of the plowed fields. When she came hurrying back with a stolen and killed chicken, Dain was sitting up.

While she guided and helped him into the boat he was unquestioning, seeming to sense dimly from her urgent mood that some kind of peril hung over them both. Later, though, while rowing with the current, she saw from the strengthening cast of his face that he was fighting to break through his fog.

"We're on a river," he said suddenly. "What river?"

"Miss'ippi," she answered. Because she needed her breath for rowing, she spoke shortly. She was setting herself a fast stroke and keeping to it, ignoring aching muscles.

Frowning, he pondered on that piece of knowledge. "Where are we going? How did I get hurt?"

"They tried to kill you. I don't know where we're going. Just trying to get away, that's all."

"Who are 'they'? When did it happen? How long have I been blind like this?" His queries were gathering force. A strong and intelligent mind, crippled, was beginning to assert itself and struggle with a multitude of strange problems.

The girl studied him as she rowed. She was having a mental fight of her own, and after she won it she gazed at him with a queer mixture of defiance and pleading that he

could not see. "I don't know who they were," she answered
deliberately. "I never saw them before. It was late last night.
It's getting near morning now."

"Where did it happen?"

"Up the river. That's all I know."

"But—but who *am* I? This boat—the river—and you . . .
Tell me everything!"

She failed to reply for a long moment. Finally she said
steadily, "I don't know. I never saw you till last night. All
I know is, they want to kill you—and your name is Dain. I—
I heard a man say it. A tall man, tall as you. His eyes are
like—like little moons. And a big black man, with a silver ring
in his ear. And one I shot with your pistol. There are others,
but I don't know them."

"Is that all you can tell me?"

". . . Yes."

He leaned toward her, his battered face ghastly in its bitter
disappointment. He moved his matted, rag-tied head in an
angry way, as if straining to replace with some other sense
the loss of his sight. "You're lying to me!" he accused her
harshly. "You hint that you saved my life—that you're helping me to get away from something. Why should you do all
this, if I'm a stranger to you?"

"Maybe *I'm* getting away from something, too," she said,
low voiced, and she shivered while rowing.

He stilled. "Are we outlaws, or have we got private enemies—or both?"

"Maybe," she answered, and said no more.

He sank back, beaten by her guarded reticence. "All right,
girl," he muttered. "You're entitled to keep your own secrets.
Perhaps I'm better off for not remembering mine! Devil
knows what *I've* been. Devil knows what kind of life I've
lived." He sat and brooded with the thought, his useless eyes
turned downward. "Dark and ugly it was, I think, and dangerous. I have that feel of it in me. Where do we go, girl? What's
ahead of us?"

She rowed three strokes before answering simply, "Devil knows!"

It was cold, and the blinded man's hands were numb on the oars. He had given his greatcoat to the thinly clad girl, and she huddled under it in the stern, guiding him in his course with now and then a directing word. Except for this they spoke little.

For days and nights they had been creeping their furtive course southward, but the fringe of a late winter had spread down from the north and caught up with them. Tight scrapes had drawn them close together, raised in them the predatory instincts of confederates against the world, and developed for them a confidence in each other.

A boat with four armed men in it had pulled out after them one evening from the cluttered wharfs of a river town. A pistol shot from Cleo had not discouraged them, but only served to confirm their suspicions. Luckily, the sky was cloudy that night. The four had searched the river for hours, rowing back and forth, cursing. After they gave up, Dain and Cleo slipped out from under the low pier where they had taken refuge, and drifted cautiously down river in the darkness.

Another night, somebody on the bank fired a signal shot as the little flat-bottomed boat passed. They worked on the oars that night until they shook with fatigue. From these happenings and others, it became clear that the river was being watched for them, not only by the unknown hunters, but by the law.

Yet both agreed that it was better to keep to the river than to take to the country roads. On the back roads, instant attention would have been aroused by their appearance, and continued flight would have depended upon the acquiring of good horses. Dain was a fearsome sight, his head bound in dirty rags, hair tangled and a stiff stubble of beard, his clothes muddied and torn. Even to the eyes of the dullest backwoods farmer, he could have passed for nothing but a desperado on the dodge. Cleo was in no better condition, and she was barefooted, having discarded her shoes after they fell apart from constant soaking.

Dain had discovered that he wore a leather moneybelt heavy with gold coin. Being hard pressed by hunger one early evening, they tried to buy food at a levee village. Cleo returned from her expedition, racing, part of a venison haunch under one arm and half of the village population swarming after her. Hearing the commotion, Dain rose in the boat with his long pistol out. Not taking time to learn that he was blind, the villagers scattered at sight of such a wild and menacing apparition.

After they got clear, Cleo told Dain that the village watchman had tried to arrest her. She had knocked the watchman down with the haunch of venison that she had bought, and fired the pocket pistol into the crowd behind him. "But I don't think I killed anybody," she concluded, more as a statement of record than of wishful thinking.

Dain laughed shortly and shook his head. "So now it's bodily assault on the majesty of the law, is it? You're a lawless young animal. I admire you very much. I wonder what you look like—plain or pretty?"

"Pretty," she admitted at once.

Dain put a hand to his eyes. Somber reaction caught up with him, tipping his mood toward impotent anger. "Then that's another grudge I hold against the skulker who bludgeoned my sight from me, hell burn him! Oh, girl, girl —why don't you quit me and go on alone? I'm a hindrance to you, and a burden to myself. Take the boat and the gold, and save yourself."

"No, I'll never leave you."

"Why? Why, Cleo?"

"I'll never leave you," she repeated. It was like a litany, the way she said it.

Life for them had taken on the elementalism of jungle lawlessness. They lived off the country as they travelled by night and hid by day; stealing their food where and when they could get it, eating it raw; avoiding all eyes and steering clear of the paddle steamboats that thumped and clanked up and down the river. Sometimes along lonely stretches they rowed on until the sun came up. Other times they hid the boat and themselves early, and shivered in the grey dawn.

Dain had expert hands with the oars, and he mused over that, seeing it as a pointer to the past that was blacked out from him. But the familiar feel of a pistol to his fingers was surely no mark of a sailor. Without sight to aid him, he found that he could accurately load his pistol, measuring the powder by feel and deftly thrusting the wad and ball home. His hands knew and remembered. His nose and ears could analyze odors and sounds. His mind retained impersonal knowledge—a grasp of geography, history, a comprehension of the state of the world at large, and a slightly cynical evaluation of human nature. These things were still his. But no knowledge of himself, of his place in the world. It was as if death had struck away a part of him and left a remnant, a zombi shorn of all recollection, only the imprint of past experience surviving in his mind.

At all times, an obscure awareness of urgency and peril pressed upon him. Often with it came a dark flood of anger which he could not fathom, that had little connection with the present. It came, unreasoning, a vestigial emotion from his past. He had left behind him something big and fiercely alive. The nature of it he did not know, but he could feel that it was there, a sinister presence behind a black veil. Big. Dangerous.

He thought: "*I* feel dangerous, too. I think I could kill. Perhaps I *have* killed. Lord, Lord, what am I? What have I been?"

He rowed with long, powerful pulls. The blades of the oars skimmed the water, dipped into it with a turning motion, and each tugging stroke was hard and clean. He could hold to a straight course despite his blindness. He had the

feel of the water, could almost gauge its depth by the sound
of the oars and some kind of instinct that had its depend-
ence upon small evidence not consciously noticed.

A wind was springing up, intermittent and boisterous,
sweeping the river and slapping little waves against the boat.
The booming throb of a paddle steamer reached his ears,
between gusts of the wind. Cleo had been silent for some
time, and it occurred to him that she must have fallen asleep.
She was worn out. He didn't wish to waken her back to the
nagging misery of cold and hunger, and he decided to nose
the boat toward the east bank without her help. The paddle
steamer was coming down river, he could tell, and that meant
that it would hold a course west of the channel. Whether it
was moonlight or not he had no means of knowing, but he
was confident that he could drift over to the east bank without mishap or notice from the steamboat.

But the dull booming ceased, and he rested on the oars
and listened for it. It was possible that the steamboat had
pulled in to a landing somewhere up the river beyond a
bend. He accepted the thought and returned the boat to its
course, as near as he could judge, and rowed more slowly.
Still listening, he heard only the wind and slap of the waves.
Soon he detected a new element of sound, a rushing noise
in the water, growing louder. He stopped rowing.

"Cleo—are you awake?" he muttered. Then, with a sudden realization of what the rushing noise portended, he
called her name sharply: "Cleo!"

The girl woke with a jump. Her reactions were immediate.
She looked behind over the stern, and what she saw brought
a screamed warning from her.

"Dain! Swing over—quick!"

Monstrously, a steamboat came gliding at them through
the darkness, engines silenced, no lights showing, running
on the wrong side of the river. When the girl screamed, a
man's voice barked a short command from the hurricane
deck. The engines throbbed alive and the great side paddles

commenced threshing. Half rising onto his feet with the wrenching effort, Dain dug the oars in deep and swung the little boat hard over.

Ponderously, deliberately, the steamboat also changed course. While Dain strained at the oars, the girl could do nothing but stare up in horror at the onrushing murder ship. It seemed certain that the little boat must be rammed and plowed under, and she wanted to leap overboard, but she only crouched there in the swinging stern. Then the wide, snout-like bow of the steamboat was sliding by, so close that she could have reached out and touched it. She caught a glimpse of a tall, cloaked figure leaning over the deck rail, and of a pair of silver-pale eyes staring down at her.

The first high wave, ridged up by the steamer's bow, lifted the flat-bottomed boat and spun it around. A pistol emitted a brief flash from the deck, the report of it thinned to a faint crack by the roar of the side paddles. The little boat slid down the wave, stern first, sucked toward the passing steamer. It bumped her side, careened off, and returned as if intent upon self-destruction. The big paddle-box smashed full into it.

The girl had taken a leap toward Dain as she saw the paddle-box coming, her chief thought for him and his blindness, but she never reached him. The boat was butted out from under her, and she went over the side into the river. Before she had time to begin fighting the icy water, the gunwale of the capsizing boat came down on her head.

The man leaning over the deck rail fired his pistol again, but the bullet only whined off the stubby wooden skeg of the smashed and overturned boat. An oar, caught in the paddles, caused a grinding sound as it was champed to bits, and the broken little boat lurched sluggishly into the wake as the vessel swept on by.

CHAPTER TWO

W<small>HEN THE GIRL OPENED HER EYES SHE WAS</small>
lying on land. It took her a moment to recall what had happened. The horror of it rushed in upon her again, and she pushed herself up with her arms and sat up giddily, staring wildly about her for Dain. His hand pushed her down again.

"They're searching for us," he muttered. "They've stopped and they got a boat out. Searching for our bodies, likely!"

He lay close by her, shivering with cold, his head raised and face turned toward the river. The slow throb of engines sounded plainly. The steamboat, with paddles reversed against the current, was holding to a stationary position in midstream. Some men were rowing a boat back and forth, and peering overside.

It took the girl some time to realize that the man beside her was following the movements of that boat. "You—you're . . ." She could not finish. She was afraid.

He brought his face toward her, and she shrank from his smile. "They did something for me, this time," he murmured. "Shock—strain—cold . . . God knows what did it. I was blind when I hit the water. When I beat my way up and got my head clear, I could see! Lucky for both of us. You were . . . What are you afraid of? Me? Why should you fear me?"

"Can you—remember—too?" she whispered.

"No. My memory is still botched. I reckon it always will be." He peered at her narrowly. "You seem glad to hear that!"

"No—oh, no! I was just—surprised—and glad. Glad you can see again. I'm glad you can see, Dain!"

He continued his sharp scrutiny of her. His grey-green
15

eyes were speculative, and touched with a tinge of sardonic skepticism. "I took a good look at you after I dragged you ashore here," he told her. "Your face brings nothing back to me. I wonder if it should? I wonder how much you really do know about me? I wonder what you're hiding—and why—and what you're hiding from? I wonder . . ." He caught himself up short. "No, I'll not try to pry out your secrets. I owe you too much."

He saw her as a dark-haired girl, with long, slim legs and rounded arms. Not of coarse-grained texture, but neither was she too finely spun. Rather, there was about her the smooth, firm structure of a cat. This feline quality also appeared in her facial features, which had that same smoothness and were faintly blunted. Her eyes were of an odd brown hue, bronze and transparent. A strikingly handsome girl, and a strange blend of feminine depth and masculine directness, of bold candor of gaze and an almost Oriental air of subtlety. She was terribly cold, but she had the faculty of overcoming her own suffering; it went deeper than stoicism. Under Dain's long regard, a sultriness crept into her eyes, and Dain was able to imagine how her skin could be warm and rich in color.

"You came close to giving me one truth, at least," he said. "You're pretty. That word doesn't fit you, but I can't think of one better. We'd better crawl off and get to walking, or we'll freeze. Those devils are likely to search all night."

She followed him obediently, and after they had crawled up over the bank he gave her a hand to rise—a casual act on his part, accepted by her with manifest pleasure high in proportion to the small courtesy. They came to a wagon road that followed the river and they trotted along it together, trying to work up some warmth. The girl's free gait carried further the impression of her catlike suppleness, and the gravel under her bare feet brought no mincing flinch from her.

A log shack showed up in a clearing, off to the river side of the road. They slowed and studied it, and without exchanging a word they cautiously left the road and approached it. Dain drew his long pistol. The powder charge in it was wet, but he trusted to the threat of it to command fear in the event of trouble.

Cleo touched his arm lightly. "They've got a fire," she breathed, gesturing up to the shack's smoking stone chimney. She was stepping noiselessly along beside him, and he saw that she had produced the pocket pistol.

He grinned down at her, a hard recklessness on his face. "Food, too, likely. For those things I could do murder tonight!"

"So could I!"

Dain rapped the pistol on the leather-hinged door. The only response from within the shack was the muffled sound of movement and the deep growl of a dog, followed by complete silence. He rapped again. The silence continued. Waiting no longer, he put a shoulder to the door and burst it wide open.

There was only one room to the shack, flickeringly lighted by the log fire in a smoke-blackened clay and stone fireplace. On a few rags in a corner lay a shrunken-cheeked old woman, risen up on her hands and glaring. By the fire knelt a gaunt old man and a weedy youth with hair straggling to their shoulders, both engaged in loading a flintlock musket from a powder horn and ball pouch. The firelight played over their bony features and dry, dirty hair, and cast shadows that filled their cadaverous hollows. The dog, a rough, big-headed cur, rose bristling under the split-log table and came out in a rush at the intruders.

Dain struck with the barrel of his pistol. The snarling brute yelped and retreated to the filthy pallet, skulking down behind the hag and whining. The hag fell to mumbling oaths, while the man and youth stared dully.

"River rats!" said Cleo contemptuously.

Dain watched the man and youth put down their musket and edge away from the fire, and he felt that he had experienced the like of this before, that this was not an unusual episode in his life, but merely another link in a long chain. Danger and violence, he felt sure, must have played dominant roles in his past, for he knew instinctively how to handle himself.

He motioned Cleo toward the fire. "We'll make the best of this. Dry your clothes and warm yourself. Smells like food in that pot on the hearth. What is it?"

"Hominy and meat, I think."

"Good—then we'll eat." He clinked two gold pieces on the table, and nodded curtly to the old man. "There's your pay for what we take. I want that horn of dry powder, for one thing!"

Cleo knelt facing the fire, her back to the room. Without any shrinking modesty she slipped off her thin, wet clothes and held them before her to dry. The weedy youth gaped at the fire-lighted outline of the slim young body, while the old man blinked at the coins on the table as if he had never seen gold before.

Dain dragged a tattered blanket from the pallet, ignoring the unintelligible mutterings of the hag and the shuddering growls of the frightened dog. "It's not much of a bedroom robe, but it'll do to shelter your young charms," he commented, and shook it out to spread over the girl. "Even river rats are human, I suppose, and you're altogether too pretty to . . ."

He broke off, his eyes fixed on her bare back and shoulders, shocked speechless by what he saw there. Half a dozen long stripes marked the white skin. He examined them more closely. The skin had been cut. These were recent scars of a brutal lashing.

"How did you get those?" he rapped. His voice was harsh and peremptory.

She turned her dark head and looked up quickly at him. She reached up with her arms, took the blanket from him,

and covered herself with it. "From a whip!" she answered.
"Who did it?"

She shook her head and turned back to the fire. "It doesn't
matter now." The firelight glowed on her face, and her eyes
shone more than ever like transparent bronze. "It'll never
happen again. Never!"

"By the Moloch, I'll see to that, girl!"

She bowed her head, concealing her eyes from him, and in
that pose she looked small and pitiful, and yet voluptuous,
too. When she at last raised her eyes to his, they were sensual
and full of secrets. "I know you will," she whispered. "I know
you will, Dain!"

They ate from the pot on the hearth, and warmth crept
into them. Dain loaded the pistols from the powder horn.
"Those men who are after us—what did you say they looked
like?" he asked Cleo.

She studied his face for a moment before giving him a
careful reply. "A tall man. Thin. He's pale, and his hair is
white. His eyes are almost white, too. There are others, but
he's the head of them. He's rich. He's got a big black man
with him always—a half-witted slave who does as he's told to
do. Please don't ask me anything more." Her eyes begged
him. "Please don't, Dain!"

"Just one more question. What would happen to *you* if
we were caught?"

She gave him no direct answer to that. "Let me keep the
little pistol," she asked him.

He gave it back to her, and stood and meditated. "We've
got to get away from the Mississippi," he decreed. "Likely it's
being watched for us all the way down to New Orleans, as
badly wanted as we seem to be. If we could get up into the
Arkansas or the Red River, and get hold of some other
clothes, and . . . Where the devil are we, anyhow?"

He turned on the old man. "We passed a big town up the
river, a few nights ago. What town would that be?"

The old scarecrow was still blinking at the gold coins,

fascinated by them, but not yet daring to pick them up. He worked his scraggy throat. "Memphis, reckin."

Dain considered it. He found it no difficult feat to conjure up a mental picture of the geography of the country, and again he was struck by the vagaries of his injured mind. "Then we can't be far from the mouth of the Arkansas. You got a boat?"

"Aye."

"We'll take it. Here's another yellow-boy." Dain threw him a third coin, and knelt behind Cleo to whisper to her. "We'll lie low here till tomorrow night, and then try for the Arkansas. If we can get hold of some presentable clothes along it, we'll take a chance and board a steamboat up to Little Rock."

"Can we get out of the United States that way?" she asked.

"You mean out of reach of United States law? Is that it? Lord, girl, I wish I knew your past! Well, let's see. From Little Rock we could travel overland to the Red River, and when we crossed the Red we'd be in Texas."

"Isn't that in the United States?"

"No. Texas is a province of Mexico—a Mexican territory. Now, how do I know that?" He shook his head. "I can't recall ever being there, or of even looking at a map of it. Yet I know its shape and where it is, and I know it belongs to Mexico. I know . . ."

"Please," she said, "let's try to get to Texas. I want to get away from—everything. I want to go where things are different. Where I'll never be found. Where nobody will know me. I want us both to go there, Dain!"

He scowled into the fire. "It's not what *I* want. What I want is a hide-out where I'll have time to grow a good beard and change my looks, and get new clothes. Then I want to come back and find that white-eyed devil you speak of. Trap him off somewhere alone. Make him tell me everything. Choke it all out of him!"

His words were bringing fear to the girl. He said no more. For the rest of the night they took turns sleeping. Toward morning Dain had an ugly dream. He thought that he was peering down through a gaping hole, into a great chamber that was so dimly lighted that its limits were invisible. Howls and shrieks came up to him through the hole, along with a fetid odor; and from this hell of filth and horror, glistening faces glared up at him, scores of them, contorted and despairing.

He woke and sat up, filled with an unreasoning fury and revulsion. The old man and the youth shrank from the look on his face. The hag ceased her everlasting mumbling, and the cur dog, that had ventured out, whined and took cover again.

He said savagely, "I've got to know! I've got to know who I am—what I've been! That dream—it came from something I've seen and lived. For God's sake, girl, tell me all you know!"

Cleo huddled in the tattered blanket, and again she bowed her head from him. "I can't," she said stonily.

The tall, weather-beaten man in the coonskin cap squared off and took aim at the mark, pegged up at a hundred yards' distance. He was evidently somebody of considerable renown, for the competing crack shots of Little Rock watched him respectfully. His rifle, a very fine Philadelphia piece, steadied in his brown hands. His shooting eye was confident. To judge by his manner of speech, he was a Tennessean, and he wore the garb of a backwoodsman, but about him hung an air of worldliness and distinction.

He fired, and the ball spotted the mark, dead center. "There's no mistake in Betsey, gentlemen," he remarked casually, and patted his splendid rifle.

Some of the onlookers whistled admiringly. It had been a marvellous shot. The tall Tennessean, Dain suspected, was more pleased with it than he cared to evince. Dain idly wondered about him and decided that he was probably a naturally modest man, a trifle spoiled by fame that had somehow come his way. He was evidently a newcomer to Little Rock, but had a reputation. These Arkansans looked up to him.

"Could you do that again, Colonel?" somebody ventured.

The Tennessee Colonel shrugged. "Oh—about five times out of six," he answered airily, and then Dain knew that the man was cutting a big figure.

Since quitting the Mississippi, Dain had managed to make some good use of his gold. He and Cleo had secured new clothes, and when they unobtrusively boarded a steamboat coming up the Arkansas River they were accepted as a gentleman and his lady travelling for their own private reasons. This morning they had disembarked here at Little Rock. While Cleo kept to her room at the best tavern, Dain was circulating around and trying to discover if there might be any way of conveniently slipping off into the back country without arousing too much attention. It would not be long, he thought, before the pursuers came tracking up here.

But there was a perverse streak in him that offered him a reckless joy in taking chances. He was not fashioned for furtiveness and restraint, and a moody restlessness was upon him these days, the result of constant defeat in his attempts to unveil his past. All in all, he was in a ripe temper to play with mischief and to challenge the presumption of any man.

He spoke up deliberately, pointedly, bringing many eyes to bear upon himself. "I'd be a surprised man to see that done just *once* more!"

The Tennessean wheeled around, one eyebrow cocked, not at all pleased. "I'll do it," he drawled, "if any gentleman here will first match that shot of mine. Can *you* oblige, suh?"

They were both tall men of much the same breed—like chestnut burrs, rough to the unguarded touch and hard to handle. They stood and took each other's measure and they lined their lips straight, both satisfied that here was a match for fight or frolic.

Dain inclined his head. "If I may use your gun—?" he suggested, and calmly helped himself to it. He loaded it, taking his time.

The Tennessee Colonel critically inspected the process, plainly jealous of anybody else handling his beautiful firearm. He was an arresting figure in his coonskin cap and flapping buckskins, his carved powder horn and pouch slung from shoulder thongs and a long skinning knife thrust in his belt. But for all his backwoods hunter garb, he was plainly a man of travel and experience, and he appeared to accept as his right the title of Colonel by which the others addressed him.

Dain fitted the greased patch, pushed the snub-nosed ball home, and gave it a final light tap with the hickory ramrod. He set the priming and cocked the lock. "The head of the mark, Colonel, right over that bull's eye of yours," he called pleasantly, and took aim.

He fired, peered briefly after the smoke drifted clear, and handed back the weapon. He had correctly called his shot. "Not a bad gun. A heavier stock would give it better balance, and I'm of the opinion that the frizzen takes too much priming for the charge. But let a good gunsmith work it over for you, and you'll have a fair piece of iron, Colonel!"

The Colonel reared back his head and snorted like a stallion. "I'll have you know, suh, that this rifle is the finest that ever came out of Philadelphia!" he stated. "It was presented to me by the people of——"

"Ah, a gift?" Dain murmured politely. "Well, in that case its defects should not be noticed, of course. Will you fire now—ah—Colonel?"

The Colonel reloaded, his eyes snapping. He was so irritated by the slur upon his cherished weapon that he spilled a ball from his pouch. Reaching down to pick it up, he inadvertently dug the muzzle of his rifle into the dirt, which brought a muttered oath from him.

Dain commented sympathetically, "The stock *is* a little light, isn't it?"

The Colonel opened his mouth to give a blistering retort, closed it grimly, and fired at the mark. Dain concealed his amusement behind a carefully blank face. The rifle was perfect, but the proud Colonel had shot a little before he was ready. No third shot appeared on the mark.

An Arkansan spectator cleared his throat. "I reckin, Colonel," he opined, "you done missed that time!"

The Colonel refused to believe it. "I warrant you I never miss!" he insisted, and paced like a hurrying Indian toward the target, a small crowd following. He was ahead of them, and after a moment of fingering the bullet hole in the center, he smiled and nodded at them.

"If you'll dig into that hole, I wager you'll find *two* bullets in it. My second shot followed the trail of the first, slick and clean. And that, gentlemen, was my intention!" He cast a cold look on Dain. "Are you satisfied, suh, as to the craft of my eye?"

Dain doffed his hat in mock respect. "To the craft of your eye, Colonel—and the dexterity of your hand!" he said solemnly, and the Colonel stared sharply at him.

That night Dain stood the drinks in the taproom of the tavern, thereby interrupting an eloquent political discourse of the Colonel, who was making out a scathing case against half the politicos of Washington.

The Colonel followed Dain outside, later. They fell into step, strolling down a path toward the river. The Colonel had his fine rifle under his arm, and he stroked it. He looked sidelong at Dain, and grinned. His grin made him a lot more human and engaging, and when Dain grinned back it placed them both on a companionable footing.

"Any man is li'ble to miss his shot," observed the Colonel

meditatively. " 'Specially when somebody fuddles him the way you did me. But when a man's had his trumpet blowed loud by fame, he can't afford to miss. Not once. Suh, I 'preciate you keeping quiet about that. I reckon you was the only one who caught me poking that second ball into that hole with my finger!"

They laughed over it. "I don't believe I've heard your name spoken, Colonel," Dain remarked. "What is it?"

He was a little surprised at the Colonel's reaction to that. The Colonel pulled up and faced him, eyebrows cocked high. "You don't know who I am?"

"Sorry—no. Should I?"

"We-ell. . . . Ahem! Perhaps not, suh, perhaps not. It's like the feller who met President Jackson and says to him, 'Seems like I seen you afore, some place.' To which Jackson says, 'Likely enough. I'm General Jackson, who whipped the British at New Orleans.' Feller took a long look at him, and says, 'Ye do say! Tell me, how did ye keep all them guns a-shootin' an' a-bangin' by yerself? I allus figgered ye musta had a couple o' boys helpin' ye!' " The Colonel chuckled at his own little joke. "As for me, I don't claim to've won any battles by myself. True, I fought in the Creek war, and I was at the burning of Black Warrior's village, and the Battles of Talladega and Horse Shoe Bend—but I was just a common ord'nary mounted volunteer under Gen'ral Jackson. Later, suh, the Gen'ral and me fell out over politics."

He gazed at Dain in the moonlight, evidently expecting some dawning sign of recognition. But Dain only nodded, so the Colonel continued.

"After the war, I was made a magistrate of Tennessee, and then elected to the legislature. Twice elected, suh, and finally to Congress—twice again. But the Gen'ral and me still didn't see eye to eye over politics, and we still don't. The Gen'ral is a right sturdy enemy, and his power's consid'rable—pretty consid'rable. And he's got men in his camp who don't fight politics the way soldiers fight wars. I was rascalled out of my last election. Yes, suh, rascalled out of it, I say, or my name's not Colonel David Crockett!"

"Crockett," Dain repeated. "Crockett of Tennessee." It had a familiar sound. As had become his habit, he strained to recall definite facts, but drew only dim impressions. "Aren't you somewhat out of your territory, Colonel?"

Davy Crockett shrugged. "War knows no boundaries. I'm on my way to Texas."

"To war?"

"Yes, suh—to fight for my rights!"

"What rights, may I ask?"

"Why—ah—the right of liberty and self-rule for Texians, for one thing."

"But you're not a Texian, are you?"

A buckskinned arm waved that point aside. "A mere quibble, suh, a mere quibble! Tell me, who are you?"

"My name is Dain. Don't ask for my history—I can't give it."

Crockett nodded confidentially. "I respect your discretion, Mr. Dain. Many a good man's got his reasons for leaving his history behind him, and a lot of them are heading for Texas these days! H'mm—should I venture to ask if that's where you're bound for?"

Now that they were on a fairly candid basis of friendly understanding, Dain liked the famous backwoodsman, hunter, soldier, and turbulent prince of politics. The man was a natural champion, full of restless energy and sweeping convictions, on his way to a new battleground. "My destination," Dain said noncommittally, "has not yet been decided upon."

Lighting a cigar, Crockett glanced keenly at Dain by the light of the little tinder glow. "Like the farmer's boy who was told to plow the field to the red cow, suh? Two days later the farmer caught up with him in the next county, still plowing. Boy said he'd plowed nigh up to where the cow stood, but the critter got scared o' the plow and wouldn't

stay still, and he hadn't yet caught up with her! I'm not following any red cow, m'self. Texas is at the pitch of war and
calling on all good fighting men and patriots to come and
help her. I'm to join Colonel Travis at a place called the
Alamo. I'd like your company, suh."

Courteously, Dain thanked him for the invitation. "I'm not
well acquainted with the facts," he admitted, "but this affair
has somewhat the smell of a filibuster, to me. Mexico owns
Texas. It would seem that she's got a right to rule it."

"But not to misrule it!" countered Crockett. "Texas was a
wilderness. It has been colonized mostly by Americans. They
were invited to settle there by Spain, when it was a Spanish
province, and were guaranteed certain rights of self-government. Those rights were later denied them, so when Mexico
broke away from Spain, Texas helped to run the Spaniards
out. And now Mexico denies Texas her rights! It has reached
the point where Texians must choose between armed revolt
or humble obedience to tyranny—and we Americans, suh,
have never been particularly humble!"

"I'm afraid the call of patriotism—if it can be called that—
doesn't reach me very loudly," Dain observed. "I regard myself as a man of no particular country. I give allegiance to
nothing but my own interests, and I may add that I already
have considerable trouble of my own."

"I wager you're a man who can be stirred by rank injus-
tice, nevertheless," vowed Crockett. "Bear in mind, too, that
Texas is a vasty land where nobody inquires where you came
from or what you left behind you. Some day it'll be a free
state, a land of free men. Finally, let us trust, it'll take its
place as a part of our great United States."

"You sound more than ever like a filibuster, Colonel!"

"By no means, suh, by no means! By what title does Mexico lay claim to all territories that Spain once held on this
great continent?" The Colonel was getting warmed up. A
certain grandiloquence began coloring his phrases. "Each
province of New Spain fought for its freedom from the Span-

ish yoke. The Texians rose up and threw out the haughty Spanish overlords, and by so doing they earned the right to liberty and self-government. They fought for their soil, and they won it. Yes, and they still found strength to help Mexico fight for *her* freedom! Mexico talks of Texian ingratitude. By Harry, the ingratitude is all on the other boot! And now for years Mexico has been going through commotions and revolutions, with first one government and then another, until the Mexicans themselves are in a hobble and don't know what to look for next. Here she has this rascally Santa Anna with his boot on her neck. A military dictator—a tyrant of the worst stripe! A man who flouts treaties and guarantees! A man who demands that the Texians either abandon their lands, or submit to base tyranny—to taxation without representation—to a Mexican army of occupation, paid for by Texas—to the despotism of a state religion. . . ."

The aroused Colonel David Crockett of Tennessee thundered eloquently on, and Dain could well understand how it had come about that he had left such deep and spectacular tracks behind him in his career. With each passing minute, he liked the Colonel more and more. No faint-hearted partisan, this, but a staunch battler who'd always make it his business to be in at the death, whichever way the fight went.

"Colonel, what is this place that you call the Alamo?" he inquired.

"It's in San Antonio. Or near it."

"Yes, but what is it?"

Crockett gestured airily. "It's the place where a free Texas will be born—where a Mexican army, bent on invasion, will be shattered—where that damned Santa Anna will get the beating of his life—and where the flag of Texas will never cease to wave over liberty-loving men! That, suh, is the Alamo!"

"Thank you, Colonel, I'll try to remember all that."

"Mr. Dain, Texians will forever remember the Alamo!"

CHAPTER THREE

Quietly, cautiously, the steamboat edged inward to a dock, downstream from the town. She carried no lights and sounded no whistle for the landing, so there was nobody on hand to help warp her in. Commands were given in a mutter, and were obeyed without the usual noise and shouting of boisterous riverboat crew men. She was a side-paddler, squat and rounded at stern and bow, but fast. No mast or cordage graced her ugly outlines, and recent hard service had blackened her with a covering of soot from her funnels. Under her long stateroom deck the furnace fires of her open engine room glowed intermittently on the half-naked bodies of black, sweating stokers.

She wharfed and was made fast, still holding to her unnatural hush. As the gangplank was quietly run out, her captain came down from the glassed-in steerage house. His stride was quick and nervous, reflecting the state of his mind. A group of four men, moving toward the gangplank to go ashore, paused at his low hail. Four pairs of eyes impatiently regarded him.

The Captain stopped before the tall man in grey, ignoring the others. "I've either got to open the escape valves, or pull the fires, sir," he declared. "The boilers won't stand that pressure much longer."

"You will do neither, Captain," came the soft retort.

The Captain clasped his hands tightly behind his back, but retained his formality of manner. "You chartered my boat because she's got high-pressure engines and she's fast, but you know as well as I do that she's got her limits," he argued. "We've kept her at top speed, day and night, and torn her near to pieces bucking this current. And there's my crew. We've worked the hearts out of them."

"They're being paid, aren't they? And so are you, Captain —paid well, I might say!"

The Captain unclenched his hands and gestured. "You can go just so far with money. I haven't asked what business you're on. I don't want to know. I've followed your orders, and asked no questions. But I do know my boat, and I know my crew. You can't drive them much further!"

Pale eyes regarded him expressionlessly. "If your crew gives trouble, I'll handle them!"

The Captain was the product of a tough environment, but he had an inexplicable fear of this passionless man. Still, he put up a last protest. "In the name of reason, sir, let's lay up here for just one day! The crew needs rest. We all do. And those boilers——"

"Keep a full head of steam, Captain," interrupted the tall man tonelessly, and paced down the gangplank, followed by his silent trio. When he stepped onto the dock he spoke over his shoulder. "Got my pistols, Quaw?"

"Yassuh."

"Give them to me."

They moved off along a narrow path toward the few lights of Little Rock that could be seen through the trees, and were soon enclosed by the darkness. Left behind, the Captain cursed wearily and headed for the engine room to keep an eye on his mutinous stokers.

Cleo left her room, and when she walked slowly out into the yard from the rear door of the tavern she looked about at all the shadows. Standing like that, stilled and intent, she had the apprehensive appearance of a girl bent upon clandestine romance.

She had shown no stint in her choice of clothes when the opportunity came to buy some, and her taste was not cramped by too much conservatism. She wore a full-skirted dress of soft levantine satin, tight in the waist and bodice, hiding little of her supple young figure, and her dark hair was piled high in the currently fashionable coiffure. On the boat coming up the Arkansas, men's eyes had followed her whenever she appeared. It was not that she dressed in bad taste. Rather, it was somewhat too good. It set off her dark beauty to vivid advantage and made of her a stirringly provocative figure.

She was uneasy. Her bronze eyes ranged distrustfully over the shadows. Once she raised her head as if sniffing the wind. But her searching senses brought nothing back to her. It was instinct that was prodding her with foreboding and the feel of danger. It had brought her out of her room to seek Dain. From her window she had seen Dain and another man stroll off down a path that led to the town wharfs.

Something was wrong. Something was creeping up on her. She whirled swiftly, but saw nothing, and she told herself that her nerves were playing her tricks. There was nobody here in the yard but herself. Inside the tavern were men, drinking and talking. The town was undisturbed, sleepy, for it was getting late. There could surely be no peril stalking her here tonight, here in Little Rock, two hundred miles from the Mississippi. She stepped quickly across the yard, away from the tavern and toward the river path.

She refused to allow herself to look back, not wishing to give way to her fears, and so she missed seeing the four men who moved noiselessly out from behind the stable building.

They had been standing there in the darkness, gazing at the tavern windows, when she emerged. The darkness, and the girl's changed mode of dress, kept recognition of her from them, but something in her manner of walking betrayed her to two of them as she quit the yard. The tall man in grey turned to Quaw. The black giant did not nod or speak, but the shine of his eyes was sufficient corroboration.

"Go after her, Quaw!" murmured the tall man. He spoke

to one of the two other men behind him. "Go with him, Jarvis. Take her aboard the boat—quietly!"

He watched the pair leave on the trail of the girl, and transferred his attention back to the windows of the tavern. After a while he spoke again. "Farrow, go back and tell the Captain to make ready to cast off. Tell him to be ready to head the boat back down to the Mississippi."

Hands thrust into the pistol pockets of his plain, high-collared coat under the grey cloak, he paced into the lighted tavern.

Cleo followed the path and she was frightened. This fright made her furious at herself, and this in turn caused her to walk at a slower pace, perversely, than her normal gait. She was not an easy subject for physical fear to conquer, and when it came she was ashamed of its presence. She told herself that the occasional trees and dark clumps of brush lining the path were the same harmless greenery that belonged to the day, hiding nothing sinister, giving cover to nothing more than the nesting birds that belonged there. But it was hard to dismiss the sound of something that moved over the rough ground off from the path, and silenced itself for a moment, and sounded again ahead of her. Her senses shrieked. She tried to fight them down to quietness. And then another sound came to her, from behind her. At last she surrendered to the press of fear, and stopped, and looked back.

Because the man following her along the path was crouched in his creeping, he appeared to her as a thing that could not be human—all legs and body, and no head, a black form in the night. She turned and fled. It came running after her, and it did no creeping now. Its feet pounded the path, and she knew with relief that it must be a man. Then a clump of bush ahead of her and just off the path resolved itself into two shapes, one of them moving—straightening up, towering giant-like, arms apart and fingers spread. It lunged at her. There was no escape from it.

The girl screamed shrilly as the huge hands grasped her, and Black Quaw chuckled an idiot's pleasure.

"My father was an Irishman," Crockett was saying, "and he fought in the Revolution for America. I'm a Tennessean, and I'll fight in the revolution for Texas. He would've liked that. Liberty and justice are worth fighting for, any time, any place. Don't you agree, Mr. Dain?"

He was persuasive and forceful, wholehearted in his enthusiastic support of the cause which he had adopted as his own. It was not enough for him to go trekking off to a far-off Texas war, but he must beat the drum for additional volunteers on his journey there. Dain grinned. "My own keen taste for liberty, Colonel, is more of a personal trim," he confided delicately. "I'm already fully engaged in a contest to retain it!"

"Mr. Dain, a man could rid himself of such personal botherations, in the greater contest that faces Texas." Crockett chewed his cigar ruminatively, a twinkle in his eye. "Not for the presidency, itself, would I cast a word against the volunteers who're making their various roads to Texas from everywhere, y'understand. But it's a fact that war can be a considerable convenience for men whose affairs happen to be in a bad snarl—and I don't mean only these-yere soldiers of fortune like the New Orleans filibuster crowd, who'll go anywhere for a good slam-bang fight. No, I mean men who can't afford to stand still in one spot too long! Men who're looking for a new country and a new start. I include, suh, fugitives from justice."

"And busted politicians?"

"Ahem! Well, perhaps, as long as they've got the right kind of grit in 'em."

They exchanged grins again. To insist upon noble impulses was not permissible. It was more comfortable to present self interest and easy cynicism as motivating forces leading a man to war.

"Frankly, I could be tempted into joining you," Dain admitted. "But there happens to be a young lady with me. The backroads to Texas are not being travelled by members of the—er—gentle sex these days, I take it?"

"H'mm—hardly."

Dain nodded. "So I thought. However, that's a matter for the lady to judge. In the meantime, Colonel, the chances of my reaching Texas would be greatly improved by a certain amount of reticence on your part."

"That's understood," Crockett assented. "You have my bottom word for it, I'll not breathe a word about you to a single living soul. As far as I'm concerned——"

It was then that they both heard the scream.

Quaw had the girl tucked under one arm, his free hand clamped over her mouth. He started off the path with her, and her clawing and kicking only brought more low chuckling from him.

His white companion kept up a muttering. He was stocky and thick necked, a ruffian for hire for anybody's money. "Quick, ye damned ape, lively to the boat! Lively, now!" He was armed, but the girl's scream had rasped his nerves, and Black Quaw's crazy chuckling did not soothe them. "Run with her, ye blasted . . . Arrrrgh!"

He was on familiar ground again, ready for what he could understand, when two men came sprinting up the path. His pistol levelled out, and while he sighted it he dug for its mate under his coat.

Running, Dain caught the faint sheen of metal. He saw also the monstrous figure of the Negro and the girl under his arm, and there was where he sent his shot. He fired low, skimming the ground for fear of hitting Cleo. It was strange, the confidence that was in his hand, the sureness with which he touched the trigger. He knew where his bullet was going, and the matter of lining up his sights was something that he could ignore, for he was shooting by feel and sense of direction. This he had done before, in that other life, he knew; the expertness of it was a memory that belonged to his hand.

The black man howled and went down on one knee, clutching that leg and letting the girl fall. The white man fired, cursed, and took aim with his other pistol. His orders were not to kill the girl, but to bring her alive to the boat, but when he saw that she was getting away he brought his pistol slashing toward her.

Dain's pistol was a single-shot, and he had fired its load. He ran on, ducking and weaving, until he saw that glint of steel cut toward Cleo. Just behind him another gun coughed a roar, and the man with the pistols floundered onto his back.

Crockett said cheerfully, "I reckon I got that rascal, suh!"

The Negro reared up. For an instant he glared at the pair of oncoming men and at the escaping girl, now out of his reach, before he turned and crashed off into the brush. His companion got up, stumbling and awkward, still retaining one of his pistols. Dain was long and fast in the legs, but Crockett streaked by him. The Colonel lunged in. His rifle rose and fell, once, and when Dain reached Cleo there was nothing more to do than pick her up and steady her.

Dain said, holding her, "They hurt you?"

She shook her head. "No." To remain against him, his arms holding her, was all she seemed content to do.

Crockett joined them. He carefully examined his rifle all over for possible injury, and reloaded it. "If that fellow ain't dead now, he's immortal," he opined, and doffed his coonskin cap to Cleo. "Ma'am, our apologies for not getting here sooner. We came soon's we could cut out from where we was at. They won't trouble you any more. Wish we'd got that other big rascal!"

Quite unperturbed by the violence that had gone on, he gazed quizzically at Dain. "I misdoubt if the like o' this would happen in Texas. Ladies are queens in Texas!"

Cleo stirred, still clinging to Dain. "Texas," she said. "Dain—let's go there, please! We've got to get away from here. There'll be others coming. Let's start now—tonight!"

Crockett performed a creditable bow. "Your spirit, ma'am, is admirable. Most admirable. I could pretty near deplore the fact that you're not a man. Texas needs men of your spirit."

"She's right," Dain said. "She and I have got to get away from here. They've tracked us. Can't take the road to Natchitoches, though, unless we can get hold of fast horses. Have you any, Colonel?"

"Unfortunately, no. That's what's holding me up, here. I'm trying to buy one for m'self."

"Then that's not the road for us." Dain listened. "Those shots'll bring everybody here soon. Damn! If I had a boat I'd head back toward the Mississippi. They wouldn't look for us to back-track, and we could board the first steamboat we meet."

Crockett snapped his fingers. "Right! By the time they find you're not headed overland for Texas, you can be back on the Miss'. And from there you can take a Red River boat up to Natchitoches. Our tavern landlord owns a small boat, with a sail. Keeps it at the ferry wharf. Take it! Come on, I'll help you shove off."

They hurried toward the river. "You have our gratitude, Colonel," said Dain.

"By Harry, suh, I'm always ready to lend a hand to a man of the right grit!" vowed Crockett. "You got the lady with you, too. The damned rascals! Here's your boat. Pile in and run your sail up, whilst I untie her. I judge your course'll be for Texas, suh?"

Dain looked at Cleo. She nodded eagerly. "I reckon it will," he answered. "Seems like we've got to travel that Texas road to your confounded Alamo, Colonel!"

"Quarters for the lady," Crockett suggested pointedly, "can be found somewhere along your course, I'm sure."

"The lady goes to Texas, if I go," Dain corrected. "If necessary, she can dress as a man. Let me assure you she can handle herself like a man when she has to!"

With a nod, Crockett gallantly conceded any virtue claimed for the lady. "Then," he declared, "we'll fight together for Texas!"

He waved them farewell. Cleo sat in the bow, gazing forward, while Dain held the tiller. The boat's single sail caught the river breeze and she heeled to it and slanted toward the far side of the river.

The steamboat was a silent blob in the night. Aboard it the Captain glanced at a pale triangle of sail gliding by on the far side of the river, and switched his attention again to the shore. Two men came hurrying through the gloom to the gangplank. One of them sent forward a rapid hail.

"Captain, where did that sailboat come from? Who's in her?"

"Boat? Oh, that'n yonder? Can't tell who's in her. She put out from the town wharfs, I believe. Saw her when she cut across——"

"Shove off! Head your boat around and get after her!"

The tall man stepped aboard and paced swiftly to his cabin. He emerged with a rifle and went aloft after the Captain to the steering house. Quaw ran the gangplank in unaided, and stood on one leg, grinning insanely with excitement and pain the while he rubbed the bloodied calf of his raised leg.

The Captain, his commands given on the run, paused at the door of the steering house, listening to the coughing noise of the engines starting up. The side paddles began their splashing and the boat lumbered away from the dock, groaning like an irritated mammal. Steam hissed a sudden hoarse note, and a flash of fire and sparks leaped from a funnel. The groans were repeated, and would be every half minute or so as long as the boat gathered headway. With every groan the steam would hiss again, and flame and sparks would cast a glare over the surface of the black water. The water, aside the beam, port and starboard, and trailing from the stern, turned white from threshing, smearing a pale and troubled track upon the river.

The steamboat drew that troubled track in an arc as she cleared the wharf and turned about, putting her nose downstream, and the current washed and dragged it to its own pattern. With the flow of the river to aid and push her, the boat gathered headway. Her engines at full throttle, paddles thrusting at the water, she moved in dead pursuit of the little sailboat.

The Captain closed the steering-house door, and the noise dimmed. He watched the steersman for a moment, checking on him. Satisfied in that respect, he turned a disquieted glance upon his employer. "Those shots I heard reached the town," he mentioned. "Some commotion there, I'm afraid, from the sounds. If anybody's been killed, there'll be trouble out of it!"

The silver eyes flicked briefly to him. "Never mind that. My concern. Can't you make this damned tub go any faster?"

"She's at full steam now. Listen to those engines tearing themselves to pieces." The Captain scowled forward, eyes on the bit of sail. "My boilers——"

"Curse your boilers, your boat, and you!" The tall man flung open a window and rested his rifle across the sill, taking sight.

In Dain's ears the noise of the steamboat grew steadily louder. Every time the flare jetted from the funnels he could see her, all the squat and ugly shape of her, drawing closer. A shot rapped through the noise. He didn't hear the bullet, wherever it struck, and he felt for his pistol, but abandoned that intention when the ordinary noise of the steamboat abruptly changed to a tremendous roar.

"Boiler exploded," he said mechanically, the knowledge of

what had happened sure in his mind. He repeated it in a shout, kneeling upright against the tiller and staring back. "Boiler exploded! Burn, damn you—burn!"

Matching the frightful change of sound, the steamboat appeared to change shape. She sprouted a grey fullness, and this fullness ballooned until she was enveloped in it. Then a sheet of flame swept upward through the escaping steam, along with a furious sizzling. A mate to the wide flame shot up from the other side of the boat, until the upper part of the boat with its cabins and steering house was like a flattened ship sailing on a cloud of fire.

The roar came to its end. The engines had died. For a moment the boat sailed on like that in silence, blazing and majestic, drifting on under her own momentum. Then the fire shrank, leaving minor fires clinging here and there to parts of the boat. Somebody up in the steering house regained his head and spun the wheel over, sending the doomed ship shoreward. Now cries and shrieks could be heard. Those of the crew who had not been trapped below were diving overboard, some with smouldering clothes and burning hair. But the steering house had not been touched as yet by the fire, and up in there men were acting to save their lives.

"I hope they burn—I hope they *all* burn! Oh, please Heaven—let them all burn!" It was Cleo, in the bow of the sailboat, calling out that prayer.

The sailboat held to her onward course, unhurrying, unconcerned. Dain found himself cursing aloud—cursing because he dared not put about to save some of the struggling, swimming crew men. This urge, too, was an old instinct in him, a kind of law under which he once must have lived, and he had to fight it away. He turned his face from the burning steamboat, and sailed steadily on down the Arkansas for the Mississippi, two hundred miles away.

The steamboat had made the shore, ramming into it with

a crunch of wrenched timbers, becoming an earth-bound fixture until the fire should burn her down to the water's edge and the water patiently suck away what remained beneath. Her bow stuck up, her stern hung low, and both banks of the river were lighted up by the increasing flames of her.

The Captain sat in the wet weeds ashore, nursing an ankle broken by his leap from the grounded boat. Near him stood his employer and the slave, neither of them making a move toward giving help to those of the crew struggling dazedly onto the bank. Under the glare of the burning boat, the master and the slave were red-lighted symbols of evil and calamity, and that was how they appeared to the sickened eyes of the Captain.

The Captain was considerable of a rascal in his own right, short on scruples and receptive toward venal profits. But in his shocked condition he was vulnerable to a low stir of revulsion. He began cursing, until a toe prodded him contemptuously. He raised his head and stared into the cold eyes of the gentleman in grey.

"I told you she'd blow up!" the Captain denounced him hoarsely. "Damn your dirty murdering game, whatever it is! I'm finished with it, you hear? And you'll pay me for my boat, by Ned—full value and a bonus to keep me quiet!"

"Is that a threat, Captain?"

Some of the storm subsided in the Captain, and with it a degree of his nerve. But gain had always been his major incentive, and he clung to it. He muttered defiantly, "A word from me to the right quarters, and you'd have some powerful awkward questions to answer, mister!"

The tall man smiled faintly. "Yes, Captain. That has already occurred to me." He glanced at his slave, and back down at the Captain. His nod was sufficient.

The Captain began a bellow of terror, cut off before he could give full voice to it. A little later his body splashed in the river, and the black giant stood watching to see it sink.

The tall man gazed calmly out over the river. Small boats were putting out from the town, attracted by the explosion and fire. He called quietly, "Come, Quaw," and trod up the bank away from the river, the black giant limping after him and peering back over his shoulder with childish delight at the spectacle of the flaming steamboat.

CHAPTER FOUR

A<small>TOP THE BLUFF, FAR DOWN THE</small> M<small>ISSIS</small>-sippi from the Arkansas, stood the handsome little town of Natchez—Natchez On The Hill.

Below the bluff lay the other town—Natchez Under The Hill—like filth giving life to the flower above. This was a place of slaves and cotton, fevers and alligators, long knives and whiskey. This was the place where the lovely magnolia and Spanish moss tried to hide the sordid corruption, vainly. Where buzzards were the unpaid scavengers of the crooked streets, tearing their livelihood from between brothels and gambling houses. Where the only law, such as it was, was wielded by the violent body of night-riders who styled themselves the Natchez Lynchers. Where a cheating gambler was reckoned the greatest enemy of organized society, and could be flogged to death in public. Where murder was greeted with a shrug, and robbery was accepted as a normal occurrence. This was Natchez Under The Hill, notorious headquarters of riverboat gamblers and prowling semi-pirates of the great Mississippi.

In the Marietta Inn nobody any longer took much notice of the large, shaggy-headed man who sat at the battered piano, broodingly picking out scraps of tunes from the yellowed keys. When he had first appeared, a few days back, the habitués of the dive had centered some attention upon him, deeply interested in the fact that he paid for his drinks in gold. But men had soon found out that he was well qualified to take care of himself, and the women had discovered

42

that the girl who hovered always near him could unsheath wildcat's claws when aroused. They were not popular, these two, but they were left alone.

The man played softly, a little stumblingly, drifting from one unfinished tune into another. Sometimes he struck a discord, for he was more than half drunk. He had been in a haze of near drunkenness since soon after coming here. His clothes were rumpled and untidy, the collar of his shirt torn open and his knotted tie dangling. Tawny hair hung tangled over his broad forehead, and under it his eyes stared into nothingness, absorbed and somber. Dreamlike in his manner and movements, he ceased playing and reached for the bottle and glass on the piano's stained top.

The girl said patiently, "Dain—when are we going on to Texas?"

"Texas?" He came slowly out of the haze and he looked at her, his eyes still blinded by long, groping thought. "Damn Texas!"

She put a hand over his that held the bottle. "Don't drink any more, Dain."

He considered it absently, without irritation. "It's the only way I've got to find out," he muttered, more to himself than to her. "It brings all that—" He gestured with the bottle, spilling whiskey—"that unknown—up close to me. When I drink, sometimes I can nearly reach all that. Sometimes I feel there's only a thin cloud hiding it all from me. And I get dreams, after I drink enough. Some day I'll break through that curtain! I think if I could get drunk enough, long enough—enough to forget the present—I could remember the past. Just leave me alone, Cleo. Just let me drink."

His dreams were often ugly, but sometimes not. The howling faces in the shadowy pit had become familiar to him, along with dim visions of dark forests, sun-glittered deserts and brilliant blue skies. And brown, hawk-eyed men whom he knew to be enemies of mankind. And sweating horses and hard riding. Momentary flashes of armed men, desperate men, himself among them, all shadowy and unreal, plunging into some kind of bloody fight. Stilled nights when he crouched with his eyes strained upon a moonlit rise. Visions of color and gayety, and laughter and dancing. . . .

They were merely a few broken pieces, and what he sought was the whole design. If he was an outlaw, as well as the hunted prey of powerful enemies, he wanted to know it. He wanted to know the why of it, and all the things that he must have done. His had been a wild and tumultuous life, that was certain.

"Poor girl." He stroked Cleo's hand. "You ought to quit me. I'm no good."

She flushed at his touch and the half whimsical tenderness of his voice. "Never," she said. "Never, as long as you need me—as long as you let me stay with you. I'm still your eyes. Those men who're hunting us—you don't know them. I do!" She smiled, and there was a kind of glory in her face. "You need me, Dain, as much as I need you. We could get away from all this. We could go to Texas. They say everybody gets a new life in Texas, no matter what you've been or where you come from."

Dain regarded her curiously. She was as much a mystery as he was, with the exception that she knew her own past, while he was a mystery even to himself. He had said that he would ask her no questions, and he did not, but he wondered about her. He was sure that she was a good girl, in the narrowest conventional sense of the term. She was even modest, after a fashion. Yet she was haunted by some enormity behind her, something so hideous that she would not expose the nature of it even to him, whom she trusted and—he could not help knowing—loved.

The knowledge that she loved him was a trouble to him. He liked her, was deeply fond of her. She stirred his compassion and his respect. He knew that he could possess her, for her eyes had more than once betrayed the knowledge to him. But it was his fondness and his respect for her that caused him to treat her as a comrade on equal footing, not as a desirable girl who was foolish enough to love him.

He tilted the bottle and poured his drink, and was a trifle annoyed when she tugged his arm. She whispered something that he did not catch. He raised the glass, and then he heard her say with a tense calmness, "Dain, are your pistols loaded? *He's* here!"

As forcedly calm as she, he set down the glass without drinking. He had bought himself a brace of new pistols, heavy calibred percussion repeaters. They were under his coat, slung in holsters from his belt. He touched them. "Where?" he asked.

Now he was sober, but his blood raced hot and he was eager. He swung away from the piano and looked over the crowded room at the drink-blurred faces that moved sluggishly in the smoky air. Any one of them could belong to the enemy, for all he knew. Only she knew.

She retained her control. She touched a piano key, and smiled at him with a tavern coquette's smile, for the benefit of watching eyes. "The window, to the left of the door," she murmured. "I saw his face there. The white-eyed man! He's not there now. Watch the door!"

They shifted away from the piano and stood against the wall to one side of it. From no window could anyone outside have vantage of them here. They waited. The noise of the drinking dive ran on along its discordancy of slurred voices, loose laughter, slap of cards and rattle of dice. At last the door burst open and slammed back on its hinges.

But it was no tall man and giant black who entered. It was a group of five armed men. Each had his head and face masked in a white hood. They entered swiftly and lined up in rough formation, leaving the door open behind them. All noise drained out of the tavern instantly, and the hush lasted until somebody uttered a shout.

"The Lynchers!"

The keeper of the tavern was the first to make a move toward the blanket-hung doorway that led to the rear rooms and the back yard. He was a scarred ex-sailor with a peg-leg and a sharp scrutiny for all strangers. Half the customers, including some of the harpies, evinced an eagerness to follow him and vacate the premises.

A visit from the Lynchers was to be dreaded by anyone. They were the unofficial, overlords of bad old Natchez Under The Hill. In the absence of other authority, they wielded the law, and not always from a spirit of disinterested righteousness. It was whispered that the hooded men could be actuated by other motives than civic virtue, and that some of them could be bribed into instigating their periodic reigns of terror. The members were supposed to be unknown and sworn to secrecy, but the identities of many of them were open secrets, despite the hoods and masks which they always wore when in action.

Their methods of dealing justice were unconventional and extreme, embracing cowhide beatings, tar-and-feathering, dragging of the bound and naked victim through the town behind a racing wagon, and on up to straight assassination. It was natural that the owner and customers of the dive should seek distance and cover from the white-clad squad. When the Lynchers marched at night in Natchez Under The Hill, nobody breathed easily until morning dawned, for they were apt to run berserk and settle all scores, public and private, before they quit work.

A command rapped from behind a mask. "Stand steady, all, or taste trouble!"

The speaker, evidently the leader of the squad, paced forward. Shuffling feet stilled, and he waited for the hush to be complete before he spoke again. Behind the mask holes his eyes ranged about him, catching glints from the smoking oil lamps. "In the name of justice, we're after one man and a woman tonight!"

Dain felt the glance of the man touch upon him and Cleo, and slide on. He lounged at ease, and mocked the leader with silent derision. It was significant, he thought, that the man should feel called upon to pause long enough to state a reason for this sinister intrusion. True righteousness, once aroused, acted promptly and needed no excuses; but shabby rascality could be depended upon to invoke the name of justice before carrying out the crime.

"The man is the worst kind of degenerate blackguard, and isn't fit to live!" pronounced the Lyncher, somewhat pontifically. "The woman——"

It was not Dain who interrupted to cut off the rest of the accusation. It was Cleo. The spurt of her little pocket pistol put a stop to whatever was about to be added, and the Lyncher sucked in his breath and clapped a hand to his neck. The four by the door abandoned all semblance of cold omniscience. In their hands they held their guns, and they swung them into use with more urgency than coolness. The pistol shot was all contrary to the reaction of hopeless resignation usually encountered by the militant, all-powerful Lynchers.

Dain cleared his repeaters from their holsters, neatly and efficiently, no flurry in his movements. He fired over the piano top, and then there were only three masked knights of the law disputing his right to live, the fourth sinking down on one knee, the leader still clasping his throat and gasping. The peg-legged ex-sailor took up his first impulse and rocked fast toward the blanket-hung doorway. Disciples of this thought followed him in a rush. Some of them got ahead of him and there was a jam that turned into a battle.

Panic swooped in; everybody was trying to get out by any exit at hand. The three masked men were rattled. Here was no easy capture, effected with a degree of formality and smooth dispatch. This man with the brace of repeaters was for making a fight of it, and the girl with the deadly little derringer was a hellcat. They blazed at both and wrecked the piano behind which the pair had made fort. The noise and confusion of the stampeding crowd was an added barrage against cool nerves. Every window had its quota of screaming, cursing escapees. Few had faith in the Lynchers' discrimination of victims when brought to the point of battle.

A Lyncher's bullet passed through Cleo's thick hair, tugging it and bringing a small cry of pain from the girl. Hearing her cry, and seeing her drop down behind the piano beside him, Dain thought she had been hit. Fury leaped in him. In the last few seconds his contempt for the Natchez Lynchers had expanded to include their shooting ability. To his view, they were proving themselves inept as executioners. They were too skittish to be first-class gunmen. *He* was a gunman, or at least a fighter of experience. The experience was in his hands, which knew how to behave without promptings from his mind. He pulled the triggers of both his pistols.

Another Lyncher went down, and that marked the end of the visit. The remaining two about-faced and plunged for the door. They'd had enough of nonconformists who refused to bow down to lynch law. Their wounded leader, stumbling after them, chopped a last shot that ripped into the piano. The bullet flicked a string and twanged a single, sonorous note from it, and on that note the brief gunfight ended. The last of the panicked mob still milled at the rear doorway, but the combat was over.

Dain stooped over Cleo. "How bad are you hurt?"

"I'm not hurt at all," she answered, and had the courage to laugh while she rubbed at her scalp. Physical cowardice was something she rarely displayed. As long as she could see and know the nature of whatever peril faced her, and as long as Dain was by her, she was an intrepid Amazon.

He smashed out a window glass with a pistol barrel. "Let's get out of here!"

He helped her through. Her full skirt hampered her, but she gathered it up and jumped lightly to the ground like a boy. Outside, men and women were running in all directions, every dive in the vicinity emptying. Dain and Cleo lined their course toward the river, their road and their refuge for so long that they had learned to turn to it first.

Beyond the limits of the town they stopped to catch their wind and listen for sounds of pursuit. Dain pushed fresh loads into his repeaters. "I've got a mind to prowl back there," he said. His eyes blazed. "I've got a mind to go back after that white-eyed devil and settle this thing once and for all!"

The girl's deep breathing broke off. "You'd be killed! And I'd . . . Listen! They're coming—the Lynchers are coming!"

Hours later, muddy and spent, they stumbled down a cut bank and stretched out on the damp red clay. After a while the girl whispered tiredly, "Texas—it's the only place for us, Dain. We'd be safe there, wouldn't we?"

"Safe in a war that doesn't concern us! But maybe you're right. Anyhow, it's what you want, isn't it? A new life, in a new country." Dain lay staring up at the stars. "I reckon I owe it to you, after all we've been through together. I've dragged you through hell, and you've stuck by me with never a whimper."

He rolled over and gazed at her. For all her indecorous capabilities, she looked small and tired, lying there. A gentleness came over him. He patted her shoulder. "So Texas it is, girl! We'll steal another boat somewhere and cross to the west bank farther downstream. Red River can't be far from here, and we can make our way overland to it. I reckon we shouldn't have much trouble, there, boarding a steamboat to Natchitoches. Might even catch up with Crockett before he reaches the Alamo, and arrive there with him."

She uttered a soft sound in her throat, a choking little laugh of relief, excitement and pleasure. She sat up, vibrant and tireless again, and kissed him full on the mouth.

"My, my!" Dain murmured, and gave her a grin. He rose and helped her to her feet. "I think we'd better start looking for a boat to steal. Come on, fellow pirate!"

The graceful young man in buckskins sang alone in the single street of Natchitoches. The stars were growing faint in the sky, dimmed by the dawning sun that struggled against the Louisiana mist in the east. It was toward the east that the young man gazed as he sang, with a pagan melancholy and a clear, musical voice:

"Saddled and bridled, and booted rode he,
    A plume in his helmet, a sword at his knee. . . ."

There seemed little to sing about in this low-lying land of monotonous pine. The morning mist regimented the near pines to a semblance of uninspiring uniformity. Deeper back in the mist, the timber became a broad expanse of smudge that blurred into the level distance. Natchitoches, itself, could lay claim to no magnificence in keeping with its rank as a post town and a Louisiana parish seat. Its population was less than a thousand, and its most imposing building was the chief tavern.

For all that, the young man sang to the rising sun, and he was sober. Here were romance, a sensitive soul, a glory and a pensive joy. He was clean and young, careless and yet absorbed in his dreams and his singing. His beaded moccasins, fine rifle, Indian-ornamented hunting pouch and jaunty fur cap—these were popinjay marks of youth. But his handsome face was strong, and burned to a mahogany darkness. He leaned against a signpost, singing to the dawn. To the man and the girl coming up onto the street from the direction of the river, he paid no heed. His voice rang out, with no strident loudness or callow overload of sentiment, but melodiously, reverently:

"But toom cam' the saddle, all bluidy to see—
An' hame cam' the steed, but hame ne'er cam' he."

"That young morning lark," observed Dain to Cleo, "is either drunk or doesn't belong in this world, or both!"

They paused to listen, intrigued. At first amused, Dain became, in a manner, charmed. "He's beautiful," Cleo said.

There, from her feminine standpoint, she spoke the truth, and Dain nodded agreement. The singer was beautiful, physically and—judging from his half melancholy, half joyous tone—perhaps spiritually. He was beautiful in form, from cap to moccasins; in stance and features and youth; in all the finely dramatic completeness of him. He was almost too beautiful for a man—for he was a man, of perhaps twenty, and boyhood ended early in old Louisiana.

He became conscious of having an audience, but with the awareness came no embarrassment. His glance lighted on them, drifted away, returned to them. He saw Cleo. She was nearest to the hanging door lamp of the tavern. He regarded her, his eyes glad and amazed, like one awakening from a dream and finding the vision of his dreaming had followed him into reality. He plucked off his fur cap, revealing fair, curling hair. He bowed his head, his entranced gaze remaining upon her.

"At last!" he breathed. "At last you've come! Your name is Amaryllis, and I am Boniface Eden, and we meet at last!"

It was startling, incredible. Young men did not behave like this, except in old romance. But this one was so behaving, and with grace and dash. If he was a maniac, as seemed likely, he was at least unique and engaging in his lunacy.

Of what it might have led to, Dain couldn't conceive, and

he was robbed of the opportunity to view the conclusion, for just then some men came out of the tavern. This put an end to the idyllic tryst in the street, and saved Cleo from the necessity of replying to the young man's greeting. Dain had been wondering what on earth she would say to such a high-flown speech, and he regretted losing the chance to hear it.

Among the emerging tavern group was one who appeared the worse for an alcoholic night that had not been entirely slept off. He was a bulky man, red faced and in an ugly temper about something, and he carried a coach whip in his hand. For a moment he stood undecided in the street, the others grinning and watching him; spying the fantastic youth at the signpost, he got into ponderous movement again. He stalked up, as threatening and blustery as a Gulf storm. His throaty bellow resounded through the street.

"Ye're a lying scoundrel! A scoundrel, sir, d'ye hear?"

The young man bowed gravely. "I hear."

"Last night, in the presence of my friends, ye said I was a calf—a bawling calf!"

"Correct. Your memory serves you credit."

"D'ye see this cowhide whip?"

"Quite clearly." The young man handed his rifle to a tall man garbed much like himself in buckskin shirt and coonskin cap. "I see it with surprise. I think to myself, what does a calf do with a cowhide?" He drew a long hunting knife from his belt and handed it after the rifle. Dain gained a mounting respect for him. He was a cool cockerel.

The red-faced man sputtered, shaking his whip. "A calf, ye say? Ye call me a calf again?"

"If you insist."

"By—! What'll I do with the damned young scoundrel?"

"You might flog him," suggested the tall receiver of the weapons, blandly.

"That I'll do!" The bulky man shook his whip. "I'll flog ye out o' yere skin!"

"I doubt that."

"Ye call me a liar?"

"Now that you mention it, yes."

The whip whined through the air, but never finished its stroke. In lightning time it changed hands. The enraged man lay puffing on his back in the street, and the young romantic resumed his careless position against the signpost, cracking the lash experimentally. Dain's respect mounted higher. Here was no popinjay. This was a man of icy coolness and decisive action. This was a *man!*

The bystanders let out a shout of laughter. Laughing, they picked up the mortified fire-eater and carried him back into the tavern.

Dain said conversationally, "Well, Colonel, is this as far as you've got?"

The tall, buckskin-shirted man, returning the rifle and long hunting knife to their owner, wheeled sharply. "Bless Bess, it's you, Mr. Dain! How are you, suh? And you, ma'am." He bowed, eyes alight. "So you've caught up with me, eh? By Nelly, I've worritted about you. Knew you'd join me if you could, though. Knew you were of the right grit. Yes, this is as far's I've got. Had trouble getting a horse, back there in Little Rock. But I push on tomorrow."

He waved an arm. "Mr. Dain—ma'am—permit me to make known to you my young friend here, Boniface Eden. A hunter an' a fighter. Knows the country. Knows Texas. He'll be going on to the Alamo with us tomorrow."

"In a fashion, we've already met," said Dain. "At least, he's made himself known to Cleo." He returned Boniface Eden's cool bow. "You've got a good voice and a good right arm!"

The young hunter surveyed him up and down, eyes narrowed. "Is Amaryllis with you?" he demanded bluntly.

"She is. And her name is Cleo—or so she tells me."

"Is she your wife?"

"Uh—h'm? Wife? No." Queerly, Dain felt almost guiltily

embarrassed under the probing look of the clear, luminous eyes.

Boniface Eden drew his head erect. Deliberately, he stroked the haft of his belted knife. "I don't think I like you, Mr. Dain! I think I would like to kill you!" He bowed again to Cleo, stared bitterly at Dain, and wheeled and stalked noiselessly off on his moccasined feet.

Crockett coughed. "Very remarkable young man. I reckon you'd call him one o' these-yere idealists. Too bad—too bad. I wanted you to be friends. Don't take him too lightly, Mr. Dain. The boy's pretty consid'rable of a fighter, most partic'ly when—hem—there's a lady concerned. Lady's honor, y' know —that shape o' thing. Pity—great pity. We'll all be travelling together, from here on."

"In that case," Dain commented dryly, "maybe I'm the one who should be concerned about the lady!" He eyed Cleo critically. "You're just too damned pretty, that's what's wrong! Better get into man's clothes. Anyhow, something a little less fetching than what you're wearing now. It'd never do to have to kill that beautiful young man before he gets a chance to die for Texas, would it, Colonel?"

"No," Crockett agreed seriously. "We need every man. The latest news says that Santa Anna is marching up from San Luis Potosí with a pow'ful big Mexican army. We've got to push on quick, if we want to be in at the death."

"The death?" Dain echoed humorously. "You ring a somber note, Colonel!"

"The death of Santa Anna's tyrannous invasion, is what I mean," amended Crockett. "If I thought otherwise for a single minute, I'd certainly not let the lady go with us. Nor would you, suh, I'm sure."

"The lady is endowed with a mind of her own, and it appears to be made up," Dain confided. "I doubt if Santa Anna himself could keep her out of Texas!"

CHAPTER FIVE

THE MEXICAN ARMY OF CAVALRY AND marching infantry, with its heavy transports and artillery, moved northward across the desert toward the Rio Grande and rebellious Texas. Up ahead, surrounded by his staff officers and his hand-picked dragoon bodyguard, rode His Excellency, General Antonio López de Santa Anna, soldier, political adventurer extraordinary, and president-dictator of the Republic of Mexico.

Big and robust, possessed of piercing black eyes and a stout frame, His Excellency was of the right type to inspire awe and confidence in his peon troops. To most of them he was a demigod. To several of his more discriminating officers he was something more earthly and mundane.

It was as Brigadier General Rubio remarked to Colonel Duncaerlie, privately: Santa Anna really should have emulated Iturbide and proclaimed himself Emperor of Mexico, if only for the sake of consistency of behavior. "Not," amended the Brigadier hastily, "that I wish it. Heaven forbid! We want no more emperors in Mexico. But how natural it would seem to bend the knee and address him as 'Your Majesty!' And with what sublime grace, I suspect, he would accept it! But of course he is a very great man," he added cautiously, glancing at his brother officer.

Colonel Baltasar Duncaerlie nodded absently. They both were riding well behind Santa Anna's coterie of favorites, back in the dust of the column.

In his grave preoccupation, Colonel Duncaerlie looked much less Spanish than Scotch. He was remembering the days when he had fought alongside Santa Anna at Tampico in the war against Spain for independence. Those had been great days. Nobody could have foreseen then that an obscure officer like Antonio Santa Anna would rise from them and grasp the reins of a freed Mexico. But perhaps even then Santa Anna had carried the vast ambition secretly in his mind, while he shouted fiery words about freedom. In the light of events since those days, Duncaerlie could well believe that no series of political accidents could be blamed for Santa Anna's rise to power. Rather, that rise had come about as the result of a scheming brain—Santa Anna's brain.

Duncaerlie could concede that Santa Anna had displayed touches of genius here and there on the battlefield; what he condemned was the turning of that same genius toward equally sanguinary political intrigue. Of noble but impoverished family, Santa Anna had risen from cadet to lieutenant colonel in the Spanish army before he was thirty. By that time, too, he was also a friend of the Spanish field marshal and the viceroy. The friendship did not deter him from plotting against them both and going over to Iturbide's camp in the Mexican revolution against Spain. Luck favored him in this, the first of many bloody gambles. But after the Treaty of Córdoba and the triumph of the revolution, he had not been content when rewarded by Iturbide with only a full colonelcy. By the following year Iturbide had had himself proclaimed Emperor of Mexico, but in that same year the dissatisfied Santa Anna plotted and led the revolution of another malcontent. Emperor Iturbide finished up before a firing squad, regretting the meagerness of that colonelcy reward.

From then on, the fortunes of Santa Anna had risen and fallen in pace with the rapid changing of his allegiance from one party to another. Revolt was the sport of the day. Guerrero, Bustamente, many others—all came to know him in turn as friend and dangerous enemy. His turn-coat adventures were never actuated by any such intangibility as a fixed principle, and his consistent devotion to self-interest finally brought him his reward. He at last reached a springboard from which he leaped up into the presidency. From that eminence it was a relatively simple matter for a man of his attainments to kick Congress into submission and become supreme dictator of all Mexico and its provinces, as well as commander-in-chief of all its armed forces.

Yet, for all his shady intrigues and unscrupulous use of power, he was always convinced of his own rightness. Even his bitterest critics—and Duncaerlie was not bitter—admitted that his loud and stamping patriotism was not merely a pose. Santa Anna's fault lay in his concept of himself as the Great Patriot of Mexico, and in this conception Mexico became somewhat the shadow and Santa Anna the substance. A slur at Mexico thereby became an insult aimed directly at his august self, at his own splendid ego, and only indirectly at the honor and majesty of his country. Because of this, as well as for more subtle reasons, he was personally leading the Mexican army against the defiant province of Texas.

Duncaerlie's thoughts turned into another channel. He rose in his stirrups and saw that the long column was about to be slowed down again by a sandy river bed ahead that would bog the transports and gun carriages. He muttered impatiently, and Brigadier Rubio inquired concernedly, "You have worry?"

"For my daughter," admitted Duncaerlie.

"Ah. Are those Texians truly as rough and crude as I hear?"

"Truly. Ruffians and barbarians!"

"Ah!" The Brigadier had thought as much.

A humorless, one-sided man, Colonel Baltasar Duncaerlie was honest in his opinion of Texians. Although he had lived in Texas, he had never gained any intimacy or understanding with his neighbors there. That they were mostly Americans did not help toward building in him a liking for them. Their irreverence for established authority, their impatient informality, their careless, combative attitude toward life as a whole . . . everything about them grated upon his strict soul, and bore out the bitter opinion of Americans that his father, Ian Duncaerlie, had handed down to him.

Ian Duncaerlie had been a rigid and outspoken Tory in the American Revolution, to his cost. When things grew too hot for the King's men in the embattled colonies, he had found it necessary to flee to Canada, leaving a handsome estate behind him. There he waited for a year and a half for the expected defeat of "those damned rebels," only to learn finally of Washington's victory. When the British Crown politely rejected his claim for reimbursement for his property—lost to him, as he pointed out, because of his loyalty to his King—his disillusionment was complete, and his Scottish blood boiled. He shook the dust of British Canada from his feet and went to Mexico. There he married a Spanish lady and settled down for life, nursing an animosity for all Anglos. To his Mexican-born son, Baltasar, he repeatedly denounced British ingratitude, and to his last day he swore in Scottish-flavored Spanish at the North American rebels.

Baltasar Duncaerlie, obtaining an army commission, a Spanish wife, and a Texas land grant, moved up to Texas and became a *ranchero*. There, his wife presented him with a daughter, and died while he was arranging passage south for her, back to her warm, beloved Mexico City.

"To me it appears strange that you left Texas without bringing your daughter with you," commented the Brigadier.

"I had no other choice," replied Duncaerlie, stiffening at the implied criticism. By birth and training, fealty and manners, he was Mexican. In appearance and thought processes, he was Scottish. A long-jawed Scot with grave and intolerant eyes. "My daughter was not then in Texas when I left," he added reservedly.

He had fought for Mexico against Spain, and served with Santa Anna at Tampico. A colonelcy had been his reward, too, but unlike Santa Anna, he had been content with it. He had not fought for rewards, but for Mexico. After the revolution he had gone back to his Texas ranch as a retired officer.

There he had raised horses, cattle, and his daughter, until called back into service during the Long Filibuster, again during the Fredonian Revolt, and finally into permanent service after Mexico closed the Texas frontiers against further American immigration. He had been placed on duty at the port of Anáhuac at the head of Galveston Bay, under the notorious John Bradburn, renegade American soldier of fortune serving in the Mexican army.

Bradburn, hard and arrogant, took with a heavy hand his authority as collector of customs. By temperament he was as little suited to diplomacy as was Duncaerlie. The Texian colonists, roughly humorous, fiercely independent, had a fixed idea that the earth belonged to those who gave it value, and by tradition they abhorred anything that smacked of unfair taxation—or any kind of taxation, if it came to that. They resented Mexican military garrisons and Mexican law by proclamation. Their resentment took the form of playing practical jokes upon garrison and port commanders, to which Bradburn and Duncaerlie were peculiarly vulnerable.

Things went from bad to worse at Anáhuac. Soon, armed clashes flared up. Bradburn, more overbearing than ever, arrested several prominent colonists. Then he and Duncaerlie found themselves and their Mexican soldiery surrounded in the Anáhuac fort by a mob of belligerent Texians, and there was a battle. In the end, the fort fell, the prisoners were freed, most of the Mexican garrison got to schooners and put out to sea, and Bradburn and Duncaerlie had to escape in disguise to Mexico. The aroused Texians had showed their teeth.

The indignity of that forced flight rankled in Duncaerlie. To his mind, the Texian colonists were interlopers on Mexican soil, originally permitted to enter and settle the country by the grace and blunder of past Spanish and Mexican governments. He saw them as ungrateful guests, blackguardly predators who, having received Mexico's hospitality, now sought to repay it by robbing her of her northern province. As a Mexican patriot he bedamned the Texian rebels. As the son of his embittered father, he expected nothing better from Anglo-Americans. As a soldier of Mexico, he was ready and willing to do his duty and help put down the uprising.

"Your daughter was not then in Texas?" inquired the Brigadier, elevating his eyebrows. "That appears strange."

Duncaerlie compressed his lips. Stiff and reserved, a man of few friends, he was known for his reticence. But he could not avoid, now, the giving of brief explanation. Besides, he wished to make use of the Brigadier's superior authority, and elicit a favor.

"My daughter had a whim for education," he said. "Many better class colonists of Texas send their children north to school. She desired that same for herself. It was not of my wish, but I allowed her to have her way. A daughter, *señor*, can be most persuasive. She was in the United States when the trouble occurred at Anáhuac. Since, she has returned to my home in Texas—also, I may say, not to my wish."

"Is she not safe in your house, although in Texas?"

"In my house, yes. But when we began this march, His Excellency inquired of me if I could use my Texas connections to our advantage. It seems that a force of rebels and volunteers is gathering at the town of Goliad. His Excellency wished to discover their strength and their plans, if possible." Duncaerlie blinked rapidly, a habit of his when embarrassed. "So I sent a message to my daughter, suggesting that she go quietly to Goliad and there make use of her perceptions."

"To spy?"

"I did not think of it so, at the time. Since, I have thought of it so. And I have worry for her. Much worry."

"The news, then, is bad?"

"Worse than bad," replied Duncaerlie. "There is no news. No word from her. No messenger. Such a silence brings fear to me."

"It has implications," agreed the Brigadier. "Were I the father of a daughter in such unknown peril, it would be my desire to learn of her fate and perhaps to save her."

"That," said Duncaerlie quietly, "is my desire. Will you speak to His Excellency for me? Our army marches fast, but slowly for me. With the leave of His Excellency, I would ride on alone much faster."

The Brigadier pursed his mouth. "Such a thing has danger. Many Texians, I presume, know you by sight?"

"Many." It was not necessary, in Duncaerlie's opinion, to add that he was known as one of the two "renegades of Anáhuac." To the Texians, prone to judge men by their appearances, he was not a Mexican, but another Bradburn, a traitor to his own race. Any Texian would consider it a constructive day's work to put a bullet into him.

"It has danger," repeated the Brigadier. "Yet, if your unfortunate daughter is in Texian hands—*que lástima!* It is to be dreaded what could befall her, when those rebels see our army sweeping through the country. I feel for you."

"*Gracias.* Then you will speak to His Excellency on this matter? I will shed my uniform, of course, before entering Texas."

"If you wish it, I shall obtain leave for you. Now?"

"If you are pleased to do so."

The Brigadier returned at an easy lope from his audience with the Commander, and reined in alongside Duncaerlie. "You have leave. It is the order of His Excellency that you obtain such information of the enemy as may be possible, while attending to the search of your daughter. Comprehend?"

"Comprehend. I start at once."

"And you will arrange to communicate with His Excellency by the time our army reaches San Antonio de Béxar."

"San Antonio. Yes."

"Fortune attend you, Colonel."

"And you, General."

The narrow trail through the cane-brake was like a tunnel, for the tall and slender reeds arched their tops over it, forming a bowered avenue into which the filtered sunlight shone greenly. The little party rode at a walk along it in single file.

Now they were seven. The persuasive Davy Crockett had picked up three more volunteers for Texas—one in Natchitoches; and two in the buffalo plains below Nacogdoches. With a penchant for succinct nomenclature, Crockett had conferred upon them nicknames which they accepted. Each had his own reasons for desiring anonymity. Markedly dissimilar, and from widely different backgrounds, they observed a scrupulous lack of curiosity in each other, to which the rest of the party subscribed.

The Natchitoches recruit, a lanky individual in shabby genteel attire, flaunting a big white Vicksburger hat that was badly soiled, juggled absently with three silver thimbles and a dried pea as he rode along. A picayune gambler, a blackleg from the Mississippi, he spoke not of whatever pressing necessity it had been that had caused him to quit a muddied life along the muddy old river. He was amiable and thoughtful, and invariably polite. He had merely given a wry smile when christened Thimblerig by Crockett, and gone on playing with his thimbles.

Of the two picked up on the buffalo plains, one was a rawboned, elderly man, dressed in a sailor's jacket, with a tarred round hat on his head. His whiskers covered most of his face, and his hair was long and black, tied up in a queue. He had a deep scar running down from forehead to nose, and more scars on his arms and broken-knuckled hands. Crockett named him the Pirate—a jocular jibe that developed indications of being a true shaft when the tough old seadog made casual mention of Jean Lafitte and the buccaneer stronghold of Campeche.

The other, not as dark of skin as the Pirate, was obviously of a different race. He was clad in dirty cotton shirt and pantaloons, but his feet were bare and his head was shaved. Stocky and small, compactly built, agile of movement, he ap-

peared young until closer study of his finely lined face posed
a question as to his years. He spoke rarely, and then only in
stripped economy of words, in a murmuring voice without
tone or inflection. Occasionally, listening to the talk of the
others, a flickering trace of dry amusement touched his thin,
flat lips. For want of better knowledge of him, they called
him the Indian and let it go at that.

As the sun went westward, the light in the reed-arched
trail dimmed and slowly lost its greenish tinge. Although they
knew that it must still be daylight in the open country, it was
hard for the seven travellers to believe so, and when they got
through the thick cane-brake it was like coming into another
day. They came out onto grassed prairies, rolling, dotted with
widely scattered groves of cottonwoods. When they topped
the first rise they could see bands of horses grazing in the distance. Wild turkeys burst from the groves as they passed, and
they sighted deer bounding soundlessly off to safety.

"What a country, by Nelly, what a country!" Crockett kept
exclaiming. In his hunter's rapture he was like a boy running
a fever over his first rabbit. "Why, it's—it's a land for the
gods, I tell you! I'll certainly stay here!"

He was so worked up that, when they called a halt to rest
their horses, he unpacked the fiddle that he had brought
along with him from Tennessee, and played until ready to
push on again. Next to his rifle, the fiddle was his greatest
treasure.

They hoped to find a stream before sundown, and there
make camp, but sunset found them still in their saddles. Boniface Eden, who had never before ridden this deeply into
Texas, said that he had heard mention of a ranch somewhere
in these parts, and that perhaps they could come upon it and
find hospitality for the night. He was proven right about the
existence of such a place, at least, when, just before dark,
they rode over a low range of hills and looked down at what
appeared to be a small settlement in a shallow valley.

It was park-like, the valley; a pleasant and peaceful sur-

prise of low, thick-topped trees, fenced fields, and long meadows spread out farther up and down the valley. The travellers straightened up, sighed their deep satisfaction at the
promise before them, and followed a descending path. Even
the tired horses pricked ears and raised their drooping heads.

"I do declare, I think those are fruit trees," Crockett mar-
velled, as they drew nearer. "Apple or peach, you reckon?"

"Peach?" murmured Thimblerig. He passed the back of a
hand across his mouth. "Let it be peach, I pray. Peach
brandy! But even hard cider . . . Eh, Mr. Dain?"

"If stored in a cool cellar. And served in large stone mugs.
With cigars. But first, of course, the roast fowl, the corn and
sweet potatoes, the——"

"Mr. Dain—*please!*"

On closer inspection the fences proved to be in bad repair,
and the fields were weed-grown and unplowed, although it
was past planting time. What had seemed a settlement became one establishment: a large ranch house built with two
wings so as to enclose a patio, a stone and mud wall com-
pleting the square, the outbuildings off to one side of it. The
whole style of the place was Spanish, the *hacienda* of some
wealthy colonist. The trees, both apple and peach, had been
planted on the south side, and there were more planted inside
the patio. No light shone anywhere, and nobody came out to
greet or challenge the party.

Boniface Eden rode up to the gate of the patio and looked
in. "How lovely!" he cried in his unaffected way. "Look,
Amaryllis! When the moon comes up—and it will be up soon
—how beautiful this will be!"

He persisted in calling her Amaryllis, and when he spoke
the name the aggregation of soft syllables made melody. His
attitude toward her had been variously colored by changing
hues of perspective, corresponding to the struggle of his emotions, interesting to watch from Dain's viewpoint.

The stern pain of disillusionment, occasioned by his shocked
conception of the relations between Dain and Cleo, had at

first chilled the young hunter to stony formality. From this he had descended to a less lofty pinnacle, from which he sent out dark references about scoundrels who preyed upon innocent girls. Thence to an exquisite role of gentle brotherliness toward Cleo, who frankly encouraged him to come farther down to earth. Having successfully guided him down through an emotional spectrum, Cleo now enjoyed the experience of having a buckskinned young knight for her devoted attendant and scrupulous protector.

It was not possible to know whether Boniface Eden had revised his belief that Cleo was an angel wronged. Being all that he was, in his hunger for perfection he erased from actuality all flaws not visible. By that process, Cleo was flawless, a dream princess. She was Amaryllis, the ideal. Dain was the ravening dragon, to be guardfully watched at all times, and lanced to death if necessary. The fact that the princess indicated no desire whatever for the dragon's ears was beside the point.

Obediently, Cleo gazed with Boniface into the patio, and agreed that it was beautiful. In the twilight the fruit trees were rounded and friendly, standing modestly back from the stone-flagged walks that invited entrance into the patio. There were oval and diamond designs of flower beds, and from a grotto of rocks sounded the tinkling splash of a spring, feeding a rock-banked pool overhung by willows. Still, Cleo would have preferred a melon patch, or something equally useful.

The rest pushed by and entered the patio, leaving their horses outside. Their footsteps clattered on the flagstones, disturbing the hush, and they trod more quietly, even the Pirate taking to the grass, which was high and old. Like the fences and the fields, the patio underwent a change when viewed at close quarters. The trees were ragged, the flagstones uneven and broken, the flower beds nothing more than mounds of earth overgrown with dead weeds. The place wore the air of a shabby and dissolute old dowager, fallen from grandeur and sinking into degeneration behind walls.

"Good-bye, peach brandy!" sighed Thimblerig. "Farewell, hard cider—in a cool cellar, served in large stone mugs. With cigars. *After* the roast fowl and . . . What else was it, Mr. Dain?"

"We'll forget that. This place has gone to hell." Dain glanced at Boniface Eden. "When the moon comes up, how beautiful this will be!" Hunger and thirst and tiredness made him caustic. "So go your dreams, dreamer! Pirate, kick on that door, will you? Damned place seems dead, but maybe we can raise the ghost of the manor."

The double doors of the main entrance were weathered grey, the massive panels carved. Like the columns and casings of the high Spanish windows, which were shuttered, the doors had evidently been brought up from Old Mexico. The Pirate brushed his wiry whiskers on the doors, peering closely at them, and he grunted, finding San Miguel and minor saints depicted upon them. He kicked San Miguel in the shins.

The boom of the Pirate's foot resounded in echoes and died away inside the house. The Pirate grunted again, kicked again, and got the same barren results. He drew his huge flintlock navy pistol and hammered with the butt. Dain and Crockett made the rounds of the windows and found them all shuttered and locked on the inside. There was a second story on the main wing, and some of its windows were un-shuttered, but to climb up there presented a problem which they were not in the mood to tackle.

"Locked up and deserted—nary a soul to home," Crockett condemned the place. "Place is like a burying-ground. Spooky. Kindly stop that infernal pounding, Pirate. It's—it's sacrilegious or something, burn my boots if 'tisn't! Let's try the outbuildings."

They left the patio. Dain bumped into the Indian in the dark. The Indian had turned to look back at the house. He said musingly, "Empty? No. No, not empty."

Dain scanned the upper windows. "What did you *see?*"

"Nothing."

"Then why d'you say it's not empty?"

The Indian did not answer. His lips twitched a faint derision and he turned and followed the others. Dain experienced an inordinate irritation at the man.

They found a granary shed whose door was amenable to force, but scamperings and thin squeals inside decided them against it as a shelter. It was alive with rats. As if he had already known what the decision would be, the Indian was gathering wood and building a fire outside, and it was there where they finally settled their camp for the night. While the rest set to work getting a meal ready from their scanty supplies, Dain and Crockett watered the horses at the patio pool and staked them out.

Later, Crockett wandered off and returned with a discovery. "There's another spring yonder over on the west side," he reported. "They've built a pen around it, but the gate's down. It's a water pen. There's fresh horse tracks there."

Boniface Eden looked up from the fire. "All those bands of horses we saw today—they weren't wild horses, then. That is, they haven't always been wild. They belong to this ranch, and some of them still come in to water at night. It's a pity the *ranchero* isn't here. We could buy fresh horses from him. Ours are playing out."

Dain cocked a sardonic eye at the painfully honest young hunter, and then at Crockett. "How do the ethics of the matter strike you, Colonel?" he queried.

Crockett donned the judicious pose that must have stood him in good stead during his earlier days as a Tennessee county magistrate. "If those horses belong to a good Texian, he'd be only too glad to let us have what we need, seeing we're—ah—embarked upon the cause for Texas," he proclaimed. "I take that to be self-evident, conclusive and—hem—irrefutable."

"Point one for the claimants, Colonel!"

"On the other hand, we must as honest men consider the opposite aspect of the case," Crockett debated. "If he's not a

good Texian, what is he? Why, he's either a Mexican or a
blackleg—in which case, to hell with him! Gentlemen, it's
my considered opinion that we're entitled to take what horses
we need. Case closed! Question now before us—how the blink
do we catch 'em?"

Thimblerig, who on occasion displayed rare talents, had an
answer to that. Rig a trap at the water pen, with a long rope
tied to the gate. When the horses came in for water, jerk the
gate shut with the rope. "I've—uh—seen it done," he said
modestly. "Very simple. Just keep quiet till they come in. If
they get wind of us, they'll be off."

Having satisfactorily disposed of ethics and settled upon
practice, they finished eating. Thimblerig, elected captain of
the horse trap, chose Boniface for his helper and both set off
with all the ropes available. The moon came up like a new
silver dollar, and the rest of the party spread out their blan-
kets and stretched out to listen for Thimblerig's success as a
horse thief. Everybody agreed that Thimblerig was a valuable
member of the party—except Dain, who privately bedamned
the gambler for bringing up the subject of peach brandy.

From thinking about peach brandy, it was not a long step
to consideration of the possibility of there being some, after
all, in the cellar of the locked house. The fact that the house
was so strongly locked presumed the premise of there being
something in it worth locking up. The longer Dain entertained the thought, the larger grew the possibility. Not that
he contemplated burglary, exactly, but it did seem a pity to
let good peach brandy lie wasting in an abandoned cellar.

He moved restlessly and cursed himself for allowing such
a virtueless temptation to haunt him, but the old brooding
query was nagging at him again tonight. In the end he rose
from his blanket and drifted over to take another look at the
house.

For some time he stood in the gateway, inspecting the
patio. He thought of Boniface Eden's reaction to his first sight
of it, and smiled with little humor. That high-minded young

idealist had a lot of bruises coming to him before he would learn to mistrust his romantic wings. Lighted by the moon, the patio was more than ever a broken promise of beauty, and the shuttered house looked sad and desolate. He thought it likely that this was a casualty of the Texas rebellion. A colonist empire was in revolt, and its effects were far reaching.

His mind returned impatiently to the lure that had drawn him here, and he shook his head at himself. "I wonder," he muttered, "if I'm a drunkard?"

"No," spoke a muted, toneless voice, "you are not a drunkard."

He whirled and met the dark eyes of the Indian, standing behind him. The Indian had his arms folded, and his eyes were remote and gently quizzical. In some manner the night and the moonlight placed upon him a mantle of age, and with it he had donned a dignity that was conscious and a little mocking.

"You are not a drunkard," he repeated. "Not yet. But you could become one, if you persist. The pity of it is, that road is blind. Pleasant, yes, but it leads nowhere. The ancients explored it thoroughly, many centuries ago, but they discovered nothing of lasting value or reality along it."

"Interesting," Dain commented. He was taken aback by this metamorphosis in the swarthy little man, and annoyed by what he felt was cool presumption and insolence. "You speak from experience, no doubt?" he added.

The Indian twitched his lips. "I believe I can say that I do, yes." He gave an impression of acting a part; of not only acting it, but of gently clowning with it. "To a very limited degree, Mr. Dain, you are on the same dark road that I travelled long ago. I could help you, possibly, but we have such a very short distance to go now that it would be wasted effort."

"What d'you mean?"

"I mean, Mr. Dain, that our road ends here in Texas. Of our party of seven, not one will escape death in Texas!"

"You're still speaking from experience, of course?" Dain inquired dryly, and only then did it occur to him that the Indian was using the speech of an educated man.

Again the amused twitch of the thin lips. "Let us call it, rather, the reflection of experience. Isn't the future, after all, merely a reflection of the past? More—it is basically a projection, a continuation of what has already happened over and over again. It is a mathematical certainty that a cause must have an effect, and that the nature of the effect was predestined by the cause. That is elemental. Therefore, all that has happened in the past could not have happened in any other way. And so, the future being merely an extension of the past, what is yet to happen, *must* happen."

Dain blinked, caught the elaborate proposition by the tail, and hauled it in for inspection. Somewhere in the broad logic he felt that there had to be a specious flaw, but at the moment he couldn't place his finger on it. He half suspected the man of laughing at him, of building the extraordinary thesis for entertainment. "According to that," he countered, "prophesy should be possible. Do you by any chance call yourself an occultist?"

The Indian flicked a disdainful finger. "Always this insistence upon rigid words, this slavery to names, this attempt to pin down every element and object with a conjugation of letters from an alphabet!" he murmured painedly. "Occultist! You speak that one word, and at once it conjures up in your mind the picture of an idolatrous figure garbed in sorcerer's cap and gown, mumbling incantations in the night—a sort of counterfeit Cagliostro. No, no—connect me not with the weird brethren of demonology and black magic. If you must name me, call me a mathematician. I have had other names in other parts of the world, but that one will do here."

It was disconcerting to be bombarded with such a fluent barrage of verbal fireworks by a man who, up until now, had voiced himself in only short gutturals and sibilants. Dain had some difficulty in adjusting himself to the surprising meta-morphosis. "You've done considerable travelling, then?" was all he could find to say for the moment.

"A long time ago I came from what you probably call the Far East," explained the Indian calmly. "Yes, I have travelled —physically and spiritually. It has been a pilgrimage, a seek-ing along a dark road to find myself. Some people believe in a Hereafter of golden temples, some in Mahomet's Paradise or in Nirvana, and some in the Inner Circle of the Unknown. I found my faith in all of them. They are all one. I found that I had lived many lives, and that life itself is an illusion—an illusion concocted of all the possible and various experiences that can befall man. Only after we have suffered or enjoyed every experience, is the illusion broken. Then we go to—what shall we call it? Heaven? Paradise? Nirvana? The Inner Circle? The name we try to pin to it does not matter. It is all one and the same place."

Where, during the journey through the cane-brake country, the Indian had been a self-effacing nonentity, now he sud-denly loomed as a positive and dominant personality. And where, a moment ago, his manner had been tinged with mock-ing humor, now it was gravely canonical. His dark eyes grew luminous and piercing. He had not altered his pose, still stood with folded arms, but he seemed bigger, taller, an imposing figure. His round, shaved head and bare feet did not detract from his dignity. They added to it a patriarchal fittingness.

"I have crowded experiences into this life," he said. "I have been priest and giver, and thief and murderer. The long road is nearly done. My escape from the illusion is close at hand, and I am eager to go. But one last experience remains to me. I must die by violence in a holy place, my body to be burned, my bones never buried. It shall happen in a land of two languages, and of revolt and war. And I must go there in a company of seven, who shall perish in that same land."

He brought his luminous eyes to bear upon Dain's face,

and he smiled. "The Alamo, my friend, was a church before it was a fortress!"

Dain shook off a spell that had crept upon him. The man was a crazy fanatic, a victim of self-hallucinations. He had dreamed too much, perhaps over an opium pipe. Illusion of life and many lives—the Inner Circle—death at the Alamo and a company of seven . . . Balderdash!

"I'll take peach brandy!" he growled, and moved on into the patio, angry at himself for having listened so long to the fellow.

The Indian called softly after him, the mocking humor back in his voice, "Try the end window of the east wing—and may good luck guide thy search!"

CHAPTER SIX

Purposely and perversely, Dain tried all the lower windows before following the Indian's advice. Their shutters were tight. But when he finally got around to the end window of the east wing, he found that its shutters had warped a little and did not come together, leaving a crack that invited the insertion of a knife blade.

"So that son of India was prowling around here ahead of me, was he?" he muttered, and drew his knife.

The shutters were fastened on the inside with a wooden bar. He located the bar through the crack with his knife, and thrust upward. With some trouble, he managed to lift it up out of its slots. It fell, clattering, and he swung open the shutters. The glassed window inside presented no problem at all. He broke out a pane, and found the brass bolt and released it.

From across the valley the sound of a slammed gate reached him, followed by terrified squeals and stampings of horses. Thimblerig was making good on his horse trap. A crash of a broken fence and pounding hoofs then went far toward cancelling the gambler's triumph. Some of the horses were promptly breaking out again. Dain grinned and climbed on through the window.

It was very dark here inside the house, no moonlight penetrating except through the window by which he had entered. He felt his way around and located a candlestick, almost knocking it off a table, and he spent a moment making a light from his flintbox. The candlestick was triple-branched, a graceful article of carved and polished lignum vitae, with brass cups fitted into the sconces and each cup holding a finely moulded candle. The candles lighted, he looked about the room.

The ceiling was low, the rafters massive, and the walls were austerely bare except for a *santo* niche near the fireplace. Conforming to Spanish taste, there were few pieces of furniture, but these were heavily built. A pair of long wooden chests, leather topped, the side panels carved with a simple diamond design, stood by the low table and served as seats. Goatskin rugs were on the floor, and a bench, also leather topped and carved, was before the fireplace. A tall American clock stood silent and incongruous in one corner, darkly varnished and ornamented with spindly towers that stuck up above its face like ears cocked in perpetual astonishment.

For the country, this was a house of comparative wealth, even of luxury, Dain judged. Only the very wealthiest of colonists could afford to import an American clock, and then think so little of it as to put it in a corner of what appeared to be a rarely used guest room. Such extravagance connoted a *ranchero*, a lucky possessor of one of the great land grants, or a moneyed *empresario*—a land speculator. It also offered reasonable grounds for expecting a well-stocked cellar. Dain picked up the lighted candlestick and found the door.

In half an hour of diligent searching he learned his way around the house, became familiar with the diamond design which he found most of the furniture wearing, and, in abstract fashion, admired the craftsmanship that had gone into the building of the house and its effects. But his approval cooled when he was forced to the conclusion that the establishment lacked a cellar. It was possible, he mused, that such refinements had not yet been introduced into Spanish-Texian architecture.

"But they must have *some* place for the stuff," he muttered. "Upstairs? Well, Crockett claims the dons do everything backward. . . ."

He pursued his search to the upper floor. This part of the house was small, little more than an apartment built onto the main wing, and the American influence was more in evidence here. He entered a room furnished with a glass-fronted bookcase and desk, a mahogany-framed mirror, and even a couple of rush-bottomed chairs. Many of the books in the case, he noticed, had English titles. But the only bottle in sight was a Bristol potpourri flagon, so he passed on.

A recurrence of confused noises rose outside from across the valley, and he thought he heard his own name being called, but the closed house muffled the sounds. Floor boards creaked under his feet, and those outside sounds were wiped out. He began to regret breaking into this house. The search had tended to shift his mind from its brooding plane, and his desire for brandy had become blunted, so now the act smacked of sneak thievery. It jabbed at his self-respect to see himself in the role of crib-cracker, prowling through a strange house in the dead of night, with no more excuse for it than a thirst. He decided to quit the house. But he was standing before another door; to look into or forgo one more room would neither heighten nor mitigate the offense. He opened the door.

The candlelight fanned into the room, and he stopped short on the threshold, embarrassed for an instant and half expecting a feminine scream. He grinned at his automatic reaction to the sight of a lady's bed chamber. "Maybe I'm something of a gentleman, after all!" he muttered. "It's an encouraging sign."

A four-poster bed, its heavy curtains drawn partly back, cast shadows over the floor and to the top of the wall beyond it. Garments hung in an open wardrobe, and a lacquered table at the foot of the bed held a miscellany of feminine articles. The windows, unshuttered, overlooked the patio and the valley. Dain set the candlestick down on the floor, and stepped toward the window to see if he could observe in the moonlight what the rest of the party was doing.

A tiny rustle of movement snapped him motionless, one foot before the other, and he stood listening. It came again, and he located it. He kept his eyes fixed on the high head of the bed, while his right hand slid under his coat, and he thought, "So that damned Indian *did* see something!"

The girl behind the bed was so terrified that she could not move or speak. For what had seemed hour after hour, she had listened to the progress of the prowler in the house, knowing that at last he must reach and enter this room where she waited alone. The quiet opening of the door had been her cue to shoot, but her hands were too cold and shaking to obey.

Through the parted canopy curtains she had full sight of him—the tall prowler. His face was dark and scarred, and, the candlelight now behind and below him, he looked gigantic and his shadow covered half the room. His eyes, level and deep-set under the slanted brim of a wide hat, were twin green lights that stared unblinkingly in her direction.

For all the bad days that she had been here alone in this dead house, this had lurked in the background of her thoughts as a haunting possibility. The coldness of her hands spread all over her. And then a calm desperation came to her, and she forced herself to speak.

"I'll shoot!" she said. Her voice was strong. "I'll shoot if you come any closer!"

Oddly, Dain's sensation upon hearing that feminine voice was one of acute embarrassment. That the unseen speaker was implying that she had a loaded gun, and would use it on him, was only a side circumstance. To be caught in the act of entering a lady's private chamber, by the occupant, like a petty thug or worse—that was the real and rotten core of the situation. It was degrading. He was horribly ashamed of himself.

"I beg your pardon!" he mumbled, and backed hastily toward the door. Such ordinary and formal apology sounded too slight, to his own ears, as compared with the crime. "I mean—I'm really sorry. Mistake. I had no intention . . ."

One of his backing heels kicked the candlestick on the floor and knocked it over. The candles spilled from the little brass cups. They rolled and went out, while he stooped and snatched at them.

Over the head of the bed, the girl's pistol flashed in the darkness. The report rang very loudly through the house, and Dain ducked and stepped on one of the candles. His foot shot out from under him and he sat down hard on the overturned candlestick. He swore.

The pistol clicked. Dain got up hurriedly off the candlestick, pained and mad. Damn the female! Was she getting ready to take another shot at him? "Hey, hold off, there!" he barked, and dodged low around the foot of the bed.

The girl sprang out ahead of him. He got a sight of her in the moonlight near the window, a white-gowned figure clutching a big pistol. She used both hands to point the pistol at him, and he took a long, low dive and clamped an arm around her. Both crashed into the tall wardrobe, bringing down a soft mass of garments upon them, and for the next minute Dain had an impression that every entangling garment contained a fighting, scratching, kicking girl. It seemed hardly credible that just one girl could deal him punishment from so many different directions.

A flickering light shone into the room. "Dain! Who's that? What are you doing?" It was Cleo, her voice near to screaming pitch, a lighted pine knot in her hand. "Dain! Stop it!"

Only too glad to, Dain shook clear and retreated to the bed. "Watch out for that crazy female—she's got a gun lying around somewhere! Lord!" He felt his face, keeping a wary eye on the heaving pile of dresses. "She pretty near ruined me!"

The feline suggestion was strong in the way Cleo glided swiftly up to him. "What were you doing?" she demanded.

"H'm? Oh—just looking around the house."

"What were you doing with *her*?" She was actually glaring at him.

"Don't be a fool!" he said roughly. "I was trying to keep her from killing me." He heard the others shouting around the house. They hadn't yet discovered the open window. "Shut that door. We don't want . . ."

He stopped talking, abruptly. The girl had disengaged herself and was on her feet, a slim young girl with face flushed and fair hair dishevelled over her shoulders. Her high young breasts rose and fell with her hard breathing, and she was very angry and very beautiful. She was such a wondrous sight, so splendidly vivid in her beauty and her blazing anger, that Dain could only stare.

And then the whole vision of her took hold of him, and his throat ached strangely, and suddenly he was almost drunk with the wanting of her. Curiously, a corner of his mind brought forward the recollection of how Boniface had reacted to his first sight of Cleo; now he understood how a man of strong impulses could be affected like that, on the turn of a minute.

He watched her snatch up one of the fallen dresses and wrap it around herself swiftly, and he realized that she had been garbed only in a night dress. For some reason his sense of shame left him then. He was glad, desperately glad, that he had broken into this house. He felt his chest pounding, and he had to force himself to speak in an even tone.

"I'm sorry," he said. "Why didn't you scream, or something, when I opened your door?" The presence of Cleo irritated him now, and although he didn't look her way, he knew that she was watching his face.

The girl brushed tumbled hair from her forehead with quick, trembling fingers. Her eyes were stormy, the grey-blue of a cloudy sky. She had to wait to catch her breath. Cleo's presence had obviously quieted her fear, and wrath alone was coming into play. Even with the dress wrapped haphazardly around herself, she succeeded in donning icy dignity. "What right have you here?" she demanded.

Dain picked up the candles and relighted them from the pine knot. "Not a right in the world," he admitted. "The truth is, I was looking for—er—some medicine."

"Who's in need of it?" Cleo snapped skeptically.

"I am!"

The others could be heard tramping downstairs inside the house, still calling. Dain bowed formally. "My name is Dain. This is Miss Cleo. We're of the party you hear downstairs. It so happens that we're travelling to San Antonio, and made camp on your property for the night. We thought that the owners must be absent, when nobody answered our knocking. Accept my apologies, please."

He was a little bewildered by the girl's reception of his words. Something that he had said had brought about a change in her. Her expression altered and reflected a reversal of thought and mood. She regarded him strangely, dubiously. The doubt faded. Her flush returned in full color, and suddenly she was smiling at him, and it was like unexpected sunlight. Dain caught his breath, held onto his poise, and smiled back at her. But he couldn't wholly control his eyes; didn't wholly try, and he knew that she could read them well enough. Yet she smiled on at him, her gaze held by his, and he hoped enormously that she might be discovering him a little to her liking.

"You're going to San Antonio?" she exclaimed relievedly. "Then you must be volunteers for Travis! I—I thought you were bandits when I heard some of you trapping our horses. You see, I've been all alone here for nearly two weeks, and I've been expecting . . . I mean, I was afraid. I'd been to New Orleans. When I came back home I found the house locked up, and all our *Tejican* servants and *vaqueros* were gone."

"Your what?"

"Our *Tejicans*—Texas Mexicans. I thought they'd be back

soon, so I dismissed the carriage and escort that I had hired to bring me from Anáhuac. Then I found a message waiting here from—from a member of my family, requiring me to journey on to Goliad. But I've had no way to travel. Our horses have become very wild, and I couldn't catch one. Our *vaqueros* must have left a long time ago."

The rest of the party was coming upstairs. Dain called through the closed door, "Everything's all right. We'll join you outside in a few minutes. We've—hem—just met the lady of the house!" He turned back to the girl. "Do you want us to take a message from you and see that it reaches Goliad?" He was very polite now, on his best behavior. He was thinking: Lord, she's a lovely thing! God bless Texas!

Her brows creased faintly. "I am afraid a message would hardly do," she said slowly. "But if you have succeeded in catching any of our horses, I would very much like to go with you—" Her flush heightened at his involuntary look. "With your party, if they are agreeable, of course. As far as Gonzales. From there I'm sure I can arrange a conveyance to Goliad. Would you mind?"

Cleo, her eyes grown hard and challenging, asked bluntly, "Why didn't you answer us when we knocked on your door?"

Their eyes met, clashed, and Cleo's challenge brought a swift response. "I have already said that I thought you were bandits."

"You said you thought we were bandits because we helped ourselves to your horses. We were here an hour or more, before that. We knocked on the door like honest folks. We camped and cooked out there. You must have seen us from your window. Did we look and act like bandits then?"

"Yes—some of you!"

"Didn't you see me among them?"

"Yes—and I was reminded that this country has sometimes been a refuge for bandit women as well as men!"

Dark cat and fair cat, claws unsheathed. Such quick

animosity between the two girls placed Dain in the role of peacemaker. He sent Cleo a look of rebuke, and turned to the girl. Meeting the girl's eyes again, he smiled and held her gaze until the storm warnings subsided and she looked away.

"We'll be very happy to escort you to Gonzales," he told her, speaking the truth for himself, if not for Cleo. "You'll be a welcome addition to our party, believe me. And please do accept my apologies for breaking into your house. I trust I didn't hurt you?"

The corners of her mouth hinted of laughter. She was adorable. "I trust I didn't hurt *you!* But I fear I did, a little. When you kicked over the candles, I thought—I was sure . . ."

"You needn't have," Cleo broke in, her tone deliberate. She picked up a silver comb from the lacquered table, and examined it critically at arm's length. Just by a tilt of her dark head and a lift of one shoulder, she contrived a look of voluptuousness that fitted her well. "Dain, I like silver combs," she purred sweetly. "They look so nice in dark hair. The next time you buy me some clothes, get me a set, will you?"

Dain coughed. "I think we'd better go." He bowed to the girl. "Until morning. By the way, I don't think you mentioned your name."

The girl hesitated. Her glance ran between them, and her cool dignity returned. "Suela Caerlie."

Going downstairs, Dain repeated the name. "Suela Caerlie." He scowled down at Cleo beside him. "Pretty name."

"Yes." She nodded. "I wonder why she has other initials on her silver combs? They're engraved 'C.D.'"

"What're you hinting at?"

"Nothing. Nothing at all. She's a lady. I'm not. It wouldn't be seemly for the likes of me to talk against her, would it?" She stopped and faced him. "You fool!" she hissed. "You blind fool! You—you *man!* Can't you see she's hiding some-thing?"

The armed men of Gonzales cheered in a party of eight riders, and, because they were surprised and glad to observe that two of the riders were women—young, Anglo-American, and very kind to the eyes—they made the cheers extra long and loud.

The sprawling little Texas town had become a general rendezvous for bands of volunteers, many of them newly arrived from beyond the Sabine frontier. They were drifting in, singly and in groups, all highly individualistic, comba-tive, and determined to do as they pleased. Hadn't they come hundreds of miles to make Texas free? And wasn't personal liberty the main pillar of a free country? Well, then!

News travelled slowly over the pony trails and vast dis-tances. Rumors grew fast. Nobody knew of any master plan of campaign, of whether it was to be offensive or defensive, nor the precise locations of the main Texas forces. Every-body knew how the war should be conducted, most of the theories embracing a smashing invasion of Old Mexico, not to be halted until Mexico City capitulated and Santa Anna met a tyrant's end, *à la* Julius Caesar.

Tomorrow, perhaps, Sam Houston or somebody would come and lead them to battle and victory. No hurry, though. Everybody knew that Mexicans took a year to march a month. In the meantime the convivial swashbucklers of Gon-zales enjoyed clean air, lowered the whiskey supplies, shot for wagers, and turned out to cheer in all newcomers.

"Fine fellows!" Crockett approved heartily, taking it upon himself to bow in all directions for his party. "The old fightin' stock. And"—he added a bow toward the two girls— "they very plainly know beauty when they see it!"

"And fame," Dain appended, for the sake of the Ten-nessee champion's honest pride.

"In the present dazzlin' company I find m'self," gallantly

responded Crockett, "I doubt if even Gen'ral Jackson would spare me a look to know me. I do indeed." He swept off his coonskin cap and sat straight and tall in his saddle. He cocked an expectant eye about him at the friendly crowd, but his joking words began acquiring truth. Nobody shouted his name. A little crestfallen, he replaced his cap and sat not quite so straight.

So Dain called loudly to him, "What? I wager there's no part of the world where Colonel Crockett could pass unknown!"

Somebody caught the name, and yelled, "Wal, burn my britches if it ain't ol' Davy Crockett! *Yee-ee-hoo!*"

It was noisy disorder after that. They bore Crockett off, he happily protesting that he was "just an ord'nary volunteer like y'selves, gentlemen!" They passed bottles to the rest of the party, who protested not at all, and they had hot arguments as to who should give up their lodgings to the ladies. There were dozens of claimants to that honor. The town was overflowing. Men were sleeping in stables, wagons, in the streets, anywhere.

A swaggery, rawboned man, slightly drunk, wearing a sailor's knee-breeches, got a wrong impression of the whole thing. He leered up at the girls, grabbed the bridles of their horses, and began leading them off. "Come along wi' me, duckies, I'll see ye . . ."

Dain hit him. He swung his horse forward and hit him with the barrel of a pistol, and turned a darkened face to the crowd. "A man can make a mistake—but not that one!"

A New Orleans gentleman of fortune, rakishly debonair, swept off his hat. "Accept our apologies for the lout," he begged. "Quite unforgivable. You should have killed him, sir. We—a party of us—picked up that seacock off the New Orleans waterfront to cook for us, but the scruffy swab can't even dish up a bite fit to eat. Now, about respectable quarters for the ladies. You must allow me. . . ."

The upshot of it was, Suela and Cleo acquired a fine room

in the house of the town's leading merchant, looking out onto the camp-crowded plaza. Crockett vanished with a mob of new friends and admirers, and Thimblerig and the Pirate inserted themselves into that party, lured by the prospect of plenty to drink.

Dain grinned at Boniface and the Indian. "Looks like we're elected to tend the horses," he remarked. "It's my guess we won't be seeing much of the Colonel till we're set to push on to San Antonio in the morning."

For once falling in with Dain's humor, Boniface opined that this war was using up a powerful lot of whiskey. "But if they ever run out of that ammunition and get down to hard business, they'll raise smoke. It *is* a fighting crowd."

Dain conceded that they all looked capable in that respect, but their blithe and shiftless attitude toward the war struck him as comical. Some other streak in him, more rational, caused him to view it all with a professionally disapproving eye, even while he enjoyed its genial cheerfulness. This was not war, nor the way to win a war. It was a spree. He hoped that the Mexicans were bringing the same sportive frame of mind to it, on their part.

His hope did not stem entirely from unity with the Texas cause. He was no rabid partisan, as was Crockett. His destination and his alliance had been the choice between two evils. But he liked to see any fight conducted upon more or less equal terms. As he sized it up, if the Mexicans came in good strength and military cohesion, they could break and slaughter the uncombined Texas irregulars.

He thought of the current news that was going the rounds, about San Antonio and the Alamo. Old San Antonio de Béxar had fallen to the Texians. From all accounts it had been an amazing battle, the Battle of Béxar, plunged into impetuously and carried through without benefit of military plan or strategy. The town had been held by the Mexican General Cós, who had marched up with an army division from Matamoros and occupied it. A motley mob of Texians, spoiling for a fight, had then camped outside and waited for the word to attack. That word never came.

Far from the zone of combat, the newly formed provisional government of rebellious Texas was in grave assembly, busying itself with important matters of legislature. As a very young and self-conscious government, it leaned over backward in observing correct parliamentary procedure. It elected a Council, a Governor, and passed a Bill of Laws. It drew up a solemn Declaration of Causes for Taking Up Arms against Mexico. That done, in due course it took official recognition of the fact that there was a war on by making provision on paper for the organization of a Texas Army, and voted that the command of it should be given to Sam Houston.

It was all very proper. But the Texians outside San Antonio de Béxar, having little respect for politicians and none at all for punctilio, ran out of patience. They had no field commander, but that lack was soon and simply filled. They elected one from among them. He called for a council of war, which convinced some of them that they had elected the wrong man. They only wanted a commander for the looks of it, anyway, and the army already had its mind made up as to what it was going to do. Why talk about it?

The council of war was just beginning to get somewhere, when Benjamin Milam, a fiery old war horse, broke up the whole consultation. He shoved his pistols into his belt, gave his hatbrim a yank, and stood up.

"Who'll go with old Ben Milam into San Antonio?" he bellowed, and they all charged joyously into town with him.

It took them five days to do the job, but they got it done. They used logs to smash holes through the walls of the adobe houses, and they went through the holes at the enemy. They smoked General Cós out of town. He made it to the old fortified mission of the Alamo, across the river, with the remnants of his army, and they smoked him out of that. He surrendered, and they let him march back to Mexico. Some of them thought that they'd ended the whole war, then and there. They were a boisterous crowd, given to rough humor and quick wrath, preoccupied with the jollity of the moment. But incapable of sustained malice. They had too keen a sense of the ridiculous. So they let Cós march away to fight again another day, and they celebrated.

After that came a chaos of cross-purposes. The Governor fell out with the Council, and the Council fell out with itself. Everybody wanted to run the army, the army had its own various ideas of what should be done next, and Sam Houston was a voice in the wilderness. The conquerors of San Antonio, hearing of another Mexican army coming up, decided to go and meet it at Matamoros before it got into Texas. Even that decision was not unanimous. Some stayed to garrison the Alamo. Others bethought themselves of their spring planting, and went home.

The Council, entirely ignorant of the happy-go-lucky expedition to Matamoros, by a coincidence made plans for a similar venture. Houston protested, but the Council was inspired and full of military geniuses. It got a regular army organized and handed the command of it over to James Fannin, with orders to go and whip the Mexican army at Matamoros or thereabouts. The Governor didn't like that, so they threw him out.

Texas was in high confidence. Victory was certain. One good Texian was worth twenty trained soldiers of Mexico— or of any other country, if it came to that. And volunteers were hurrying into Texas to get into the fight—New Orleans filibusters, gayest and toughest of the tough; independent fighters from the northern United States; wanderers and adventurers and soldiers of fortune from everywhere. Men of grit and men of greed. Of high drama and laughing carelessness. Men who talked much and looked brightly ahead, and men who spoke little and looked carefully behind from habit. All for Texas. If not for Texas, for an escape from unsatisfactory lives elsewhere.

It was a gay war, a holiday, a lark. The world looked on,

entertained. It was said that up in Washington, Old Hickory Jackson wagged his head and wished he were again a foot-loose Tennessean free to tramp off down the pike with a good rifle in the crook of his arm. That way lay the real glory of a man. Maybe he thought of Davy Crockett, that doughty but defeated political enemy, and envied him. By gravy, the boys were sure going to have their fun in that big old Texas, down there!

Due to the gay advance of the San Antonio army, the Alamo fortress—that had been thought would be the scene of a major battle—was now far in the rear of the war zone. Lieutenant Colonel William Barret Travis—"Bob" Travis—left in command of the Alamo, looked wistfully southward and cursed the duty that held him here while all the signs in-dicated that there'd be a slap-up fight down Matamoros way. His command was small, but big in able fighters. He thought it a damnable shame to waste such men in humdrum garrison work, he said.

Decidedly, Dain considered, this was an unconventional, harum-scarum war—on one side, at least, if not on the other.

At dusk a green-painted wagon trundled into Gonzales. It was topped with new canvas, drawn by a team of six fine young mules, and a pair of saddle-horses jogged behind, bridles tied to the tailgate. A good outfit. The outfit of a moneyed man.

It pulled into the plaza. Campfires were dotting the dusk, reddening the yellow tan of adobe walls. The customary cheer greeted the wagon, and a young Texian lieutenant walked over to it.

"Swing over there a bit and you'll have space to camp."

"Yassuh."

The driver was huge and black. Seated well back under the forward peak of the canvas top, the shine of his eyes was the only visible part of his face. A silver earring caught a shifting glint of firelight. He handled the mules as if they were dogs on a leash, with no effort.

The young lieutenant walked alongside. "Come far?"

"Yassuh." The wagon halted.

Inside the wagon a different voice spoke. A cultured voice. "Climb in and join me in a toast, won't you? I still have a few New Orleans cigars left, too."

The lieutenant climbed up into the wagon, congratulating himself. Here was common politeness paying big dividends. The light from the campfire reached only weakly into the wagon's interior. He found his host reclining on a built-in bunk—a man garbed in grey, with very pale eyes, his face barely distinguishable. A gentleman, obviously, from his voice and manners.

"Forgive me for not rising. A slight indisposition has temporarily laid me low. The sea voyage from New Orleans—the Gulf was quite rough. And then the journey up here from Brazoria. But I shall be all right again soon. Won't you be seated, Mr.——?"

"Hocker, sir—Lieutenant Hocker—at your service."

"Thank you, Lieutenant. Let me introduce myself as Mr. Falconer. That is not my name, frankly, but it must do while I am here in Texas. It might create official embarrassment for General Jackson if my identity were revealed. He expressly warned me on that point before I left Washington. I am here in a position of unofficial observer. You understand, of course? I am sure that I can depend upon the discretion of a Texas officer."

The lieutenant was both flattered and greatly impressed. The United States Government at Washington was maintaining a careful neutrality toward the Texas revolt, not wishing to commit itself one way or the other. But it was generally whispered that President Andrew Jackson—everybody still called him the General—was following the affair with keen private interest. Here was proof of the General's personal sympathies—the sending of an important observer, incognito, to keep him informed.

Mr. Falconer brought forth a large metal flask, metal cups, and a box of cigars. His travelling equipment bespoke a man accustomed only to the best, without regard for cost. He filled the cups, opened the box, and proposed a toast.

"To a free and independent Republic of Texas!"

Lieutenant Hocker drank, batted his eyes, and privately wondered how it must feel to be rich enough to buy such excellent old Demerara. He lighted one of the cigars, inhaled luxuriously, and his cup was courteously refilled. "To the health and long life of the General, sir!" he toasted, and emptied it again.

He settled himself more comfortably. The Demerara was better still on the third drink, and like rich old wine on the fourth, inserting its potency under cover of a bland and deceptive mildness. The night grew darker, the campfires brighter, the murmur of voices more genial in the plaza. It was a wonderful world and a grand war. He became sentimental and fierce, both. "Damnation to Santa Anna and his cohorts, and Heaven bless Texas!" he pronounced with a little difficulty, and lifted his cup, which had somehow taken on the delightful attribute of being always full when he wanted it.

Mr. Falconer was saying something. The lieutenant listened attentively to the hospitable, charming, splendid Mr. Falconer. "Outside of yourself, Lieutenant—whom I trust fully, of course, not to reveal my purpose in coming here—there is only one man who might unwittingly expose my identity," Mr. Falconer said.

Lieutenant Hocker thrust out his jaw. "Who is he? Name his name and I'll put him to quiet!"

Mr. Falconer made a deprecatory gesture. "The man may not have arrived here yet. That is what I wish to know. You see, he was once a member of the United States legislature. Having spent some time in Washington, naturally he would know me at once. In his pardonable excitement he might blurt my name. His name is Crockett."

"Davy Crockett? He got in today."

"Er—alone?"

"No. Wi' party. Eight." The lieutenant reflected solemnly and repeated, "Eight—'cluding the ladies. That's right. Eight. And one of 'em . . ." He wagged his head and stared out at the campfires. "Damnedest thing!"

"Indeed?" murmured Mr. Falconer. His eyes were like polished white marbles now. "Eight? They told me at Natchitoches . . ."

The lieutenant brought his eyes back from the fires. "The damnedest thing," he said heavily. He reached unsurely for his cup, and Mr. Falconer deftly filled it ahead of his groping hand. "Mr. Falc'ner, you've gave—given—taken me into your conf'ence, an' I'll take you into mine." He bent closer and whispered tragically, "Spy! One of 'em a spy—for Santa Anna, curse him!"

"You mean one of Crockett's party?"

"'S what I said." The lieutenant swayed back upright. "Damnedest thing. No mistake. 'S what I was sent here for. Fannin sent me. To watch, see? We got word. I didn't believe it—never would've—till I saw today wi' m'own eyes. Ridin' wi' Davy Crockett's party! Hell, huh?"

"Very bad. Another drink, Lieutenant?"

Not long later, the black driver had to assist a young Texian lieutenant whose head had not been conditioned to resist the power of red Demerara rum. He helped him down out of the wagon, and watched him fall before he had gone fifty yards. Some laughing volunteers picked up the Texian and carried him off.

Mr. Falconer called softly from inside the wagon, "Quaw, come in here."

The black giant clambered in swiftly and stood stooped over, the canvas top too low for him.

"You mustn't be seen, Quaw, understand?" Mr. Falconer

said distinctly, as if to a child. "They're here." He saw the huge hands begin to work and writhe, and he shook his head. "No, Quaw. Too many here to see. Put that keg outside. Then go to bed under the wagon. Be ready if I call you."

He waited until Quaw had placed the keg of rum on the ground and gone under the wagon. Then he sat up and called an invitation to the nearest campfire group. "Would any of you gentlemen care for a drink? Sorry I can't join you, but I'm not well. Just help yourselves from the keg."

They were New Orleans men. They advanced promptly.

Mr. Falconer listened to them drinking. Patiently, he waited for their voices to thicken. Rum was so useful. He had always found it a valuable commodity.

CHAPTER SEVEN

D<small>AIN ENTERED THE HOUSE ON THE PLAZA</small>
wherein the girls had obtained quarters. The few belongings
of the party had been taken up to their room, and he needed
his razor. He went up the stairs and found the door of their
room open, and there, with a hand raised to tap on the door
frame, he paused.

Suela was alone in the room. Her back was toward him
and she stood at the window, gazing down into the crowded,
noisy plaza. Sunlight slanted through the window and fell
across the front of her, while her back was in shadow; from
where Dain stood she appeared to be outlined in a golden
light. It touched her hair, and showed up the curve of one
cheek and a rounded shoulder.

She turned from the window, suddenly aware of him.
Although the sight of him standing silently at the door must
have startled her, she tried to keep all sign of it from him.
He saw her even breathing check and deepen, and then her
fingers slowly closed. For his part, he tried to be natural. He
said humorously, "Don't shoot, please. May I come in?"

"Of course. Cleo has gone out with Boniface, to look at the
town."

He left the door open behind him, and joined her at the
window. "It's a wild crowd," he said, nodding down into the
plaza. "A gay crowd."

"Yes. Too gay, perhaps. I wonder if they realize . . ."
She did not finish.

He turned and looked down into her face, and found it
grave. During the long journey from her home, he had
found that she had these grave moods. They came upon her

92

suddenly, sometimes in the midst of warm, low laughter. He regarded them as an intrusion, and he did so now. They were part of the mystery of her, and he had become impatient of mystery and unanswered problems. He wanted to understand her completely, to know all her moods and reactions.

"Perhaps they do," he said. "They know there's risk ahead —they must know. But they're not letting that make them too solemn before the time comes."

She brought her gaze to his, and asked seriously, "Am I too solemn?"

"Only sometimes. Like now. It would seem to indicate a troubled mind. At least, a preoccupied mind. And I don't want you to be preoccupied, not right now, at any rate."

He had surprised her. "Why?" she asked, and immediately closed her lips, and he sensed that a tiny panic had leaped to life in her.

"Because," he said swiftly, "I am about to tell you that I love you." He had decided upon reaching this point the instant he saw her alone at the window. He could wait no longer. She had to be his, and be damned to everything else.

She was caught off guard. She continued to gaze at him, her presence of mind routed by his swiftness. Her lips opened and she gave a quick little breath, and while she stood like that he took her in his arms.

Her hair was a soft, sweet cloud in his face. For a moment she surrendered to him. He felt her hands, warm on his hard wrists, and she brought her face up toward his, without protest, without struggle. Yet, abruptly, while he bent to kiss her, she was pushing him away and murmuring, "No— no—please. . . ."

She had caught her gaze on something down in the plaza. He looked that way, impatiently, and saw Cleo coming with Boniface toward the house. "Damn!" he muttered.

The bright, trembling moment was gone. He looked at Suela. They stood apart now, embarrassed, an unreasonable feeling of guilt between them. He said, "I meant it. I love you. And I think you love me."

She avoided his eyes and said nothing, looking down into the plaza at Cleo.

Dain decided that night that it was high time to have things out in a straight talk with young Boniface Eden.

The dark looks and ominous silences of the young hunter were getting on Dain's nerves a little, causing him to remit payment in caustic barbs which he always regretted afterward. Often on these occasions Boniface stroked the hilt of his long hunting knife, his face stiff. Now that they were nearing the last lap of their journey to the Alamo, Dain reached the point where he thought it decent to clear the air of animosity and bitterness. He guessed that the youth's strong flair for self-dramatization had burned out—that there was nothing left in him now but love and hatred and suffering. In this he was right.

Boniface Eden wanted to kill Dain. He did not think of it as an urge arising from blind jealousy. It was an affair of honor, the honor of Cleo—of Amaryllis, rather, for he had never ceased to think of her and call her by that idealistic name. As such, he justified the impulse to himself, giving it an almost holy background of motive. That he had so far held himself back from putting it into execution was a puzzle to himself. He had come closer to doing it, or trying it, than Dain knew. The truth was—and he suspected it without admitting it—that he liked Dain. But, because of his love for Cleo, he hated him on principle and silently cursed him for a thief and despoiler of virtue.

He was startled and suspicious when Dain suggested that they take a walk together, but after a brief hesitation he nodded. It was significant that he picked up his rifle to take along, and Dain grinned wryly. The boy probably suspected that he was being lured out by the knavish rival to attempted assassination in some dark spot.

Of privacy there was none in the crowded town, and Dain steered the way to the outskirts, and slackened pace. "Do you know why I've brought you out here?" he queried.

Boniface stared straight ahead. "I think I do!"

"I think you don't," Dain disagreed calmly. "And you can rest your finger off that trigger! I've got not a reason for killing you. Fact is, I like you. That is, when you act like a human. Most of the time, though, you're a pretty objectionable pup! It's a misfortune that you had to tumble so far for Cleo. But perhaps not. If Cleo hadn't come along first, likely you'd have plunged for Miss Suela—and then we *would* have had good reason to sharpen up our knives!"

"What?" Boniface turned on him. "You—you dare, now, to —to have designs on Miss Suela?"

"Designs? Well, that's not the word I'd choose, but I suppose it'll do."

"So you'd throw one aside and go after another! Why, you——!"

"Swallow that, please!" Dain cut in curtly. "I'd like to finish this talk without bloodshed, if possible. It so happens that I'm not throwing anybody aside. True, Cleo thinks she loves me—but I think that's an outcrop of other feelings. If I didn't think she would get over it, I certainly wouldn't be talking to you now. Understand me?"

He fastened a stare on the younger man, and he said slowly, distinctly, "Cleo and I have gone through a lot together. I'm very fond of her. I respect her. If I thought it would really make her lastingly happy, I'd—yes, damn it, I'd marry her tonight! But she knows I don't care for her enough that way. I've never lied to her. Get that into your head. There's never been anything between us—in the way you think."

"But—but you and she—travelling together. . . ." Boniface Eden's voice trailed off.

"Don't judge too much by appearances. They're not always reliable. Incidentally, you're not paying her any compliment, either. In fact, I could say that your opinion of her is not as high as mine."

"I'm sorry. I'm . . ."

Dain gave him a friendly shove. "Let's get back. She likes you, d'you know that? I think maybe she could like you to the limit, after I get out of the way. I think. . . . H'mm, here comes our hairless Indian. Now, how did he know where to find us?"

As mild and unobtrusive as ever, the Indian came up to them. Like an insolently superior servant feigning humbleness and purposely carrying it too far, he bobbed his head before Dain. "Miss Cleo expresses an urgent wish for the effulgent felicity of your presence, sire," he breathed, and his lips twitched.

Dain itched to kick him. Not for the gentle derision. He understood that, and it no longer grated upon him. What would be malicious satire in anybody else, was merely amiable playfulness on the part of the Indian. But such a message, so worded, was unfortunate in the light of what Dain had just been assuring Boniface Eden.

To the Indian, Dain had learned, oblique ridicule was humor. He travestied the popular Anglo-American idea of Far Eastern extravagant politeness. He caricatured cleverly the various roles of Hindu mystic, Tibetan sorcerer, and tooth-sucking Japanese monk, playing each according to his whim. But only to Dain and Cleo did he display his acidulous humor, usually, and sometimes Dain regarded that as a compliment and a mark of friendship, and sometimes not. Sometimes, Dain felt that there were sardonic little devils grinning at him through the dark, heavily lidded eyes—wise little devils that knew all about him and could tell him everything if they wished.

Oddly, the Indian and Cleo got along like father and daughter. She believed implicitly all that he said, and accepted seriously his outlandish behavior. He aimed no sharp barbs at her, reserving them all for Dain. He liked her, was kind to her. To all others he was a blank, a nonentity, a queer little brown man of no known tribe, with his hair shaved off and his feet bare. A brown brother. An inferior who responded only to direct address, and generally in half incomprehensible gutturals.

On occasion he held himself withdrawn behind that stolid mask, even from Dain, refusing to understand English, his eyes slumberous and remote. At such times, Dain was almost of the opinion that the man was a Seminole, or a wanderer from some other coastal tribe. "Gone blanket, eh?" he would remark.

The Indian would grunt, or take no notice. But he was just as apt to blink like a man awakening, and reply with an acrid quotation from Bodinus, or the *Gesta Romanorum,* or some sage who, he would explain if asked, had died four thousand years ago—"In the approximate period when your ancestors developed the stone club as proof of their superior intelligence over the other animals. Which proof, I might add, they sadly needed!"

There was no doubt but that he had travelled and studied, and acquired a wide education. Dain never knew what to expect from him next.

Boniface Eden levelled an uncertain stare at Dain, to which Dain replied with what he hoped was a frank and encouraging grin, and they started back, the Indian padding along behind them. The plaza was all firelight and movement, groups of men loafing and talking around the fires, their horses and mules picketed around the square, and here and there a wagon belonging to some band of volunteers who'd had the foresight to cart their own supplies in with them.

Somebody sang out, "Hey, there!"

Dain looked toward a green wagon that he and his two companions were passing. A little crowd was gathered around a tapped keg, drinking from tin cups. They'd built a fire there, and some of them were leaning against the wagon, their faces flushed and blurred, eyes lacking clear focus. One, seated astride of the keg as if it were a saddle, raised a hand that held a cup and motioned for the passing trio to come on over.

"Let's not refuse hospitality," said Dain, and led the way to the keg.

He was in the group and picking up a cup, before he recognized the keg straddler as the rawboned seacock whom he had knocked out of action earlier in the day. He nodded to him, received a nod in return, and all friction appeared to be forgotten. The seacock was drunk, although not so drunk that he couldn't lean down over the front of the keg and draw himself a drink without either vacating his seat or falling on his head. He had evidently elected himself master of the keg. Dain filled his cup. Boniface and the Indian followed suit. They raised their cups.

"Here's to Texas." It was the customary toast.

"An' hell burn all blacklegs," appended the seacock.

He drank, wiped his mouth on his shirtsleeve, and surveyed Dain regardfully. "What d'you think o' dirty blacklegs who'd spy for Santa Anna?"

"Shooting's too good," responded Dain.

"Uh-huh. That's the way we figger, too. Shootin's too good. Right you are! Oughta be skinned alive an' burned in a cactus clump. Huh?"

"Something like that."

"Yeah, somethin' like that. An' by 'struth, mister, that's what we figger to do with him!"

"D'you know of one?" inquired Boniface, sipping his rum.

"Yeah."

"So? In this camp?"

"Yeah."

"Who is he?"

The seacock swung a leg off the keg and stood up. He squirmed his lips and spat. "Well," he drawled, "it could be you!"

Boniface dropped his cup. Before it bounced on the ground

he had his rifle levelled, thumb lapping the lock. "Say that again!"

"There's no need for that, if you're on the straight!" spoke up one of the group, and it came to Dain that they all had been listening in silence while the seacock worked up to his point.

The speaker rose from squatting by the fire. He had the down-drawn mouth and reckless eyes of a man who has seen a lot of tough service in his life. A filibuster. A free-lance sabreur who followed war as a sport and a profession. There were many such, here in Gonzales. His right hand rested on the pistol butt at his belt. Several others had their hands in that same position. It was suddenly a grim, menacing squad.

Dain kept his cup in his hand. He ran his eyes over the group, and his estimate of trouble here ran high. Something besides rum was prodding these swashbucklers to wrath. He looked aside at Boniface Eden, and in the glance that flashed between them they made mute acknowledgment of peril. The young hunter was cool. It took action to wipe away his dreaming, dramatic youthfulness. The Indian had apparently sunk into one of his reflective moods.

They looked at the filibuster, and he said, "There's solid talk of a blackleg in your party. Hocker let it out. Lieutenant Hocker, from Fannin's army. We've been tallying your party. It wouldn't be Crockett, that's sure. It wouldn't hardly be that gambler, nor that old Lafitte wolf. Roughly, we know where they come from. That leaves you three. We can leave the Injun out, I reckon. That leaves you two. How about it?"

Young Boniface laughed at him, and lowered his rifle. "Somebody's put you on a false scent. We're square. I've been hunting Louisiana and the Sabine country since I could tote a gun. If there's anybody in this camp from Natchitoches way, he'll vouch for me, I'll lay to that."

"That leaves one!" put in the seacock. His stare had not

wavered from Dain. "It leaves the one I said it would! Where do *you* come from, mister?"

Dain raised his cup and drank. The final point had been reached—a point already decided upon, the steps to it only a preliminary approach, the course guided by the vengeful seacock. "From nowhere, like a good many others," Dain answered.

"So-oo!" The filibuster shifted his right hand. His pistol came free. Groups of men at near-by fires stood up. They had caught the drift of the talk, and they began moving in. The seacock stepped around behind the keg, and without pausing he picked up an axe.

Somebody called, "Give him his chance, boys! Let's call a trial on him—he's got a right to that."

Another voice, low and distinct, spoke a single word inside the green wagon. Underneath the wagon, a long bundle rolled over, threw off its covering blanket, and crawled out. It was the shifting glint of the silver earring that caught Dain's attention, and Cleo's meager description of the tracking enemy leaped to his mind—a pale, tall man with white hair and near-white eyes; a black giant with a silver ring in his ear. At once this affair became stark and simple. It brought a tingle to his neck-hairs and a jerk to his hands.

The seacock bellowed, "Watch him!" He swung up the axe to throw it, and the filibuster thumbed back the hammer of his pistol.

A gun cracked a report, and the effect of it was as if Santa Anna himself had dashed into the plaza. The seacock twisted slowly from his hips, the axe still held aloft. Everybody was shouting, running toward the group, few with any idea of what was happening, all drawn by the prospect of seeing what they thought was a private fight.

The seacock fell across the keg, and his axe came down on him. The filibuster with the pistol got off one hurried shot—hurried, because a shaved-headed little brown man was coming at him with a knife, and because Dain was wrenching out a pair of long repeating pistols.

Dain could have shot the filibuster, but the little brown man intervened his leaping body, so he fired into the green wagon instead. "Run for it!" he called to Boniface, who was knocking a man down with his rifle. "Come on, Indian!"

He broke through a scattered group of shouting onlookers, adding to their confusion, and looked back to find Boniface right behind him and the Indian darting after them and catching up fast. From the direction of the green wagon a wedge of men split the crowd, among them a giant figure that towered above the rest. Dain's neck-hairs bristled again, and then the glimpse was gone. He was racing with Boniface and the Indian down a short and narrow street, away from the light of the plaza fires.

Half an hour later, the Indian was thoughtfully wiping clean his knife. Dain said to him, "You're a livelier hand in a fight than I thought you'd be."

Boniface Eden uttered a warning hiss. A couple of horsemen went thudding past in the darkness, and when the hoof beats faded to a hollow tapping, the distance-dulled noises of the town grew audible again. Gonzales was on a man hunt.

They had taken hiding in an empty burro stable, in the yard of a deserted Mexican shack. The pale blur of Boniface Eden's face turned toward Dain. "It was a mistake, wasn't it?" he asked. "I mean, that talk of you being a spy."

"A certain party is after us—after Cleo and me," Dain answered. "I didn't think he'd follow us this far. I reckon he was in that green wagon. He was behind it all. He couldn't murder us in a crowded town, so he set that gang of fools onto us to do the job for him."

They were silent again for a while, listening. "You'll never get them to believe it," murmured Boniface finally. "You'll never get the chance to try, if they catch you. We left two dead men back there. Who was it shot that cook?"

"Not I. The shot came from somewhere off the plaza. Crockett, maybe. Sounded like his rifle."

"He gave his rifle to Amaryllis to take care of it for him while he liquored!"

They stared at each other in the dark. "Her room faces the plaza," Dain muttered. "If they trace that shot, it means trouble for her! I'm going back!"

"No, I'll go."

"Why should it be you? This isn't your affair. I got you into it."

"If she is in trouble, it's my affair. It'll be better for me to go." Boniface barred Dain's exit. "You couldn't go into town without being seen and killed. I can walk in openly, and tell them I ran because I lost my head. They'll hold me till I can get Crockett and others to vouch for me, but I'll be in no danger. I'll curse, and tell them you fooled me as well as you did Crockett, and that I've come back to get my horse and join in the hunt for you."

"What about Suela and Cleo?"

"If they're already in trouble that can't be talked away, I'll get word to you—and we'll do what we can. I promise that."

"All right. But if you don't come back here in an hour, I'm coming in."

In less than an hour, half a dozen riders came trotting down the path that ran by the shack, and turned off it to come directly at the burro stable. Dain, expecting not more than one, drew his pistols and kept them aimed until a tall and familiar figure took shape in the lead. The riders dismounted. They had two extra horses with them.

"Well, suh, you surely got y'self in a fine hobble this time!" declared Crockett. Hands on his hips, elbows out, he stood wagging his head at Dain. "Whole town is bubblin' a-boil! I tried to tell 'em they're hunting the wrong bear, but they're too infernal mad to listen even to me. They figure you must've pulled the wool over the eyes of poor old trustful

Davy. Worst of it is, I couldn't zackly vouch for you much, for it's mighty little I know about you. All I could tell 'em was, you got the right shape of a man to me, and you'll stand up to your rack with anybody. I went on to tell 'em you was consid'rable of a thundergust in a fight—and, suh, they more'n agreed with me! They 'low you went through the plaza like a wolf in a sheep pasture. And the Indian, he 'pears to've worked his knife on a fellow and cut him to a flitterjig. After this, Mr. Dain, you can't expect a fair shake in Gonzales, no matter——"

Dain stemmed the tide with an apology. "Sorry, Colonel. They ganged us."

"Huh!" snorted Crockett. "Way I hear it, you ganged 'em! They was going to hold trial on you, but you went wolf. And then, by Aunt Sadie's slippers, if a certain young lady didn't plant a bullet in the seacock! With my rifle!"

"Do they know that?"

"Not yet, but they'll get around to it, never fear. So here they are—Miss Suela and Miss Cleo. We had to give 'em men's fixin's to wear, to get 'em out of town without notice. Miss Suela, she's bound to go to Goliad, she says."

Dain found that one of the spare horses was his own, and he stepped into the saddle. Everybody got mounted and ready to leave. Cleo nudged her horse up alongside Dain, and spoke to him. She, like Suela, wore shirt, pants, coat, and a low-crowned beaver hat that was too big for her. "I saw them," she said. "I saw the black man from my window, and I sent the Indian to look for you. We could have killed him and his master during the night, somehow. Could have shot at them from a window or a roof, and nobody would've known who did it. We could've got free of them. Free!" There were actual tears in her eyes. "Why didn't you come? Oh, why didn't you?"

"I'm sorry," he muttered. "A keg of rum and what I thought was an invitation to drink—I fell for it. I had no thought of that pair."

"And now we're running away again," she said bitterly. "Even here in Texas—where everybody gets a new life, where nobody cares what you are and where you came from! We're still what we were. Curse that white-eyed devil! Curse him! Always, he's got everybody helping him. The law is always on his side. It always will be."

She had never been like this before. Dain tried to find encouraging words, but she went on without hearing him.

"Dain, I'm tired. I'm tired of trying and hoping. I didn't mind when it was just us two. Sometimes it was hard, but I didn't mind that. There was Texas. There was you. There was hope." She laughed a husky, hard little laugh. "Here's Texas. We're here. I wish we'd never come! I wish we were back on the Miss'ippi—hiding in the mud. Hungry. So tired we don't feel the cold. Yes, and you blind and hurt. Even that. We had something then that we haven't got now. *I* had something. I had hope."

Her head came up and she looked at Suela Caerlie, riding a little off to one side. Her bronze eyes held no sharp hatred, nor any of the elemental feline challenge. It was a somber, weary look.

The Pirate, who had been riding well up ahead with Thimblerig, came trotting back. He growled something to Crockett, who reined his horse abreast of Dain. "All roads out are being watched for you," he muttered. "There's a couple of fellows waiting farther on. Sit tight and say nothing. Give your hat to the Indian and tie your kerchief round your head, and you'll both look different in the dark. Bunch together, everybody."

A quarter of a mile onward, they came upon Thimblerig halted before the black silhouettes of two horsemen who held rifles across their saddles. The gambler sat clicking his silver thimbles, trying to engage them in a game. They were claiming that the chances of spotting the elusive pea were already loaded against them, even in broad daylight or under lamps.

Thimblerig, it seemed, had spent a profitable evening prior to the plaza hostilities.

Crockett rode up to the pair and inquired in a loud voice if they had seen anything of "that rascally blackleg," and he went on to say that he and his friends intended to scour the country for him till morning. While he was stating in gory detail his intentions toward the fugitive, the rest of the party rode on by. Crockett finished his speech. Thimblerig gave up trying to promote a game, and they caught up with the rest.

When well along the road, Crockett called a halt. "Here's where we break off company, Mr. Dain," he announced regretfully. "Just like we had to do before, back at Little Rock, eh? You and the ladies and the Indian ought to have no trouble getting to Goliad. The rest of us are s'posed to join a crowd out along the San Antonio road, where I told everybody you'd most likely gone. From Goliad, you can cut northwest to San Antonio and join us at the Alamo.. We'll head direct by the west road, so I reckon we'll get there well ahead of you. You'll find some provender in the saddle bags."

"Thanks for everything, Colonel. Sorry we've got to part again, but I'll be seeing you at the Alamo."

They shook hands all around, making their farewells. Boniface Eden dismounted and went to Cleo. Looking very young, very handsome, very much the knight in buckskins, he took off his fur cap and gazed up at her. "Until our next meeting, Amaryllis—good-bye," he whispered. "I shall be praying for this war to end soon."

Hearing that, Dain recalled what he had said to the young hunter. It had been wrongly given, that encouragement, although honestly intended at the time. He had instilled hope in the youth, and stored up more hurt for him. But, seeing Cleo's eyes in the darkness, he wondered. He saw that the hard weariness was gone from them. After all, adoration was a sweet thing.

Cleo leaned down toward the young hunter, one hand

outstretched to him. He stepped closer, stood taller, trembling, and she kissed him. He still stood there, cap in hand, when the eight split into two fours, one going southward. Crockett's farewells rang out above the others.

"Good luck, Mr. Dain! Good-bye to you, ladies! And you, Indian—you're all of a man!"

The southbound four rode at an easy trot, and for a long time they had nothing to say. Dain looked at Cleo, and he saw the tears again in her eyes. She gazed back at him defiantly. "I was kind to him," she said. "Maybe it wasn't right—maybe it'll only hurt him, in the end—but I couldn't help it. I was kind to him. I wanted to. He was—so fine."

He nodded. He knew that Suela was looking at them both, but he kept his gaze away from her. The kindness of Cleo's act was a mistaken kindness, perhaps, but he thought it splendid. Even in her own weary loss of hope, she could still be the giver, the compassionate one. Deliberately, he threw away his own hopes. He reached out and took her hand, and held it while they rode side by side. "We'll be married in Goliad," he said.

Hours later the Indian reined in and held up an arm. They drew in and listened with him. At first there was nothing but the night's silence. The stars were out, and the world was like a vast and empty blackness. Then they heard it—an intrusion of low, steady sound, a drumming mutter far away.

"Crockett didn't quite fool 'em. They're after us!" Dain touched his horse forward. "Cleo, why didn't you send your bullet at the black man? I could've stopped that seacook with my pistols."

"I would've," she said, "but Suela had the rifle. It was Suela who fired that shot!"

CHAPTER EIGHT

GOLIAD, LIKE GONZALES, WAS AN ARMED camp, but with the difference of possessing a recognized military commander, and a fortification that had been hastily erected and dubbed Fort Defiance. One of the first things that Dain noticed about Fort Defiance was a brass six-pounder cannon, for its position struck him as faintly bizarre. From the roof of a stone house a wooden bridge had been built, extending across the main street to one of the fort's bastions, and on this bridge was mounted the cannon.

It was in a fine commanding position to mow down any enemy advancing up the street. What the inspired gun-crew had ignored was the possibility that the enemy might also do some shooting. Even in late evening, as now, the cannon sat up there in plain sight like a chicken on a roost, visible for a mile. But then, Goliad was said to be full of volunteer companies of men-at-arms from the Southern States, and those fellows regarded this Texas affair as a bright period in the Golden Age of War. Of war fought with a flourish in the grand manner. Of the singing cavalry and the cheering charge, and the saber scar to show to the folks back home. Soldiers were the proud men, and Mars was a white knight in shining armor.

It had been a hard and killing ride from Gonzales, with short halts. The horses that Dain and his three companions rode into Goliad were stumbling on their last legs, heads drooping, smothered with sweat-caked dust. The riders them-selves were saddle-sore, famished, sunken-eyed from loss of sleep. But they hoped that they had left pursuit far behind, for no dust had been sighted in the rear since yesterday. It was possible that the pursuers from Gonzales had played out their horses and been forced to abandon the chase, or else had gone scouting off the road in the hope of obtaining fresh animals somewhere.

It being nearly dark, few in Goliad noticed the signs of hard travel that marked the four incoming riders, and those who did paid little heed. Bands of volunteers were constantly drifting into Goliad from everywhere, dusty and tired, but eager. Lights shone from windows here and there, and men's voices rumbled comfortably from the houses. Most of Goliad was at supper.

"Hope we can get hold of a couple of fresh horses here, so we can push on to San Antonio in the morning," Dain said to the Indian.

"What about us?" Cleo asked.

"I'll find quarters here for you, before I go."

She rode up close to him. "But Dain, before you go—you said . . ."

"Yes, Cleo," he said gently. "We'll be married first."

She drew a long breath and looked squarely at Suela, and smiled. It was a smile of triumph and compassion, both. In antagonism she was merciless, but mercy came with victory. And Suela Caerlie, a silent girl since leaving Gonzales, smiled whitely back at her.

The man who came out from an alley, across from the fort, stepped back quickly from the light of a near-by window and stood in the shadows to let the riders go by. As they passed into the window's light he scanned their faces. His guarded scrutiny ran over first one and then another, and stopped. He caught his breath. His iron self-control slipped from him.

"*Consuela!*"

Seeing the stranger come striding at them from the alley, Dain automatically dug for a pistol. He heard Suela utter a cry, and he got the pistol out, for it sounded to him like a cry of startled alarm. Then she was sliding off her horse into the arms of the stranger, and Dain felt foolish as he put away the pistol. He peered at the man, and he hated to see him with his arms around Suela.

The man said huskily, "*Querida, yo he . . .*" and stopped himself. And then in English, "My dear, I have searched everywhere for you! Tomorrow I would have gone on to——"

"You shouldn't be here!" she interrupted. "You know how dangerous it is for you. I never dreamed you would come back to Texas! I thought . . ." And then she, too, broke off. The man was staring over her head at the three onlookers. His hand tightened on her arm.

"These are—friends?" he questioned. His eyes held a cold alertness.

She drew away from him and turned toward them. "Yes. They brought me here. Mr. Dain and Miss Cleo, and—er—the Indian." She was agitated, and unable to hide it. "This is my father, John Caerlie. I—I was surprised to find him here. I hardly thought——"

"Let us get off the street," cut in her father rapidly, and it was noticeable that he kept out of the light.

Dain elevated an eyebrow. Having become familiar with the vigilant habits of the hunted, in himself, he recognized them in this John Caerlie. This man of the metallic voice and dour eyes had his reasons for using dark alleys, although unmistakably a gentleman. That, coupled with the fact that he was Suela's father, inclined Dain strongly to a comradely feeling for him. Any man was likely to have enemies who kept him on the alert. He bent down from his saddle and spoke confidentially.

"Could you guide us to any place where we might afford to sleep without—uh—fear of disturbance? There may be certain men on the way here from Gonzales, whom we prefer not to meet."

The dour eyes darted to Suela, who nodded. "Come with me, all of you," said John Caerlie. His tone had not warmed.

Dain got the impression that he would have much preferred to take his daughter off alone.

It was a stone and adobe cabin that John Caerlie led them to, a mile or more west of the town, along the river. The San Antonio River ran by Goliad, and Mexican settlers of the poverty class had built small farms along the bottomland. Most of these homesteads were deserted, their owners having fled. This one was on the edge of a cottonwood strip that acted as a windbreak and gave it some isolation from the road north of the river.

"It is neither clean nor comfortable," remarked John Caerlie, "but I have found that it has the virtue of privacy. Turn your horses into the yard with mine. There is some grain, and you can get water from the river."

They ate a packet of bread and meat which their host supplied, and stretched out to sleep on the hard-packed mud floor of the cabin. "What are the chances of getting hold of a couple of fresh horses here, Mr. Caerlie?" Dain asked.

"None," responded John Caerlie. "Every animal has been requisitioned by the Texians."

He was a discouraging kind of man, stiff and stilted in manner and speech. Dain began to find his company a little depressing. "What's a Texian army doing here in Goliad?" he inquired. "And what do they expect to do with that fort? I understood that the battle would be somewhere down on the border, around Matamoros."

For a moment he got no reply. John Caerlie cleared his throat. "There will be no Matamoros battle. The Texian force that marched south out of San Antonio has been utterly defeated by the Mexicans at San Patricio. Annihilated! It never reached Matamoros. Santa Anna is already well within the Texas border, and coming north." He gave his information with a stony lack of emotion. "Fannin, when he heard of it, halted his army here and has gone into camp. He is waiting for further orders from Houston or the Council, they say."

"Hell and Halifax! How are things at San Antonio?"

"A small garrison remains at the Alamo, I believe."

"Have any reinforcements been sent there yet?"

"Not as far as I know."

"The fools!" Dain exclaimed.

"Yes," murmured John Caerlie.

After that Dain lay listening to Suela and her father talking in whispers. He thought that they were speaking in Spanish, but he couldn't be sure, for their whispering was low and indistinct. If they were, it had no special significance. Many Texians spoke Spanish as well and naturally as they did English. Still, it was a little strange.

He recalled that John Caerlie's first greeting to his daughter had begun in Spanish, and that he had called her Consuela. The name Suela, then, was a contraction of Consuela. But why hadn't she mentioned that? Cleo had vowed that she was hiding something. Well, she had been, evidently, and it had to do with her father, who had either law or enemies on his track, or both.

"Like me," Dain mused drowsily, and let it slide from his mind. He thought, "Got to get hold of fresh horses somehow, first thing in the morning. Won't be easy. Probably have to steal 'em. . . ." That was his last waking thought. He slept.

Two men in the cottonwoods, watching the dark cabin, conferred together in low murmurs. "Well, he finally got his callers," observed one. "Four, no less! Wonder if that's all of 'em?"

The other shrugged. "Might be more coming tonight, yet. Damn! I wouldn't have believed Texas had that many blacklegs. They didn't look like Mexicans, either. You'd better cut out and tell the Major. Tell him to send a squad here, and we can jump that spy-nest as soon's it gets light enough to shoot."

Dain woke early. It was still dark and for a while he lay without moving, gathering his thoughts. There was a matter pressing upon his mind, and he recollected what it was. Horses. The sooner that was attended to, the better. He rose quietly, eased past the other sleepers, and left the cabin. The sky was faintly greying in the east. He would have to hurry. He went down to the river, splashed his face and drank, and struck off along the bank. As tired as he had been last night, when following John Caerlie to the cabin hide-out, he had detected unmistakable stable odors behind the stone house where the brass six-pounder was mounted, and he had registered the fact in his mind.

He kept to the river bank until well below the town, and came up behind the stone house. Unaware of the locations of possible sentries, and not sure how vigilant they might be, he crouched against the wall of the yard, listening and taking stock of his surroundings. No challenge rang out. Goliad had not yet awakened to another day of waiting. He caught the top of the wall, raised himself up, and looked into the yard.

It had once been the wagon yard of a merchant or freighter, he guessed, from the size and layout of it. The back of the house—more of a warehouse than a dwelling— led directly into the yard, and its heavily built porch was a loading platform. A slanted roof had been built flush to the top of the left wall, to form a shelter for the animals, and this shelter was partitioned into stalls. Every stall held a horse, and saddles and bridles were racked on the enclosing pole bars. Satisfied, Dain moved on to the wide gate. It was bolted on the inside.

He climbed the wall, dropped lightly into the yard, and carefully unbolted the gate before moving on to the stalls. His first choice was a big bay horse with powerful legs. He lifted down the saddle, let down the bar, and the bay turned his head and eyed him interestedly.

The bay made no objection to the saddle. It twitched its ears, listening to Dain's whispered cajolings, and good-naturedly refrained from crowding Dain against the side of the stall when Dain punched him in the ribs. It snorted fussily at the bridle, knowing that the bit should be uncomfortably cold to its mouth this early in the morning. But Dain had taken the chill off the steel by holding it tucked under an armpit while putting on the saddle. He coaxed the bay into taking it, and the animal relaxed.

Saddled and bridled, the bay backed out of the stall. Its hoofs made some noise, but to wrap sacking around its feet might have unsettled its placid temper. Dain led it toward the gate. He would leave it outside, ready for a quick getaway in case of emergency, and come back for another. He pulled open the gate.

For a moment, then, he stood with one hand holding the gate and the other holding the horse, stilled by the sight of three men before him in the gateway. The three men had pistols levelled.

"You can turn loose the horse," soberly said one of them. "And I reckon you better put up your hands and step along with us. The Major wants to meet you!"

The Major sat in a small room with a door open behind him. On a table before him was a lighted lantern and a hand-drawn map. Except for the chair and table, the room was bare. The Major had long brown hair, a long nose, and a pair of inquiring eyes that were set deeply under prominent brows.

He looked up from the map. "You say you came into Texas by way of Nacogdoches. Are you an American?"

Dain nodded. His arms were tied behind him and the rope cut into his wrists. "Is it necessary to keep me tied?" he asked.

The Major looked him up and down. "Yes. When were you last in Mexico?"

"Never, as far as I know. What's that got to do with trying to steal a horse?"

"What? Oh—the horse." The Major smiled perfunctorily. "Come, now, you must know you're not under arrest for that.

The horse affair is—er—merely incidental to the main crime."

Dain frowned. "What crime?"

"Treason!" said the Major, and then amended the term. "Espionage, I should say. We know that you're one of Santa Anna's spies. You see, we've been expecting you. At least, we expected somebody. Not as many as four of you, I admit, but we suspected a rendezvous when we spotted Duncaerlie looking the town over. And then there's that message we intercepted weeks ago, from him to his daughter telling her to come here on a spying mission. We read it, let it go on to her, and waited."

"What in blazes are you talking about?" Dain snapped. "Are you referring to John Caerlie and his daughter?"

The Major looked pained. "My dear man! We know that the young lady received the message. True, we didn't know that her father would also come here. Very rash of him. And we weren't sure if the young lady would come, either. After all, she's a Texian, even though her father is a citizen and soldier of Mexico. So we waited. Our department of intelligence is very limited—in fact, I'm practically all of it. But I pride myself that I've raised it to a fair standard of efficiency, considering that I've had no previous experience in such work."

Obviously starved for praise, and not getting much of it from the blunt-minded officers and men of the fighting forces, he was reduced to the resort of modestly bragging a little to anybody who had to listen. He added, "I'm a lawyer by profession."

"And a fool by natural bent!" appended Dain.

"Abuse won't help you. A full confession might." The Major had flushed. "After we discovered Baltasar Duncaerlie was hiding here, we looked for his daughter to arrive. It occurred to us that there might be others, too, so we kept Duncaerlie under constant watch. We also watched the Gonzales road. The fact that the girl did come speaks for itself. Very well, we know those two. What we wish to know now is, who are you? Who are your other companions? What are your orders? Are there any more belonging to your spy ring—and, if so, who are they, where are they, and what are they doing?"

"Quit your catechism and listen to me!" Dain was holding his temper with an effort. "I came into Texas with Crockett and some others who're in the Alamo by now, where I'd be headed for if I'd got away with that horse—and where you dallying daisy-pickers ought to be, instead of warming your seats here in Goliad! As for who and what I am, I don't know. My memory's gone. You won't believe that, of course, but there it is. As for Miss Caerlie and her father, they're no more Mexicans than I am. Why, the girl is fair-haired!"

"Her mother was a Spanish blonde," countered the Major. "Baltasar Duncaerlie was born in Mexico, and he holds a commission as colonel in the Mexican army. His father was a Tory from the United States. We know all about him. Now, how about that confession?"

"The more I see of Texian staff officers, the less hope I have for Texas!" declared Dain. "I suppose you've got word from Gonzales about me, and your mind's all made up. I ran into the same damned hobble there, and had trouble with some whickerbills who lacked even your intelligence."

"And you murdered two of them!" The Major turned to the open door behind him. "Mr. Falconer!" he called, and into the little room paced the pale-eyed man.

One look at those pale eyes, and Dain jerked so violently that the Major clapped a hand to his pistol. "Steady, there!" he motioned Dain back. "Mr. Falconer, this man appears to have seen you before."

Dain said tightly, "No. This is my first sight of him. I don't know who he is, nor what he is. But I think he's the devil I've got to curse for nearly killing me and wrecking my memory—and that didn't happen in Texas!"

The pale eyes flickered. "What a remarkable liar the rascal is! Major, I could not help hearing your charge against him.

It corresponds to what I heard in Gonzales, from a Texian officer—Lieutenant Hocker. Perhaps you know him?"

"Quite well," assented the Major. "In fact, I had him sent to Gonzales to watch for Consuela Duncaerlie. He knew her by sight."

"A very fine young officer," approved Mr. Falconer. "As to that, I can honestly say, *en passant,* that I have never in all my experience met such brilliant and inspiring officers as those which Texas so fortunately has in her service."

The flattered Major rose and bowed. "We do our poor best, sir."

"Lieutenant Hocker," continued Mr. Falconer, "informed me that he had recognized a spy in Crockett's party. Somebody must have overheard him. Suspicion fell upon this rascal, here, and he became alarmed, as guilty men do. He and his Indian confederate shot a splendid young volunteer in cold blood, knifed another, and escaped with their two women companions in disguise. I joined the pursuing party and we kept after them until we exhausted our horses. The others then turned back, but I and my servant came on as best we could. My indignation had been aroused by the murders. He will be shot, I presume?"

"He'll be tried as soon as possible," replied the Major. "If found guilty, he'll certainly be shot, I assure you!" He tapped on the table for the guards.

Dain glared at the pale-eyed man. "Some day," he swore, "I'm going to get you! I'll . . ." He turned on the Major. "Do you intend to arrest my friends on those wild charges?"

"They're already under arrest!" said the Major, and motioned for the guards to take the prisoner away.

CHAPTER NINE

THE INDIAN WAS IN A FRET. USUALLY SO
serene that he gave off an irritating air of aloof contempt for
circumstances, he now sat cross-legged on the floor and glowered like an acrimonious Buddha. He fidgeted constantly,
clicking his fingernails and occasionally letting out an ex-
plosive little hiss between his teeth.

The clicking and hissing got on Dain's nerves. "I wish
you'd put yourself in a trance, or go blanket, or something!"
he snapped, and realized as he said it that he himself had
been pacing up and down for an hour. "Sorry. Pay no heed
to me."

The Indian raised bleak and unfriendly eyes to him for an
instant, and dropped them again. "I pay no more heed to you
than I would to an ant!" he retorted. "That, perhaps, has been
the point where I erred. Even an ant—microscopic, but bother-
some—may be the means of wrecking the fine timing of
destiny."

"Even the ants grow big here in Texas," Dain remarked
irrelevantly.

The Indian continued clicking his nails. "Because I allowed
myself the small entertainment of observing you and your reactions, I became interested in you as a study. Because I was
interested, I was tempted into putting a finger into your affairs. I should have remembered that such a process is dangerously cumulative."

The gently ruminative tone of his soliloquizing was not
overly deceptive. He was reviewing aloud the steps of his
descent from lofty contemplation, and a smouldering rage
within him was feeding upon it.

"Because I foolishly yielded to temptation," he went on, "I am the prisoner of fools! I let slip from me my control of circumstances, and so I have sunk level with the helpless, scurrying, roaring mob—a grain of dust in the desert—a pitiful plaything of chance. To regain control demands much time, care and opportunity. It is hard to win, and easy to lose. Time, care, opportunity—where are they here? This rabble intends to kill me. The blind gullions will take me out and shoot me, along with you, and bury my body! Ah, how the shrieking keepers of Karmaluka will laugh to see me come tumbling into their hands! This is their triumph. They watched, and when I wandered off the path, they trapped me with this! *They* know —*they* know! I should be at the church of the Alamo, not here!"

"That stands good for both of us," Dain mentioned. "I'm overdue there, myself." He had got into the habit of half ignoring the brown man's crypticisms.

The Indian exploded a hiss through his teeth, a sound that was not only slightly repulsive, but took the place of an insulting epithet. "You to the Alamo! The ant to the altar! A thing of chance and mischance. What does it matter where or how *you* die? You are still only a child of life, with a long road before you and many lives yet to be endured. But *I* stand at the end, between the Inner Circle and the boiling black pit of Karmaluka! If I stumble and fall to the left, I am lost. *Lost*, I say, for all eternity!"

He drew back his head, staring at Dain, but the dark eyes looked through and beyond to visions known only to them. "*They* know the end of my road! Death by violence in a holy place, my body burned, my bones never buried! And *I* know. I have divined and calculated and verified it. It must be so! It *must* be so!"

He was trembling, sweating. The sweat beaded his shaven head and forehead. His nails clicked together in a ragged tattoo of dry sound, and he squatted there on the floor with his mouth open, staring.

It was weird and gripping, and unearthly. Dain had never before seen the brown man so agitated. He had a moment's struggle to restore himself to cynical disbelief, and he said roughly, "Hallucinations! You've been staring at a bright light too often, telling yourself to see what you want to see. There's another name for it. What is it? Mesmerism?"

The Indian came out of his trance-like horror. Anything in the nature of a faulty intellectual opinion could be counted on to arouse his prompt challenge and merciless confutation. He sighed, wiped his face and head with a sleeve, and regarded Dain owlishly.

"Friedrich Mesmer," he stated sententiously, "was a blundering ignoramus, meddling with forces too great for him to understand. Mesmerism! As well endow the whole solar system with the name of the first biped who glimpsed a star! Mesmer discovered that if a patient gazed long enough at a bright object, sleep was induced. How astonishing! His technique, which he developed upon that, was to wave his hands slowly before the patient's face and command him to go to sleep—which the patient would have done in any case. Bah! Mystic quackery! Later, other practitioners of the trick commanded their patients to stop having pains, and they had some success. Later still, others discovered that the patient— or subject—would obey other commands, within reason. But the practice is falling into disrepute, due to wrong usage. The ancients went through much the same phase with it."

"Thanks for the lecture," Dain said solemnly. "Am I to presume that you're a master of the art?"

"Oh, I have dabbled with it at times," acknowledged the Indian airily. "The technique is not difficult. The subject is induced into a receptive mood, and charmed to sleep by the practitioner—just as a child is charmed to sleep by its mother's stroking hand and soothing voice. The automatic resistance of the subject's wakeful consciousness is thereby eliminated, and by various simple tricks the practitioner reaches his inner mind. Commands are given, and the subject obeys—like a sleepwalker. The technique is founded upon perfectly natural laws. There is nothing mysterious about it."

Again, here was this plausibility, this knack of hauling apparent mysteries out into the light and presenting them as simplicities that agreed with reason. Tolerant in his general skepticism of most anything that the Indian said, Dain shrugged and went back to his accusation. "I imagine you've also dabbled in self-mesmerism, haven't you?" he hinted.

The Indian conceded that with a nod. "Many times. But only to release my spiritual mind—my egoic self. It is a liberation, not a mesmeric ecstasy."

"Have it your way. I only wish you'd mesmerize these damned Texians into letting us go!"

"Unfortunately, the subject must be willing to be mesmerized. I doubt if these Texians would be receptive to the suggestion!"

They were together in a tiny room under the roof of the stone house, opposite the fort, guarded night and day. No trial had yet been called to decide upon their guilt and execution. The army of Goliad was too busy preparing for the expected coming of the enemy. It was said that Santa Anna had reached San Antonio de Béxar, had cut off all approaches to it, and was besieging Travis's little band of diehards in the Alamo.

In the next attic room paced one prisoner, kept in solitary confinement because of his importance. From his square little window, high above the street, he could see the nose of the brass six-pounder jutting out from the wooden bridge, a brave menace to the enemy. He could stare up dourly at it, and from his long military training he could condemn as reckless madcaps the men who had placed it there.

His condemnation, however, was professional rather than personal. Let the Texians make their mistakes, and the more the better. He did not hope to live to see them pay for their sins, but of their eventual payment he felt assured. It would

come swiftly, the smashing of this revolt. Swiftly—ah, so swiftly! The fools. The criminal fools! To dare to do this thing—
to stab the mother country, Mexico, that had given them free-
ly of land. The ingrates! He never failed to grow hotly indig-
nant at the thought.

Mexico. He loved even the sound of the name. He had
never liked Texas. Although his land estate lay here, he had
never thought of it as really home. As for the people. . . .
No, no, they were not his people. He disclaimed them. His
were the people of formal courtesy, stiff pride, punctilio.
Ladies and gentlemen of Mexico. *Señoras grandes y caba-
lleros.* The land of his dead wife and his mother, the land of
his birth, the adopted land of his father—that grave, proud
Scot, to whom the elaborate manners of Mexico had been a
quiet joy, after the unceremonious ways of Anglo-Americans.

Anglo-Americans. Big, stalking men, taking their pride not
in lineage but in what they considered were the sterling
virtues of forthrightness, truculent independence, straight talk
and plain living. Plainsmen. Frontiersmen. Mountain men.
What could one expect of such half-civilized people! Proud,
they were—actually, incredibly proud of their wilderness manners. Hah! Mexico had long ago passed through that adoles-
cent age. She, too, had seen the pioneering years, and what
glorious names belonged to those years! Names of old Spain's
finest aristocracy. Not rabble. No. Not commoners. Men of
noble blood, high prestige. Grandees. Those had been Mexico's pioneers.

He stepped to the wall of his room and placed an ear
against it. In that room, on the other side of this wall, was
his daughter, a prisoner like himself. Oh, they treated her
well enough. According to their own standards, he supposed,
the Texians were gentlemen. The Commander, himself, had
apologized for locking her up, had explained that she was regarded as a spy and must not be allowed to slip off to the
enemy. But they'd had the crass impertinence to make her

share her room with that girl who passed by the name of Cleo
—a person of no high class whatever!

He listened. Voices reached him through the wall. They
were muffled and he could not get the sense of them, but the
tones troubled him. It seemed to him that anger was running
through the tones. Then he caught one short expletive that
shocked him. It was not given in his daughter's voice, but in
the voice of that girl called Cleo. It was said deliberately, distinctly.

"Damn you!" said the voice.

In that room beyond the wall, two girls stood face to face,
their enmity at last a naked flame. They had tried to smother
that enmity to a smoulder under a banked layer of amenities.
Knowing the peril of it in their close confinement, they had
quenched each glow as it broke through.

They could not kill the fire. The inflammable temper of
Cleo had finally blazed, and Suela's an instant later. Past re-
pression had made the tinder of their tempers the more dry
and combustible.

"Damn you!" Cleo said. "Damn your yellow hair and your
white skin! Damn your soft hands, your soft voice, your pretty
manners! You're a lady, aren't you? Damn ladies!"

"And gentlemen?" Suela thrust in swiftly.

"*He* isn't a gentleman, if that's what you mean! He's my
kind. He's mine!"

"So I presumed. From what I could not help observing, I
gathered the opinion that young Mr. Eden was also yours—
or should it be vice versa?"

"What d'you mean?" Cleo inquired dangerously.

Suela held herself straight to keep from trembling. There
was no fear in her, but here was a scene that went all against
her training and background. She wanted to remain cool and
self-possessed: a lady. And cutting and parrying, like a rapier.
But blunt insult called too insistently for its retort in kind.

There were times when she suspected that she was not truly fashioned by nature to be a lady.

"I mean," she said, "that your damnation of ladies is understandable. What we are not, we damn—as I damn promiscuous coquettes and courtesans!"

"You—you—! I'll choke you with your own yellow hair!"

"I think not. And *damn you!*"

The last of the lady was gone.

Enmity reached its flaming zenith, and for a moment they were tigers, both shaken by the force of their fury. They stood rigid, high-colored and hard-breathing, and both had beauty, and each hated the other for it.

The high flame sank between them, neither of them able to maintain it longer, and reaction struck at them. Oddly, Cleo was the first to break under it. She moved suddenly to the window and stood with her back to the room, hands clasped tightly behind her.

"It's a lie. A—muddy, cruel lie," she stammered. "That boy —Boniface Eden—he loved me. I didn't love him, but I pretended at the last. Not—not what you think. Not that. He was so beautiful. Good. Clean. He wanted me to love him. He wanted it so much. So I pretended. What else could I do?"

She turned, and she was crying, but she kept her hands clasped behind her, and her head was high. "You! How could *you* understand? You're a lady. The likes of you wouldn't do a thing like that—no, not to send a boy off happy. You couldn't. You'd think it was—was beneath you. Well—God didn't make me a lady. He just made me a woman. Thank God!"

"And he gave you a heart, Cleo."

They stood face to face again, and now they were both crying, their nerves ragged and exhausted. Suela said again, "He gave you a heart. I'm sorry I said what I did. Don't call me a lady again, Cleo, please—you make it sound too heartless. I'm not, really. Not a lady. And not heartless. I'm just what you are. I hope I'm what you are."

Cleo unclasped her hands. She wiped her face with the palms, carelessly, without bending her head. "No, you're not what I am. You can't ever be. You wouldn't want to be, if you knew. I lied—about Dain. He's not my kind, and he's not mine. Never was."

"Have you—have you been pretending with him, too?"

"No! God knows I haven't. I love him. So do you."

There was no reply to that. They wiped their faces and they looked at each other. As naturally as sisters, they slipped arms around each other's waist and turned toward the window. Ragged nerves quieted, and the room grew peaceful. Their heads came together, and they stood gazing down into the narrow street outside, neither of them seeing it.

CHAPTER TEN

H<small>IS EXCELLENCY</small>, G<small>ENERAL</small> A<small>NTONIO</small> L<small>ÓPEZ</small>
de Santa Anna, President of Mexico, Commander-in-Chief of
the Army of Operations against Texas, stared across the San
Antonio River at the scarred walls of the Alamo fortress and
decided that he would have to take it by assault.

He had cannonaded and besieged it long enough, without
result. That cursed little band of rebels yonder had proved
mule-stubborn to all blandishments, demands, threats, and
heavy gunfire. He damned them for suicidal maniacs, scowled
at their lazily fluttering little flag, and swore crackling oaths
under his breath when he thought of how they were dis-
rupting his plans for a swift conquest of Texas.

He had taken the town of San Antonio with little trouble,
but its defenders had mustered inside the Alamo. Dislodging
them was proving to be an astoundingly hard task all out of
proportion to the small force of Texians defying him. A long
siege was out of the question. It was not fitting to his prestige
that he should by-pass an irregular little fortification hardly
worthy of the name, and thus admit that he had been unable
to take it by force of arms. It would discourage his army. It
was against military principles.

Being a military genius in his own estimation, he sized up
the problem and placed his finger upon the solution. Assault.
Assault with everything that he had—artillery, mounted dragoons, grenadiers and sharpshooters. And ladders, wrecking
tools, and bayonets. Napoleon, he believed, would have
nodded approval, and could have done no better. Perhaps not
as well. After all, the Little Corporal had lost the battles of
Leipzig and Waterloo, and died in captivity on St. Helena.

He—General Antonio López de Santa Anna—was infallible, invincible, and blessed by fortunate stars. Also, he possessed the ruthless resolution so necessary to a great military leader and conqueror. These Texian rebels must be annihilated, all of them. Was he not the "Tiger of Tampico"? Yes. Did a tiger take prisoners? No!

True, he had originally sent Colonel Almonte forward under a white flag to the Alamo, to offer life to the defenders if they would surrender. But there were times when a touch of diplomacy saved effort and drew gratifying results. In this case the diplomacy quickly wilted. His magnificent offer drew a cannon shot as the only reply, which made him so angry that he cursed Colonel Almonte, who, having returned, at the moment happened to be venturing the opinion that the Texians would probably choose to fight.

He had around five thousand troops, cavalry and infantry, on the field. Five thousand trained and equipped soldiers against a pitiful one hundred and eighty undisciplined rebels. Absurd, that the smashing of this trifling little stronghold should require so much time and trouble, while all Texas lay practically in the palm of his hand. His scouts were telling him that the settlers were abandoning their homes and fleeing out of his path. The trails to the north and east were choked with scurrying refugees and their goods—women and children, cattle, horses, loaded wagons. Goliad and Gonzales were rallying points for colonists who had taken down their rifles, seen their families started for safety, and hurried off to war. It was high time to push on and strike hard, while the rebels were still disorganized.

He called to him his second-in-command. General Martin Perfecto de Cós came up and saluted. "Increase the cannonading," snapped His Excellency. He had to raise his voice to make himself heard above the roar of the bombarding guns. "We assault tomorrow, before dawn."

"Tomorrow?" echoed General Cós. "Ah—tomorrow is Sunday, Excellency."

"Assault!"

"Yes, Excellency. Assault. Tomorrow. Before dawn."

The Alamo, built for a mission, was fairly proof against small arms, but siege artillery was another matter. Its outside walls were of masonry, three feet thick, but only eight feet high. The main yard, nearly two acres in extent, could be swept by rifle fire from higher ground outside, so that its only shelter was close to the walls. The old stone chapel, roofless, was in service as a barracks, armory, and hospital, as well as a two-story adobe building attached to it. The small chapel yard was wedged into the angle formed by the chapel and the main walled yard.

This was the fortress of the Alamo, and for ten thundering days and nights Travis and his sharpshooters had held out against an army. More than two hundred shells had crashed into the Alamo. Santa Anna's forces were growing in number, as more units of his army caught up with him. Mexican companies had attacked again and again. Holding their fire until the enemy came well within range, the smoke-grimed defenders drove them back each time. The ground outside the walls was littered with crumpled dead. The Texians could shoot.

At night, some of the Texians had even sallied out and burned near-by houses which had furnished cover for the enemy's batteries, and brought back water. The siege continued. The sun rose and set ceaselessly upon the beleaguered stronghold, skirmishes and attacks flared by day and night, and the Texians spent their time between keeping their rifles hot and repairing the battered defenses. They would not surrender. One dark night, thirty-two daredevils from Gonzales had broken through the enemy lines and piled into the Alamo to fight or die alongside the defenders.

Crockett had his fiddle under his chin, his back to the wall, and was vigorously sawing with the bow. He was a good fiddler, but the Mexican cannons gave him so much competition that only his high notes were audible to the Texians lining the ramparts. The harder he sawed, the louder the cannons pounded, and at last a ragged hunter put in a complaint.

"Hey, thet screechin' fiddle ain't doin' us no good! Sounds like a tomcat wi' a fishbone stuck in its throat! Why, even the Mex'cans don't like it, from the way they's throwin' all their ironware at it!"

Crockett cocked a cold eye at him, and put away his fiddle and bow. "Music," he pronounced severely, "charms even the savage beast, I've been told, but this disproves it! What manner of beast are you—bovine or canine?"

"Neither the one nor t'other, Colonel," yelled the hunter. "I'm shaggy as a bear, wolfish about the haid, lively as a cougar, an' I kin grin like a hyena till the bark curls off a gum log! Thar's a sprinklin' of all sorts in me, from lion to skunk, an' I eat my meat raw! I vow I'll swaller Santa Anna without gaggin' if ye'll jest skewer back his ears an' grease his haid a bit! Yee-ow!"

This was the high mood of the Texians, worn out and surrounded as they were. Extremity of hardship was here, and death was closing in, but a joke was a joke. Crockett laughed with the rest, and stepped up onto the rampart between Boniface Eden and Thimblerig. The Pirate had volunteered to take a message to Goliad, to let Fannin know that the Alamo was besieged, and he had left nine days ago.

"By Nelly, it does seem like they're blasting at this partic'lar spot, sure 'nough," Crockett remarked as a cannonball thudded into the other side of the wall.

Thimblerig was juggling absorbedly with his silver thimbles. Without looking up from them, he said, " 'Pears so, Colonel. See what they've done? Fetched a cannon up to point-blank range. Got some rifle shooters up mighty close, too. Ahem—would any gentleman here care to indulge in a bet, just for a little excitement to pass the time away?"

"Why not try a different game for a change, and take a

shot at those gunners?" queried Crockett, nestling the butt of his Betsey to his cheek.

"Bullet cut off my trigger finger a while ago," the gambler responded calmly. "I'm educating my left hand to the thimbles, and I think I've got it. Come, gentlemen—is there no sporting blood in this crowd?"

They could see the Mexican cannon plainly, the figures of its crew moving fast, ramming in a fresh charge, stepping clear when finished. One of them stood up to it with a smoking match to touch it off, and Crockett fired. The gunner keeled over. Another snatched up the match and jumped to the gun. Thimblerig, without comment, handed his own loaded rifle to Crockett. It flashed its discharge, and the second gunner joined the first on the ground. Boniface Eden dropped a third, and then the gun crew gave it up and retired, but their carabineer comrades lay flat and poured volley after volley at the top of the wall.

"If those fellows could shoot," commented Crockett, ducking down to reload, "they could've picked us off like turkeys on a low limb."

"*Some* of 'em kin shoot," growled the ragged hunter, and jerked a thumb down at the ground.

Thimblerig lay on his back, arms outspread, his fine big Vicksburger hat crushed, one thimble still held in his left hand and the other two in the dirt. A dried pea rolled out of his sleeve as they lifted him, and Crockett picked it up along with the thimbles. They carried him into the chapel yard. He was dead and they could hardly believe it, for he looked no different except for the blood on his shirt. He had always had pallor and rarely any change of expression.

They felt that a few fitting words were indicated, and they looked to Crockett to say them. Crockett took off his coonskin cap and so did they. "He never told me his name, and I don't remember any burial service, but I reckon that don't overly matter," he allowed. "I don't know where he came from, but he had the right grit. He was a gambler, and he staked his life on Texas. He was a good loser, so I don't reckon he'd want any fussifying right now."

He took out the three silver thimbles and the dried pea, and wrapped them in his handkerchief. "It's not for us to speculate where he's bound for now, but one thing I'm dead right sure of." He tucked the little bundle into the dead man's vest pocket. "Wherever he goes, it'd be hell for him without his thimbles! Boys, let's trot back to the wall and get some more o' those varmints!"

Colonel Jim Bowie, down with an old ailment that had been aggravated by over-exertion and exposure, studied Travis's face as the young Commander came up beside his cot. It was a boyish face in some respects, clean shaven except for light sideburns, and ordinarily it smiled easily. Today it was older, thinned by strain and sober with premonition.

"Looks bad, Bob, eh?" said Bowie.

Travis seated himself on the edge of the cot, hands dangling between his knees, and gazed around the yard. Shadows had filled the holes in the earth where the enemy shells had fallen. The west wall was a long black bar, spaced by the heads of lookouts, silhouetted against the slowly coloring sky.

He nodded. "If Fannin doesn't come with help from Goliad tonight, Jim, we're finished."

"As bad as that?"

"Yes. I've been watching the enemy's movements. Their infantry is massing at four points. They've got ladders. I saw them. Their cavalry is spreading out. I don't need to tell you what it means."

Just before sundown the terrific bombardment had ceased, and the Texians could observe Santa Anna's brigades withdrawing toward the river. Some of the Texians raised a hoarse cheer, catching at the hope that the withdrawal might signify that the enemy was giving up. Fatigue, sleeplessness, the nerve-fraying strain of long days and nights of vigilance, had rendered them incapable of analyzing signs and portents. Any auspicious circumstance of the moment was enough to arouse their soaring optimism. In spite of their situation, few of them entertained real doubts of anything but eventual victory.

But Travis sensed what the lull signified. His fighters were worn out, many of them wounded. His second-in-command, Jim Bowie of the perfect knife, lay ill in his cot. Ammunition was running low. No reinforcements had come from Goliad or Refugio, and it was getting too late to expect any now. The Alamo was cut off by the enemy from all outside help, and he divined that Santa Anna was preparing for a final grand assault. He considered the position, saw it clearly, and guessed what the next few hours would bring.

Bowie was seized by a fit of coughing. When it passed he lay breathless, looking up at the sky. "What do the others think about it?" he asked at last.

"They don't know. They're too tired to think."

"I reckon they ought to be told, don't you?"

"Yes. Everything depends on Fannin getting here tonight." Travis rose heavily. "I'll call a muster and tell them. It won't make any difference, but they ought to know."

"No, it won't make any difference," Bowie said. "We'll be going out in good company, Bob, if Fannin doesn't come. They're all . . . What's the noise?"

Travis ran toward the wall. "Crockett!" he called. "You there? What d'you see?"

"Somebody running, and a bunch chasing him!" Crockett called from the rampart. "He's cutting for here like a . . . Bless Bess, if it ain't the old Pirate coming back from Goliad!" He leaped the wall, rifle in hand. "Come on, Eden, let's give him a hand!"

The Pirate was afoot. By some miracle he had slipped through the enemy lines. With his matted bush of whiskers and his ragged clothes flapping, he was hitting a fast, shambling gait for the Alamo, a group of mounted Mexican dragoons riding after him. He saw Crockett and Boniface come running out to meet him, but they were too far off. He stopped, spun around and dropped to one knee, and his rifle cracked. A dragoon stiffened, bumped awkwardly in his jolting saddle, and slid off, tangled in his yellow cape. The rest swung their mounts aside and lost headway. The old ruffian continued his flight, and they came spurring after him.

They were close on his heels when he dodged aside. He whirled on them like a tiger and dashed full into them with his gun clubbed. By this time Crockett and Boniface had reached the spot, and they charged into the fray. The dragoons' horses reared and plunged, taking fright. From the advantage of being mounted, the cavalrymen suddenly found themselves under the handicap of trying to control their horses and at the same time defend themselves from a berserk trio who had taken the offensive. Some of the horses bolted with their riders. The rest of the cavalrymen lost heart, gained prudence, and reined out of distance, dragging out their carbines.

Crockett and the Pirate, full of fight, went after them and were all for turning into pursuers, until Boniface hailed a cool warning. "We're cut off from the fort!"

Another detachment of cavalry had come riding in at a tangent, were spread out in a charging line on the route of retreat to the Alamo, their short swords flashing redly in the blaze of sundown.

Crockett and the Pirate had emptied their rifles. Boniface took quick aim with his, fired, dropped a rider to a crashing spill, and glanced at Crockett.

"Which way, Colonel?"

"Go ahead—into 'em!"

They ran at the oncoming cavalry line, swinging their rifles. Inside the Alamo wall, Travis shouted commands for which there was scarce necessity. Men were going over the wall and sprinting to the rescue of the trapped three.

Five minutes later they brought them in, carrying two and helping the other. The shattered cavalry detachments were riding back to the Mexican lines, leaving a littered little battlefield of eight sprawled troopers, three dead horses, and a few dropped carbines and sabers.

Travis bent over the Pirate. "What news from Goliad, soldier?" he asked.

The scarred old adventurer opened one eye and closed it again. He breathed noisily. " 'Nother Mex'can army there," he growled. "Got it nigh surrounded. I had hell's trouble a-gettin' through. Fannin, he won't be comin'! I figgered ye'd want to know."

That was all he said. He didn't see Travis straighten up slowly and stare at the wall. He uttered a grunt and an oath, and somebody said he was dead.

CHAPTER ELEVEN

Boniface Eden was shot just below the chest, at such short range that the discharge of the Mexican carbine had set fire to the front fringe of his buckskin shirt. That splendid, skin-tight shirt, tanned and bleached white, was no longer immaculate. The boy had lost his jaunty fur cap in the fight, and his thick hair lay spread out on the blanket like the tresses of a girl. His handsome young face was pale, but calm. His eyes were open.

"Colonel," he whispered, "will you play for me?"

"To be sure, lad, to be sure I will."

Crockett went and got his fiddle. He had a deep and ugly saber cut across his forehead, which he insisted to everybody troubled him not at all. Blood from it had run and dried into the creases of his gaunt face, outlining it to grotesqueness. He tucked the fiddle under his chin and poised the bow.

The boy whispered softly his song, and Crockett played as softly:

> Saddled and bridled and booted rode he,
> A plume in his helmet, a sword at his knee. . . .
> But toom cam' the saddle, all bluidy to see,
> An' hame cam' the steed—but hame ne'er cam' he.

The faint music ceased, and the night was quiet. Crockett put down his fiddle and knelt by the blanket. "Is there anything you want, lad?" he asked. "Anything I can do for you?"

Boniface Eden did not look at him, appeared not to hear him. His dimming eyes were on the sky, now velvet grey and streaked with trailing fingers of color from the west.

"Amaryllis," he murmured, and smiled, and closed his eyes. "Amaryllis. . . ."

The Texians mustered in the yard, and leaned on their long rifles, waiting for Travis to say what he had to say.

Travis looked along the line of tattered men, at the bearded faces, the bloodshot eyes that met his own, and he could not speak. He stood before them, their acknowledged leader, holding their confidence. For perhaps the first time in his life he felt guilty and afraid. These war-worn men had trusted him implicitly, given credence to his every word, relied upon his repeated encouragement that reinforcements would come. His was the task of disillusioning them and telling them the worst.

He pulled himself together. "My comrades. . . ."

He had the gift of fluency. It came to his aid now, fully, requiring no effort, yet he himself was hardly aware that they were his own words. It was as if he were standing with that line, listening with those tired men to a voice that spoke his thoughts. Phrases and sentences fitted and strung themselves together, until he found himself nodding agreement with their imagery and delineation of facts.

"I have deceived you. Not wittingly. I, also, have been deceived—by hope. I expected reinforcements. I hoped that our little band would be made the nucleus of an army large enough to repel our foes. This hope I transmitted to you, in good faith. I was mistaken. . . .

"Stern necessity compels me to make known to you, now, that we are doomed. The enemy is all around us, and outnumbers us thirty to one, or more. Escape is impossible. We have refused Santa Anna's demand for our surrender, and defied his threat to put us all to the sword if the fort is taken. We have no longer any hope for help. Fannin can't come. We dare not surrender. We can't cut our way through their ranks —they are far too strong. Santa Anna is determined to take this fort. . . .

"Then we must die! Our business now is to choose the manner of our death. Surrender? Try to cut our way through

to escape? I am opposed to either method. We've kept the
enemy busy here, and in so doing we've helped to give our
families time to escape from his path. I propose to continue
along that line to the last—to fight on as long as we're alive—
to kill as many of the enemy as we can before we die! Perhaps we can so weaken Santa Anna's forces, out there, that
Texas can meet him on fair terms elsewhere. That's my
choice. What is yours?"

He drew his sword. He dug its point into the ground and
paced down the silent rank, scoring a thin furrow behind him.

"Let those who'll stay with me, step over that line!"

The silence lasted another moment. Fatigued minds had to
struggle along after his words, grasp their import, nudge
bodies into action. A buffalo hunter, keyed to swift decisions
by years in hostile Indian country, hiked up his belt and
crossed the line. "I'm wi' ye, Bob!"

They all crossed. They made a rough game of it, shoulder-
ing one another out of the way, exchanging pungent pleasantries, laughing, cheering, crowding around Travis. Through
the din, a humorously plaintive voice kept saying, "Boys, you
wouldn't leave a sick old coot behind, would you? How 'bout
toting me over that line? Eh, boys, how 'bout it?"

It was sick Jim Bowie, grinning in his cot. They heard him,
and with a whoop they picked him up, cot and all, and bore
him over the line. He lounged like a nabob, carried shoulder
high, holding a pistol upright as a scepter. He grinned at
Travis as they set him down, and nodded.

"Well, Bob," he drawled, "looks like we're all here!"

"These men," said General Santa Anna, "are outlaws—filibusters—foreign adventurers! They have placed themselves
outside of the recognized rules of warfare!" His bold black
eyes stabbed around at his grouped officers, some of whom
gazed too steadfastly down their noses to suit him. "There
will be no prisoners taken! Am I understood, gentlemen?"

"Yes, Excellency."

He knew what some of them thought of him. To several of them he was an unscrupulous upstart, a scoundrel in the saddle of Mexico, to be nationally deplored. To others he was the ruling lord, to be followed and obeyed while his power lasted, to be promptly deserted if ever he lost his domination.

He had sat up most of the night with his staff officers, laying his plans. He was explicit and uncompromising, requesting no advice, but dictating to them what he wanted done and how they must do it. There must be no failure. This exasperating little nut of a fortress must be cracked open and crushed, ground to extinction.

He divided his infantry into four storming columns. The first was under the command of General Cós; the second under Colonel Duque; the third under Colonels Romero and Salas; the fourth under Colonels Morales and Minon. The reserves he commanded, himself, with Colonel Amat. All the columns were equipped with ladders and wrecking bars. He placed his cavalry at surrounding points to cut off all possibility of escape for the Texians. At his word, the Alamo would be crushed between four closing jaws. His plan was perfect; he saw it all in his mind and he nodded approval. Decidedly, he could have shown Napoleon how to whip Wellington at Waterloo!

At four in the morning he watched his storming columns silently slip to their positions, awaiting the signal. A faint bleeding of pearl light spread up into the hushed sky from the east, first finger of the approaching Sabbath day. A trumpet blared shrill notes into the hush, sounding the rapid call of the charge, followed by the malign threat of the *degüello*—no quarter. Then the running tramp of the columns advancing to the assault, five thousand against one hundred and eighty.

The besieged were on the alert, His Excellency observed annoyedly. The stone wall erupted a shattering discharge all along its ramparts, where men snuggled rifle butts to cheeks and blazed into the black, oncoming mass. Messengers began coming fast to His Excellency, keeping him informed. Colonel

Duque had fallen with many of his command; his troopers were thrown into confusion. The two columns charging the western and eastern quarters had come to a disorderly halt. Their officers were driving them on, beating them with the flats of their swords.

Now they had gained to the foot of the walls, but they had dropped most of their scaling ladders. Fools! Animals! His Excellency cursed such blundering stupidity. Unable to scale the walls, and under the point-blank fire of the defenders on the ramparts, the army was splitting, moving to the right and left around to the northern side. Uniting with Duque's disorganized column, they had formed one dense mob.

"Assault—assault!" His Excellency rapped impatiently.

Again the assault was made, again hurled back. All around the Alamo, His Excellency could see a thick fringe of his killed and wounded attackers. "Renew the assault! General Amador—take command!"

General Amador, a bull-voiced old soldier, went charging onto the field and led the third attack. The small brass cannons of the Alamo had fallen silent, useless against a foe that was crowded below the range of fire. A breach had been made in the wall by the Mexican bombardment of the night before, and there had not been time enough to repair it. His Excellency sent a messenger racing to General Amador with instructions.

Against the breach in the wall General Amador concentrated his attack, pouring his stormers into it faster than the Texians could reload and fire their rifles. Meanwhile, Morales and Minon headed a company that made another break in the stockade and captured a gun on the wall.

His Excellency nodded, gratified, and in his mind he framed the compliment that he would graciously present to good General Amador. The Alamo was tottering.

From his cot, Bowie emptied a brace of pistols at the killers of his friend and Commander. Travis had fallen, shot and bayoneted while trying to defend the cannon.

Bowie took command. To hold the wall was no longer possible; too many of the enemy were swarming over it. He ordered a retreat to the buildings. Using pistols, clubbed rifles, knives, fighting hand to hand, the remnant of his command backed into the mission church and the barrack building, carrying him in with them. Barricading the front door of the church, they prepared for a last stand. From windows and loopholes their guns cracked into the yard.

Crockett loaded Bowie's rifle and pistols for him, and laid them by his side. The church was clouded with stinging smoke of burned black powder, choking the lungs and bringing tears to the eyes. Bowie was in a high fever, and his coughing interfered with his swearing. The Mexican artillery had come up, and the Alamo's own captured guns were being turned and aimed against the church. Filled sandbags had previously been piled against the church walls, but the batteries were pounding them to pieces. Cannon balls crashed through windows and walls, and into every gaping hole poured volleys of Mexican musketry fire. Through the roaring explosions, thin voices of men howled a cacophony of curses, pained screams, hoarse cries of defiance.

Crockett, his face unrecognizable from powder burns, smoke, and streaks of dried blood, grinned amiably and hideously at Bowie. "Let the varmints come!" he bellowed. "Let 'em try! I can stop a whole damned regiment of 'em, m'self, long's I got my Betsey gun!" He believed that, for he was that kind of man. No cause was lost while he had his gun in his fist.

He went and peered out through a broken window into the big yard. The main gates hung wide open, wrecked by battering rams.

Company after company of grenadiers was filing into the yard at the double march, followed by mounted dragoons all a-jingle with spurs and bridle bits, trundling more cannon be-

hind them. The trumpet was pealing out the *degüello* over
and over again. The old church trembled to the tramping feet
of Santa Anna's legion. The jaws were closing.

Crockett levelled his beautiful Betsey. "Here they come,
boys—aim well!"

He had barely got the words out, when a volley from the
Mexican infantry swept a hail of bullets against the walls, windows and door. It was answered by the Texian rifles, and at
that range there could be no missing. The massed columns re-
coiled and for a moment it seemed that they might yet be
beaten back, but their officers could be seen rallying them and
prodding them onward. They charged across the yard into the
spitting fire of the rifles.

Many casualties had left the remnant of the Texian garrison with guns to spare. While the wounded and the sick
rammed home powder and ball down the heated barrels,
those at the windows and loopholes fired, snatched up a
freshly loaded weapon, and fired again. Their glaring, bloodshot eyes, smoke-grimed faces and torn clothes gave them the
look of mad bandits in the swirling haze. Battle and the fierce
joy of it had uplifted them beyond the reach of any fear.
Some were cursing, some growling, some cheering, and at one
loophole a wild-eyed lad sang a hymn as if it were a war
chant.

When only a dozen steps from the door, again the stormers
were driven back by the murderous fire, but a fresh column
came running aslant across the yard and reached the corner.
Bent over, the soldiery slipped along the wall of the church,
under the loopholes, and gained to the door. The door was
suddenly spiky with lunged bayonets, and the discharged
guns behind them shot it to ragged patterns and lighted up
the church with a sheet of flame.

A group of Texians, Crockett among them, had run to defend the door. The volley bit into them, knocked them in a
chaotic heap, and the attackers streamed in. Crockett reared
up, striking and chopping at them, and for a few seconds he

held them back alone. Others came leaping to help them. The attackers could not halt. Those behind were crowding and pushing, firing over the heads of those in front.

From his cot, Jim Bowie saw tall Davy Crockett fall backwards with a broken rifle in his hands; saw the last of the Texians struggling, outnumbered, swamped. He fired his pistols and his rifle. He forced himself to sit up in his cot, and as uniformed men closed in around him, he whipped out his long knife.

Outside in the yard, the trumpet sounded once more the *degüello.* . . .

Afterwards, many brave epitaphs were emblazoned upon the tomb that men raised in their memories to the Alamo, to the Texians who died there: *Devoted heroes . . . Patriots . . . Noble warriors . . . Deathless names of immortal Spartans.* . . .

They went all the way back to ancient Greece, to the impassable morass of the Maléan shore, and from there brought the crowning tribute: *Thermopylae had its messenger of defeat—the Alamo had none.*

The Alamo Texians would have been embarrassed. They were hard-bitten men, with not much respect for wordy demonstration. They would have preferred the brief remark of old Mrs. Bowie, and they would have chuckled grimly over it. That rugged frontierswoman, when told that her son Jim had been killed in the Alamo, said calmly, "I wager them cusses didn't find no wounds in his back!"

"Burn the bodies!" commanded His Excellency.

The sun was well up now. It was quiet again, except for the murmur and tramp of soldiers coming out of the Alamo, the groans of the Mexican wounded, and the restless jingling of bridle bits as excited horses stamped and shook their heads. Guns, fouled and still hot to the touch, were silent.

His Excellency had made a tour of the captured fort, inspected the carnage, assured himself that no rebel there remained alive, and accepted the congratulations of his more subservient officers. The Tiger of Tampico had once again displayed his military genius and shattered an enemy. Bury the dead? Nonsense. It would take days. Besides, he had a thousand dead of his own. Now he must march on northward to new victories.

So they piled up the bodies in the yard, poured camphine over them, and lighted it. It was, His Excellency pointed out, the more sanitary method, after all. The camphine instantly sent up a great pillar of flame to an amazing height, frightening many of the soldiers who had never before seen so much fire. Some of them were a little superstitious about it. But when Santa Anna marched them northward away from the place, they remembered only the victory.

They looked back at the desolate ruin, and they thought of the glory that would be theirs when they got back to tell of it to the folks at home. To tell of the charging, the shooting, the desperate fighting. The strange, fanatical courage of the Texians. The hard-won victory of Santa Anna's legion.

To tell of the fall of the Alamo.

CHAPTER TWELVE

THE BOOMING OF THE BRASS SIX-POUNDER just outside the window was deafening, but the Indian gave no sign of even noticing it. Since the news had come of the fall of the Alamo, he had not spoken a word to Dain. He sat staring before him, dull eyed, wrinkled, incredibly old. Sometimes Dain thought that his mind must have snapped, he looked so imbecile.

There were times when Dain, himself, sat brooding, thinking of the Alamo. Davy Crockett, tall warrior of the large gesture and the grandiloquent phrase. Romantic young Boniface, intense and idealistic. Silent and cynical Thimblerig. The Pirate. They had been grand men, faultful and human; they had been his friends, and now they were gone, slaughtered.

The grim news of the Alamo disaster had shocked the garrison town of Goliad. Everybody was talking about it, and rumors and speculations were flowing fast. The word was that Sam Houston had arrived in Gonzales, to take up a task whose every prospect was black. Nearly two hundred more of the best men of Texas had gone to glory. Following so soon after the San Patricio defeat and annihilation, this left Texas crippled. Such armed forces as Texas now had left to her were scattered far apart, due to the vast distances of the country and the difficulty of assembling an army at any given point. And Santa Anna was said to be moving fast.

Houston was saying that there was only one course of action left, and that was to abandon Gonzales and Goliad and retreat toward the northeast, picking up all possible volunteers en route. Not to attempt a stand until he had amassed some sort of presentable army. Better to give ground, than to sacrifice what pitiful little army he had in a hopeless attempt to halt the powerful enemy. Ground might be recovered later, but dead men could not be replaced.

Fast-mounted messengers were riding the long trails, warning the settlers to flee at once, and scouring the country for volunteers, to tell them all to converge in upon the line of retreat. Gonzales was to be destroyed, leaving nothing that the enemy could use.

Everybody in Goliad knew that Fannin, the garrison Commander, had received orders from Houston to burn Fort Defiance and fall back toward Victoria. Houston was counting heavily upon Fannin's four hundred volunteers of Goliad to make junction with his own force.

There were many in Goliad who did not agree with the plan, and said so, loudly. Dain often heard them outside in the street, arguing in groups. They declared with biting sarcasm that Soldier Sam had his map upside down and was marching the wrong way—that any damned fool could retreat. Somebody brought in a report that there was incipient mutiny in Houston's own army; defections from the ranks; men openly deserting to go home and help their families in what was becoming known as the Runaway Scrape.

It had become very evident that Fannin, himself, was reluctant to retreat from Goliad. He had sent out a company several days ago under the command of a Captain King, to go and help the settlers at Refugio. Captain King had proceeded to get himself holed up in the Refugio Mission by part of the advancing Mexican army, so Fannin then sent out another detachment under Major Ward to go to the relief of King. He refused to leave those men behind, but he compromised by sending messengers to command them to return immediately to Goliad, if possible. The messengers had not returned, but yesterday a refugee had come slipping into town with the news that another Mexican division behind him, under the command of General Urrea, had taken care of King and Ward. Captain King had perished with all his men near Copano, and Major Ward was making a running fight of it toward Victoria with the few that were left of his detachment.

A rage was growing in Dain. Partisanship, aroused by the Alamo slaughter, was replacing his abstract view of the Texas war. It was a struggle against overwhelming odds, for a cause that was taking on clarity and starkly simple definition, and he wanted to get into it. The desire tugged at him, familiar in its feel, and he could understand very well the impulse that had brought Davy Crockett trekking down from Tennessee with his Betsey rifle on his shoulder—"To fight for my rights, suh!"

He had grinned to himself at the time, but now he conceded the rightness of it. Liberty was the natural right of man, everywhere. Oppression and tyranny were like diseases that threatened the whole race. They had to be combatted anywhere they cropped up. He agreed with that thesis. His very instincts agreed with it. This war was his. It was enraging to lie cooped here in this little attic room, helpless, while the fight approached its climax and Texas needed every man.

The six-pounder boomed again, rattling the window, and he looked out. Yesterday, during the afternoon, a company of Texas cavalry had gone clattering out of town. They had come cantering back shortly after, without any look of victory on them. From the window, at an angle, Dain could see part of the river. A squad of horsemen passed into his view, trotting along the far bank, and he knew that they were not Texians. Two cannons roared furiously at them from the bastions of Fort Defiance. They spurred to a gallop and vanished.

"Mexican cavalry picket, reconnoitering," he said aloud, and nodded to the Indian. "Likely means an attack soon. They're looking over our defenses. Fannin had better make up his mind soon what he's going to do."

The Indian did not reply, did not look at him.

Another picket appeared, and another. The enemy was getting bolder. Teams of horses dashed along the bank, dragging artillery into position, their drivers standing up and thrashing the straining animals. More cavalry followed, many officers among them, buttons and sword hilts and gold epaulettes winking bright flashes. The cannons of Fort Defiance set up a terrific din, and riflemen spent a lot of powder on long shots. The guns kept up their angry clamor until dark.

It grew cold during the night, and a north wind howled through the town, bringing rain. Once Dain got up and peered out. The walls of the fort were studded with the shapeless forms of muffled lookouts, beating their hands and shivering. "Might as well be in your bunks—they won't attack tonight in this weather," he muttered. "But if it clears by morning, you'll be warm enough tomorrow!"

A little startlingly, the Indian spoke up in a dreary monotone. "I knew that the Alamo would fall. It had to. I knew that the bodies would be burned. It was the quickest way to dispose of them."

"I'm beginning to think you're a hoo-doo!" Dain growled as he lay down. "Damn your predictions!"

"You just made one, yourself."

"Yes, but I based it on things that I can see and know."

"So did I."

"Did?" Dain raised his head and looked at the squatting figure in the darkness. "Did? You mean you've lost the—er—gift?"

The Indian stirred and sighed. "There was no gift. Only the law of consequence—which you, yourself, make use of in your limited fashion. Mathematicians make use of it. If two is added to two, the predictable consequence is four. The master chess player makes use of it, more intricately, more subtly. Life has been my chessboard. Like all master players, I evolved a technique—a fundamental theory which guided my every move. It sometimes happens that such a theory, reaching its zenith of development, fails at the golden moment of its culmination—and leaves its devotee broken by the failure. I was on the threshold of my final triumph. I stumbled and failed. I live, when I should have died in the Alamo— my last move in a long, long game. I have lost everything— even my faith in the eternal laws, and in my theory and technique. And in myself!"

He was still squatting there when Dain fell asleep, and Dain dreamed again of the black hole, the contorted faces, the shrieking and the eyes glaring up at him.

The wind and the rain died, and the morning dawned in a heavy fog. The noise of rolling wagons and tramping feet came up from the narrow street. Activity was going on under cover of the blanket of mist. "So Fannin's finally decided to pull out, has he?" Dain mused. "Hope he hasn't forgotten about his prisoners up here!"

The noises drained out of the street, and for a while there was empty silence. Dain went and kicked on the door, calling the guard who was usually stationed on the stairs outside. The sound of his kicking drummed through the house, but nobody answered. He heard Cleo calling to him from her locked room, and he shouted back. Then artillery began booming from the river, and further shouting was useless.

The cannons of Fort Defiance opened up. Dain peered upward from his window at the six-pounder on the wooden bridge. It was manned by its crew, ghostly pale in the mist. It emitted a flash and a roar, and the house shook. They were firing blind, unable to see much of the enemy because of the fog. Dain thought it probable that the Mexicans had altered the placements of their batteries during the night. If General Urrea had any military sense, he must have done so.

An explosion burst somewhere in the fort, followed minutes later by another. Urrea apparently had a howitzer or two, and was systematically lobbing big grenades into the fort. The gunners on the wooden bridge worked fast, ramming in powder charge and ball, springing clear, touching the match to the hole. What they were aiming at was a conjectural matter. The mist was thinning, and they hastily changed the range of their gun, evidently catching at last a glimpse of the enemy's movements.

A key rattled in the lock. The door swung open and the scholarly Major of intelligence stepped into the room, pistol drawn. He was hatless, his long brown hair was rumpled, his eyes were anxious. "Come with me, both of you, and don't try anything!" he snapped. "We can't spare a squad to guard you, but I assure you I can shoot!"

"How about the others?" Dain asked.

"I'm taking all of you to—" The cannon blared outside, drowning out the rest. The Major trod quickly to the window, flung it open and looked out. "Are they advancing yet?" he called to the gunners.

"Their cavalry's just crossing the river!" came the reply.

"Use grapeshot!"

"Just what we're gonna do."

A grenade fell, farther up the street, and burst with a shattering detonation. The fog was trailing off in wisps now. Another explosion, and things whistled in the air. A shred of a man's scream rang out between shots. Dain said, "How long d'you expect to hold on here?"

The Major turned from the window. "It's a rear-guard action. Fannin is retiring with the main force."

"What's to keep the Mexicans from skirting the town and going after him? Then your rear guard'll be cut off, what's left of them!"

The Major motioned with his pistol. "Damn your talk, hurry! I've got horses waiting in the yard." He poked his head out through the window again. "Keep it going, men! Don't let their cavalry get——"

There was a blinding flash and explosion, and the Major came hurtling backward in a shower of glass. A body fell past the window, clearly outlined for an instant. A widening crack in the ceiling let in an uneven bar of sunlight that played upon the wall above the window. The crack yawned, and a section of the roof crashed in, filling the room with dust and burying the Major in debris. After two close misses, the Mexican howitzer had scored a direct hit.

Half stunned from the concussion, Dain groped his way over the wreckage to the remains of the window and leaned out, gasping for air. The gunners had been blown off the wooden bridge, all but one whose arms and head hung over the edge, the dead face leering down at Dain. The bridge still held, warped at this end where part of the support had been knocked out, and the muzzle of the six-pounder jutted at a lowered angle. He stared along the street. Smoke poured from most of the houses and buildings. Fannin had put Goliad to the torch before abandoning it.

The street was empty except for one man, standing in a doorway. Tall, spare, his grey garb correct and unruffled, a cloak tossed back over his shoulders, he stood observing columns of cavalry advancing onto the town from the direction of the river. It was Mr. Falconer, looking for all the world like a gentleman watching a steeplechase from his own porch. He turned and spoke to somebody inside the house. Quaw appeared with a glass on a tray, his black face grimacing excitedly. Mr. Falconer took the glass and sipped from it, and sent his attention back to the cavalry. Casually, he pulled a rag from his coat pocket and shook it out. It was colored green, white and red. The flag of Mexico.

It was too much. Dain whirled back into the room for the Major's pistol. He and the Indian pulled the Major clear, but the limp hands were empty. The Major was dead, and his pistol had been torn from his fingers by the blast and lay buried somewhere under the wreckage of the roof. The key which he had used was still in the lock, two others attached to it.

Dain thought of the six-pounder on the bridge, loaded with grapeshot, its muzzle depressed and aimed into the street. "Take those keys and let Caerlie and the girls out," he told the Indian. "Get them out of the house and wait for me in the yard with the horses."

He clambered onto the mound of wreckage, jumped upward, and hauled himself out through the gaping hole in the roof. The Mexican cavalry was changing over from trot to full gallop, the foremost column lining directly for the narrow street. He stepped onto the wooden bridge. The twisted boards creaked ominously, and he had to hold onto the upturned edge to keep from sliding off, but in the center where the cannon was bolted the slant was not so acute. As he worked toward it he saw the Mexican flag being held up and fluttered in the doorway down the street.

The six-pounder was loaded, as he had hoped, but its direction of aim was wrong. Due to the twisted slant of the bridge, the muzzle was pointed toward the opposite side of the street from where the man in grey stood. He swung it slowly on its mount, trying to get it aimed at the square of colored rag. Shouts told him that he had been seen, and bullets began tearing splinters from the bridge. The fort's artillery had quit, either knocked out of action or else the Texian rearguard had retired. To aim the six-pounder accurately, unaided, was difficult, and time was short. He got it trained as closely as he could, trusting to the grapeshot to spread, and locked the mount. The first column of cavalry was thundering into the street. He found the match in its holder, still smouldering, and he took a final look along the street.

Mr. Falconer was no longer visible. The doorway where he had stood was vacant.

Dain cursed. He waited a few more seconds, holding the match poised above the touch hole, eyes fixed on the doorway, hoping for his target to reappear. The charging column came abreast of the doorway. He could wait no longer. He thrust in the burning end of the match.

The recoil from the discharge set the weakened bridge bouncing, and a thick cloud of smoke drifted back into Dain's face. When it cleared and he could see again, he looked at the havoc. The grapeshot had ripped into the head of the column, some of it ricocheting off house fronts and road and finding targets farther back. Riders, unable to turn aside in the narrow street, had spilled and piled up against the fallen leaders. Others were fighting their horses, trying to hold them from bolting back the way they had come. The whole column was in wild disorder.

Dain heard a voice calling his name. He looked and found Cleo and the Indian crawling along the shaking bridge toward him. "Go back!" he shouted at them.

They disobeyed. They came up to him and the cannon. The Indian picked up the wet swabber, ran it down the smoking muzzle to extinguish sparks that might ignite prematurely the next charge, and tossed the swabber into the street. He moved with precision, as if he might have had some experience with gunnery and warfare. "I think," he said, "this bridge may stand the strain of one more shot. Aim more to the center of the street, please!"

Cleo handed him the powder charge. He rammed it in. She carried a load of grapeshot in her arms to the muzzle. He helped her slide it in, tapped it home, and they stepped clear.

Dain veered the muzzle, locked it into position, and took up the match. "Get off the bridge—it may not stand this one," he told them.

The Indian shrugged. "Touch it off—what matters!"

The bridge bounced again, sagged in the middle, and settled to a deeper tilt. They did not wait for the smoke to clear, and to see the results of the second discharge. They scrambled along the bridge to the house, and paused to view it from there.

"Where's Suela and her father?" Dain demanded. "Are they waiting for us in the yard?"

Cleo did not answer. He asked it again, shouting into her ear, thinking that the noise of the cannon might have deafened her. She was not looking into the street. Her eyes were on a farther point, on the stretch of land between the town and the river.

"Look!" she said, and pointed.

Mexican grenadiers were advancing in the rear of the cavalry. Two riders in civilian clothes cantered out from town toward them, the taller one holding up his right hand. A mounted infantry officer rode out and met them. He saluted, shook hands with the tall one, bowed to the other.

"There they are," Cleo said, and she spoke with the tones of a man. "Both of them—Suela and John Caerlie! Hah! The Major was right. Baltasar Duncaerlie and his daughter, Consuela. Mexican spies!"

She turned her head and looked at Dain. His expression brought her hand to his shoulder. "We've got to hurry, Dain. Come."

"If I had a rifle!" he said thickly. "If I had a rifle!"

"If I had one I'd give it to you!" she said. "Come!"

They rode across rolling ground, the three of them, low in the saddle and beating their horses. The Mexican cavalry columns had divided, circling around the town, and a detachment from the left was in hot pursuit of the fugitives. Far behind, smoke from the burning houses hung over Goliad, an abandoned town in the hands of the enemy, and no sounds of gunfire came from that direction any more.

It was easy to follow the tracks of the retreating Goliad army. They pointed northeast toward Victoria. General Urrea would find them just as easy to follow, and he wouldn't have to hamper his speed with wagons.

Cleo edged her horse up alongside Dain, and they raced side by side, the Indian a little in the rear. "We paid some of the score for the Alamo, didn't we?" she called out.

He nodded, speaking no reply, but in a minute he called back, "I'll pay off more before I'm through! Duncaerlie! Yes, and his lying daughter! And that pale-eyed devil! He's back there, Cleo, with a Mexican flag."

She gestured ahead. "We've made it—there's the army!"

The Goliad army marched in column formation, wagons and wheeled artillery in the center, rifle troops close in, mounted men in front and rear. Heads jerked around at the sound of hoofs behind. A body of riders detached itself from the rear and wheeled around. The pursuing Mexican cavalry pulled up out of rifle range and finally withdrew. Dain, Cleo and the Indian rode in and joined the column.

A Captain eyed them. "Don't think I've seen you fellows before," he commented. He failed to recognize Cleo as a girl, in her male attire. Under her big hat she wore a handkerchief tied tightly over most of her hair, and a shapeless old coat covered her from neck to knees. Her face was dirty with smoke and smudges, and there was no feminine shrinking in the look of her eyes.

"Any more stragglers back there?" the Captain queried.

"Nobody back there but the enemy," Dain answered, "and you'll be seeing them soon!"

"Are they after us already?"

"I reckon they are. Why not? They've got six times the force we have, and we're leaving a track that a blind mule could follow—and a cripple on crutches could catch up with us at this pace!"

The Captain nodded. "Right. But Fannin didn't want to leave the supplies behind. Well, we'll give 'em a fight if they do show up, eh?"

"We'll give 'em a fight," Dain agreed. "We're on this plain without a stick of cover, and if I were a praying man I'd pray for a good thick woods right now. But we'll give 'em a fight, as you say."

"Woods ahead, on the Coleto."

"I could pray they were closer!"

The column pressed on, leaving tracks and hanging dust, across the treeless prairie that lay between the San Antonio river and the low-lying Coleto creek. Two hours past noon, they were within a mile and a half of the Coleto's thick woods, their course running over a series of gentle downward slopes toward it. Because of the slopes they were leaving behind them, their view of. the rear was restricted. Mounted scouts were sent back to keep watch. It seemed a foregone conclusion that the woods would be reached. The woods offered a perfect refuge and covert for men whose fighting talents leaned toward deadly sharpshooting and independent initiative rather than to disciplined and concerted action. From in there they could slice to ribbons any army brought against them.

A scout came dusting along from the rear, riding hard. "Enemy in sight and coming fast!" he shouted.

Teamsters lashed their animals. The lines of riflemen broke into a trot to keep up with the increase of pace, and the small troop of cavalry wheeled out of line and came together in the rear to form a rear guard. Dain, Cleo and the Indian fell in with the cavalry. Nobody knew them as escaped prisoners. During their imprisonment few had seen them.

A careening ammunition wagon up front bogged a wheel in a sandy hollow, lurched halfway around, and overturned. The traces snapped and the team bolted onward. The rest of the column bunched and halted, while men sweated to right the wagon and a spare team of oxen were brought up.

The rest of the rear scouts rode in, offering urgent suggestions and warnings.

"Let the damn thing go!"

"Hey—we got to get in them woods! Enemy's right behind us!"

"Burn it an' push on, or we'll never . . . Here they come!"

The Mexican army loomed up on the rise behind, column after column, and came marching down in good order, at that distance looking like mammoth snakes winding slowly down the slopes. The Jiménez rifle battalion, the San Luis Regiment, a company of grenadiers, and several cavalry troops; General

Urrea had brought along the pick of his army, leaving the rest to garrison Goliad and try to put out the fires.

The distance was as yet far too great for shooting. The Texian horsemen spread out in skirmish line, expecting to play a delaying rear-guard action while the main force hurried on to the Coleto woods.

Then, up forward, somebody raised a yell: "Beard o' Moses —look yonder ahead!"

More troops of Mexican cavalry were riding at a headlong gallop, piercing between the stalled Texian column and the Coleto woods. They had circled around, unseen by the Texians, to cut off further retreat and force a one-sided battle on the open plain. General Urrea knew something about warfare and the value of the quick stroke. This day was his birthday anniversary, and he had sufficient vanity to want to celebrate it in a manner befitting a confirmed old soldier.

The little troop of Texian horsemen, faced on two fronts by a menacing foe, hardly knew which way to turn. On their own initiative some of them reined about and dashed for the woods, cutting across the path of the encircling Mexican dragoons. It was in their minds that a break-through by the whole Goliad brigade would have to be attempted; from the woods they could aid by harassing the enemy's rear. Dain's group thought so, too, and the Captain agreed and spoke of forming a spearhead for the expected Texian charge. The Captain led what remained of his troop back to the column for orders to lead off.

Instead, the command came: "Fort in!" There was some quirk in Fannin's make-up that made him reluctant to move out from any place where he happened to be.

The wagons wheeled, rocking and swaying over the ground, and drew together in the form of a rough square. Harness was hurriedly peeled off the teams and the animals driven into the enclosure. Riflemen and dismounted horsemen took battle formation, and the old brass cannons were dragged into place. They waited for the surrounding enemy's attack.

It was prompt in coming.

General Urrea barked commands. Colonel Morales to charge the left of the square with the rifle companies. The Jiménez battalion under Colonel Salas, to the front. Colonel Nuñez to surprise the enemy's rear with the cavalry. The General, himself, would lead the grenadiers and the San Luis Regiment, and charge the right. Bayonets fixed. Ready . . .

"Trumpeter, sound the charge!"

CHAPTER THIRTEEN

The sunlight was fading from the bullet-riddled wagons, stilled bodies and scattered men. Urrea had made his charge, and the loss was heavy on both sides. His four-point attack had broken against withering rifle fire and cannon shot. His foot soldiers split up into guerrilla bands, lying prone and sniping into the wagon corral. The men from Goliad built up their defenses with baggage and killed animals, and kept up a rattling fire.

He tried again, and led a cavalry attack that circled the entire square, hurling his dragoons at one side after another, trying to force a breach in the defense. The Texians ran their cannons to the corners and blasted rounds of shot until the guns grew too hot to fire. Furious, unable to break the square, Urrea was forced to retire with his reduced command, cursing because the reserve troops and munitions which he had hurriedly ordered from Goliad had not yet arrived.

Had the Texians only known it, Urrea was running perilously short of ammunition, his casualties were high, and his men had had about enough for that day.

But they didn't know it, and their own percentage of killed and wounded was enormous. Fannin himself had a bullet in the thigh. There was no way of transporting the wounded, in case of a fighting dash for the woods. Many of the horses and oxen had broken out and stampeded during the attacks. Others had fallen to Mexican snipers. The wagons could not be moved, to use as ambulances. The situation was desperate, and to make it worse they were almost out of water. They looked at the sun going down, at the constantly moving enemy pickets, and saw little to hope for in the coming night.

Cleo knelt behind the wagon breastworks, with a rifle that she had learned to use well during the past few hours. She rubbed her right shoulder, which the kick of the rifle had made sore. She watched Dain cleaning and loading the last of three rifles which he had kept busy, and she noticed how intently he applied himself to the task—cleaning the fouling out of the barrel with vinegar, then drying and oiling it. Measuring the powder with a steady hand, placing the greased patch of buckskin over the muzzle, and the spherical bullet over that, and thrusting it home. Setting the priming and flint with a scrupulous, almost holy care. Finally snapping shut the frizzen. And, staring at the enemy, rubbing his palm down the tiger-flame maple stock, with engrossed, deadly love.

She had never before seen him with quite that look on his face and in his eyes. Just as she always tried to analyze and understand his moods, she searched this one and plumbed it. It was a cold, killing mood. Not passionate. Not floated upon anger of the moment. She was a little afraid of it, and searched deeper for its causes. Not this fight of today—no, it wasn't just that. A fight did not chill him like this. A fight sharpened him to cool, concentrated violence—yes—but not to the extent that he could not retain a certain hard humor. The Alamo slaughter? It had its place under this mood, but it was not that alone.

Her mind impatiently pushed forward the thought of Consuela Duncaerlie. There was the main cause—that fair girl, so lovely. And so false. Riding with her father to meet the advancing Mexican soldiers. Receiving the bow of a Mexican officer. Her father receiving the salute befitting his rank as a Colonel in Santa Anna's invading army. Herself a spy for Santa Anna.

Well, she was gone forever from Dain, that fair girl with voice so soft and eyes so candid. She hadn't won. She had lost. This terrible mood of Dain's would pass, in time. If a few more killings were needed to hurry it off, she—Cleo—stood more than willing to help. It was well that it had turned out this way. She smiled her secret smile. It was well. It was good. She reached out and touched Dain, and when he turned she smiled at him. It didn't matter that his eyes looked blindly through her. He would see her again when this passed away.

She knew that she was uncomely now, in her ripped and shabby male garb, her thick hair hidden by a soiled rag and shapeless hat, her face dirty. The day would come again when she would walk in fine attire, elegant and very fetching, as she had done on the Arkansas steamboat—when every man on board had tried to catch her eye, and had scowled in envy at Dain behind his broad back.

She said, "I'll keep them loaded for you, Dain. My arm's sore and I can't shoot any more."

A man on the left flank hailed wearily, "Here they come again!"

Urrea had decided to risk one last attempt to crack the square while some light still remained, fearing that the defenders, those who were able, might break out during the night and escape into the woods. He employed the favorite tactics, a simultaneous attack on all four sides, and placed himself at the head of the cavalry. The trumpet brayed, and the last assault of the day was launched.

The dusk was stabbed with points of rifle fire all around the square, and this time no part of the charge reached to beyond fifty paces of the objective. The grenadiers and infantry began falling back, their officers unable to drive them on farther. Tardily, Urrea ordered columns to retire and keep up a slow fire with whatever powder remained. He kept his cavalry dashing back and forth to cover the retirement, and at last withdrew them and placed his pickets for the night.

"Tomorrow," he swore, thumping a fist on his saddle, "I shall smash that square, or die!"

The Texas men worked late, repairing and bolstering their defenses. By that time it had got so cold that they could not sleep, exhausted as they were. They could not light fires for the Mexican snipers to shoot at, so they huddled together on

the ground, forced to rise every few minutes, too cold to lie
still. The Mexicans had their campfires, well out of gunshot
range. The cavalry pickets kept prowling in close to get off
a few shots, and the Mexican trumpeter amused himself by
blaring false calls to keep the Texian camp awake.

Dain had scooped a shallow hole in the ground, for some
protection against the wind. He ripped a canvas off a wagon,
and he and Cleo lay under it, trying to get warmed. With a
faint touch of his old hard humor, he muttered, "How d'you
like Texas now, comrade?"

Her thoughts reverted to the fair girl, back in Goliad. Or
somewhere. Gone. Gone forever out of Dain's life. She smiled
in the darkness. "I didn't at first," she said, "but I'm beginning to."

At daybreak General Urrea inspected the rebel position and
found it to be much the same as that of the day before, with
the exception of the bolstering of the flimsy breastworks. The
rebels had made no attempt to break out during the night.
They had not abandoned their wounded. He glowered at the
square. He had by this time developed an invidious respect
for it. Well, there was only one thing to do, and that was to
try again with infantry bayonets and dragoon swords.

Rations were issued, and the General gave orders for his
badly battered command to take up position. He was about to
nod to the trumpeter, when his reserves from Goliad finally
hove into sight—a strong regiment of Garay's grenadiers,
heavy loads of ammunition, two cannon and a howitzer.

The General was so pleased to get the heavy artillery that
he neglected to hand out a reprimand for the late arrival of
the reinforcements. At once he placed them as a battery, pro-
tected by riflemen, less than two hundred paces from the
square. It was all over now. The guns were to open fire as
soon as the attack began. He added the grenadier regiment to
his own command, issued ammunition all around and re-

aligned his command for the assault. This time there could be no failure. He had everything he needed, and more.

The Goliad volunteers, too, knew that it was all over as soon as they saw the guns and reserves. Their wagon bulwarks were useless against artillery. Fannin, pale and weak from his wound, saw his course whittled down to a choice of three alternatives. He could attempt to fight his way out of the trap, losing many more men and abandoning his wounded. He could stay here and be slaughtered. He could surrender and perhaps save the rest of his command.

"Cease firing!" he ordered.

The General was most courteous. He begged Fannin not to rise, in respect to his wound. He glanced around the Texian camp and said—with sincerity—that he was distressed to observe so much suffering on the part of such gallant and worthy foes. Gallantry and courage, he added with a bow, were qualities that made all soldiers esteem one another mutually. As for the terms of surrender. . . .

Terms? He regretted the impossibility in which he found himself of granting any other terms than an unconditional surrender. Santa Anna was his commander-in-chief, and had been quite specific in his orders covering such matters. However, he—Urrea—would use all his influence with His Excellency to obtain lenience for prisoners who had formally capitulated.

"If you gentlemen wish to surrender at discretion," he said in conclusion, "the matter is ended. Otherwise, I must return to my camp and renew the attack, much as I deplore the prospect."

There was no more to be said. The General meant every word of it. He waited patiently while Fannin conferred with his officers. When they reluctantly gave him their reply, he bowed again and assured them that they had taken the only possible course, in view of the extreme circumstances. Unconditional surrender.

The General then sent a dispatch to His Excellency, reporting the outcome of the battle. He added that the prisoners were being taken back to Goliad, there to be held under guard until disposition should be made of their cases. He, himself, was taking the major part of his command and pushing on without delay to Victoria, where it was reported that rebel escapees from Refugio were congregating.

Disarmed and under heavy guard, the Texian prisoners tramped back to Goliad, and there a Yucatan Indian battalion, left as a garrison, took charge of them. Among those who watched the prisoners being brought in were two gentlemen in civilian attire, Baltasar Duncaerlie and Mr. Falconer, looking conspicuous among all the uniforms around them. Mr. Falconer was in affable conversation with a group of Mexican officers, but his silvery eyes bored at every prisoner as the line limped by.

"Duck your head!" Dain muttered to Cleo, but she had already seen the grey-garbed man, and she held her head bent. Her face was colorless under the dirt, and she wet her lips with the tip of her tongue.

With their heads lowered they plodded with the column. Dain could not resist the temptation to cast a sidelong glance, and then he made no more attempt to shield his face. The pale eyes were fastened upon him, blank and bright, while the lips below went on speaking complimentary pleasantries to the Mexican officers.

"It's no good—he sees us," he said quietly. "Maybe it's just as well, anyway. If he tells them you're a woman——"

"I'll kill myself! They'd turn me over to him!"

"Perhaps not."

"And if not—what?" murmured a familiar voice, and they turned and found the Indian pacing along behind them. The last Dain had seen of him, he had attached himself to a gunner crew.

As usual, the Indian had touched to the core of the subject. Dain looked around at the Indian faces of the marching Yucatan guards, and caught the meaning behind the murmured query. "I reckon you're right," he said. "I reckon maybe she'd better go on being a man as long as she can keep it up."

"Why in hell's name," said General Sam Houston, "didn't Fannin retreat when I told him to?"

He was a remarkable man, many-sided, tinged with mystery, every facet of his character having a spark to it. Stories and anecdotes about him went the rounds by hundreds, and he knew it. He did not have to seek fame; it sought him. Picturesque in dress, speech and manners, he appealed to popular imagination as much for his faults as for his finer qualities. His friends were as passionately loyal to him as his enemies were bitterly acrimonious. He was either loved or hated; he was never ignored.

Unlike Fannin, he had not tarried when he learned of a strong Mexican division coming after him. He quit Gonzales with less than four hundred men—the only semblance of a Texas army that he could find to command—rid himself of heavy burdens, trimmed his little force down to a light and mobile unit, and began his retreat. Most of the wagons he gave to the colonists of the vicinity, for them to carry their belongings in, in their flight. Having thus crippled his transport, he had to burn his surplus supplies to keep them from falling into the hands of the enemy. His cannon he sank in the river—an act for which, he knew, much of his army condemned him.

"They'd slow us down too much," he'd said; whereupon certain fiercely combative spirits wanted to know how fast and far he planned to run.

On the Colorado, while gathering in bands of wandering volunteers, he had received the report of the Battle of the Coleto and another crushing defeat for Texas. It punched sickeningly at his hopes of making a stand soon, and he ordered the retreat to be continued. That damned Santa Anna was moving altogether too smartly on the forward jump for a Mexican. What was wrong, anyway? Everybody had been gaily certain that the Mexican army would dally around, and here it was darting this way and that, splitting, coming together again, striking down everything in its path and taking Texas as fast as it could travel. It was bewildering, unnatural, dismaying.

Now the Texas army was at Groce's Crossing, on the Brazos. Houston thought that he might have time here to organize his irregulars into some sort of cohesive force, and he began training them. It wasn't easy. He found that the filibusters and adventurers from beyond the Sabine were an independent lot, regarding themselves as free-lance soldiers with the right to fight how and when they chose. They insisted upon electing their own officers. The Texian colonists let him know that they were critical of the way he was conducting the war, and they were suspicious of further retreat. Many of them had lost their homes and had had no news of their families. The way to fight a war, they said, was not by running away. No, nor by fooling around with all this consarned drilling and such like foolishness.

One bit of brightness in the dark picture came when he received a present—a brace of new cannon, bought by public subscription up in Cincinnati and shipped to him with best wishes. He was glad to get them, having no other artillery whatever. The donors had christened them the Twin Sisters.

"Well, Sisters," he greeted them, slapping their iron snouts, "let's hope you'll spit like wildcats when the time comes!"

But he wished he had Fannin's army here with him. Four hundred more men would have made a tremendous difference. He wondered how the survivors were faring in Goliad, and what their fate would be.

It gave him great pleasure, Santa Anna informed Duncaerlie, to welcome back to his staff an officer whom he had given up for lost. At the same time, he hinted that he regretted the Colonel's failure to distinguish himself by accomplishing any sort of valuable espionage work during his absence.

Colonel Duncaerlie stiffened a little. "My search for my daughter, Your Excellency—" he began.

"Yes, yes, of course." Santa Anna gestured briefly. He sat up in his tent, in overnight camp, his tunic unbuttoned and his boots off—a dark, sharp-featured man with lank black hair, beak nose, and down-curved trap of a mouth. So far, he had not deigned to spare more than a glance at the civilian gentleman who had been allowed entrance into the tent along with the Colonel.

"It is unfortunate, Colonel, that your daughter has been the means of your detention from all active duty in this war, so far," he mentioned. "She is now——?"

"Safely in Goliad," responded Duncaerlie shortly.

"Convey to her my felicitations. And this gentleman——?"

"Mr. Falconer, a neutral citizen of the United States," Duncaerlie introduced him stonily. "He met our army in Goliad with a Mexican flag, and he was unarmed and had taken no part in the fighting. Nor had he attempted to follow the retreating enemy. For those reasons he was not arrested. He represents himself to be the head of a business house with foreign interests, and he desired very much to accompany me and obtain an audience with Your Excellency."

"A private audience," murmured Mr. Falconer. "To our mutual interest, I trust."

The black eyes of Santa Anna met the pale gaze of Mr. Falconer, at first in haughty inquiry, then with a quickening interest. His Excellency lifted a finger to Duncaerlie, and the Colonel saluted and left the tent.

Mr. Falconer drew out an oilskin wallet. Casually, without humility, he unfolded it and chose from it a few papers which he dropped upon His Excellency's portable desk. "These will serve as my credentials and a more comprehensive introduction."

His Excellency perused the first paper, raised his head to

look more studyingly at his visitor, and carefully read the rest. He folded them and handed them back. He leaned forward, elbows on the desk, and tapped a thumbnail against his teeth. "Unless I am mistaken, Colonel Duncaerlie presented you as Mr. Falconer, did he not? Yet your papers——"

"Business, like government, often has need for subterfuge, Excellency," inserted Mr. Falconer pleasantly.

"H'mm. Please to be seated, *señor*."

"Thank you." Mr. Falconer seated himself, giving the knees of his trousers a meticulous hitch and arranging his cape. "The name is unimportant, except as a necessary pseudonym. Necessary because of the prominence of my business house, of which you may have heard."

"It is familiar to me. You maintain a branch office in Mexico City, and a large warehouse in the port of Vera Cruz, if I recall correctly."

"Yes. We have branches and agents in many parts of the world. Being merchant shippers, ours is a diverse business. We trade in everything, everywhere. Even in land. Cotton plantations, particularly. Cotton is the backbone of our trade. Much of Texas could be turned into very satisfactory cotton land, Excellency."

Santa Anna nodded politely, his eyes masked. "May I ask your reason for coming to Texas—ah—Mr. Falconer?"

"Two reasons. The first was a personal one. The second is—land." Mr. Falconer eyed the dictator of Mexico, reading him in spite of the controlled blankness of the arrogant face. "It is obvious that you will win the war. The rebels are thoroughly beaten, and it is now merely a matter of chasing out of the country what remains of them. I presume that the lands of the ousted colonists will then be opened up for purchase. Am I right?"

"Ah—I have given no consideration to the matter, *señor*, but no doubt that is correct. The purchasers would, of course, have to be approved by my Government."

"Exactly. And you are the Government. Confidentially, Excellency, my company would be willing to transfer its headquarters to a Texas that is fully governed by Mexico, and to continue in business under the Mexican flag and Mexican protection. The laws of the United States are becoming yearly more stringent, more adverse to some of my company's most active and lucrative interests. We are finding it difficult to continue in business under the United States flag. Such a transfer offers us advantages, and would by no means prove unprofitable to the Government of Mexico. Naturally, we would wish positive assurances of obtaining and keeping those advantages, before taking the step."

His Excellency took his thumbnail from his teeth and examined it. "Such assurances as——?"

"Choice of geographical position—title of full ownership—an agreed amount of taxes payable annually—no port duties on our goods—no examination of our vessels—no interference in the conduct of our business." Mr. Falconer enumerated them promptly, ticking them off on the fingers of his lean hands. "We would require at least five hundred Spanish leagues of land, preferably along both sides of the Brazos River from its mouth, and our own seaport."

Santa Anna prided himself upon the scope of his mind, but he blinked at this. "*Señor*, you ask for an empire!" he exclaimed.

"Excellency, I ask to *buy* an empire," corrected Mr. Falconer. "For it—and for the certain advantages described—I am ready to pay eighty thousand United States dollars. Half in advance, payable by bank draft in Mexico City. I request from you only one condition. It is a trifle, a personal matter to me."

"What is it?"

"There is a man among the prisoners in Goliad. . . ."

"You desire his freedom?"

"The contrary, Excellency—quite the contrary!"

Santa Anna slapped the desk, and an orderly entered. "My

compliments to Colonel Duncaerlie, and inform him that I desire his attendance at once." He turned back to Mr. Falconer. "Your proposition comes at an opportune time, and will receive our closest consideration. It is no secret that the Mexican treasury is in a deplorable condition. I have been hard put to obtain finances for this Texas campaign."

Mr. Falconer inclined his head in acknowledgment. The deal was as good as made. There would have to be further discussions, some polite haggling, a little judicious dallying on the part of His Excellency. Price would be the deciding factor. Mr. Falconer was prepared for that. Business was business, and human nature followed much the same groove in all parts of the world—a little more subtlety here, a little less there, but fundamentally the same.

Colonel Duncaerlie entered. He had retrieved his belongings from the care of brother officers, and now he was back in uniform. Erect and dour, his military dignity became him well, although the Mexican uniform always appeared a little inappropriate upon him. He was of larger stature than most Mexicans; bigger boned and less rounded of form and features, and conspicuous because of his reddish-grey hair and freckled skin. He would have appeared much more natural, thought Mr. Falconer, in tartan kilt and Glengarry bonnet.

Santa Anna drew forth paper and pen. "Lieutenant Colonel Portilla, I believe, is at present in command of the Goliad garrison and the prisoners?" he inquired.

"Yes, Excellency." Duncaerlie stared woodenly over his superior's head. "May I ask if you are about to decide upon the disposal of the prisoners? And, if so, may I be permitted to enter a plea for reasonable leniency toward them?"

"You may."

"Thank you. I wish to point out that the Goliad rebels regard themselves as prisoners of war, and it was with that impression that they surrendered. The same impression exists among the majority of our officers who took part in that action, including General Urrea. We realize that in the strict legal sense they are outlaws, and that a great number of them are foreign adventurers who have no real connection with Texas. But they fought gallantly, like soldiers. We feel that it would be a barbarous affront to humanity to mete out to them the extreme punishment which our laws demand in the case of armed outlaws."

Santa Anna heard him through. He dipped the pen. "Is that all, Colonel?"

"That is all, Excellency."

"Very well. Your plea is most eloquent and moving. It inspires in me the thought that blood and lineage may exercise as strong an influence as does patriotism, even in a soldier. No, no, Colonel—no protests, please! Your inclination toward leniency for men of your father's race does you credit. I take cognizance of it." The pen scratched rapidly over the paper.

"This is my order concerning the prisoners." Santa Anna sealed it and handed it to him. "You will deliver it personally to Colonel Portilla, and see that it is carried out. You will then return to my command. I shall expect you to catch up with us somewhere along the Brazos—so that you may take part in the last battle, at least."

Duncaerlie saluted and left with the order. Santa Anna turned courteously to Mr. Falconer. "*Señor,* we are going into the country which you desire to purchase. I should enjoy your company. But perhaps you prefer to return to Goliad with Colonel Duncaerlie?"

Mr. Falconer cleared his throat. "It would depend upon the nature of the order which you just penned," he said softly. "I trust that the estimable Colonel's touching appeal did not too greatly affect your judgment. I trust that the order, from my viewpoint, was satisfactory."

"Satisfactory, yes—*quite* satisfactory!"

"Ah! Then there remains no need for me to return to Goliad. I shall be honored to accompany your army, Excellency, as an appreciative witness to your final triumph over these rebels. And I am happy to increase my offer to one hundred thousand United States dollars."

"You are most generous," murmured His Excellency. "Generosity, *señor*, is a rare quality which, when found, should be cherished. Possessing it, myself, I admire it in others. We are *simpático*. We should be friends!"

CHAPTER FOURTEEN

CONSUELA DUNCAERLIE TOLD HERSELF
that·what she was about to do was dictated by common gratitude, and nothing else. She repressed a strong desire to hurry,
and she chatted lightly with her escort, a young Mexican Captain who was so gallantly solicitous of her that he almost bent
sidewise over her as he walked.

Most of Goliad had burned, despite the Mexicans' attempts
to put out the fires. The shelled and gutted town was a grave-
yard of blackened, broken skeletons of houses. The streets
were strewn with half-burned timbers and chunks of adobe,
and over it all hung a bluish haze that fouled the air with a
pungent, depressing odor. Against the somber havoc, ham-
mers and saws rang incongruously cheerful notes. The prisoners had been put to work repairing the fortress for the Mexican garrison.

The Captain escorted Consuela into the fort, and hailed a
corporal. "There is a man named Dain among the prisoners.
Find him and bring him here."

Consuela forced herself to assume a bored disinterest in
the men and activity around her, while waiting. The Captain
kept glancing aside at her, and two or three times she feared
that he was framing a question. It was an extraordinary thing
for the daughter of a Mexican Colonel to request an interview
with a rebel captive. Quite indecorous. She supposed that it
would give rise to some talk, and probably some scandal. She
wished that the corporal would hurry and return, before the
Captain could get his discreet questions framed.

But the Captain managed to restrain his curiosity, and he
ended his inner struggle by asking her if she wished to meet

the man in public. By his tone he implied that a gesture, at least, should be made toward shielding the meeting from the eyes of the prisoners, many of whom were bending considerable bold attention at her. Her father, disturbed by the shocking impropriety of her male attire, had managed to salvage for her some feminine clothes from the town. They were not what she would have chosen for herself, but they were respectable and they posed no doubt as to her sex.

She favored the Captain with a grateful smile. "You are thoughtful, Captain. Of course, you are right. Could privacy, perhaps, be arranged?"

The Captain glowed. Ah, girls were girls. They needed the wise guidance of men at all times, to guard them from thoughtless indiscretion. This innocent little thing—he should have been firm and advised her against committing this imprudent act. But she was very lovely, and it was quite impossible to refuse her a favor. He had, in fact, rushed to grant it before realizing the nature of it—just as he now rushed to grant her another.

He left her side and returned quickly with the information that there was a small room next to the guardroom. He had peremptorily emptied it of an occupying lieutenant, and it was at her disposal. She thanked him, entered the room, and he stood with arms folded at the doorway, wearing somewhat the air of a self-conscious Cerberus standing guard over virtuous innocence. At any other time she would have been amused, noting again the difference between Spanish and Anglo-American viewpoint. The Spaniard was apt to regard virtue as a precarious quality to be kept under watchful protection. The Anglo-American credited it with sense enough to protect itself, under ordinary conditions.

When Dain was brought into the room, he had no idea of the reason why he had been taken off work. The corporal was a Yucatan, and told him nothing. The Yucatans spoke only their own Indian tongue, understood little Spanish and no

English whatever. By contrast with the outside light, the room was dark, and for the first few seconds Dain did not recognize the identity of the waiting girl. When he did, he stopped short, and the following corporal bumped into his back and grunted annoyedly.

"Is this the man?" asked the Captain.

The look in the grey-green eyes of the prisoner sent a chill through the girl. She was glad that the Captain could not see her face too well in the gloom. "Yes," she replied. Under her cape her hands were tightly clenched, and she felt herself beginning to tremble. "May I have the privacy now, please?"

The Captain had not intended the exclusion to extend to himself. He drew his brows down, and cast a glance over the tall, unkempt prisoner. "You think it safe?" he demurred. "This man——"

"It is perfectly safe, thank you, Captain."

"Very well. But I shall be within call if you need me." Reluctantly, the Captain dismissed the corporal and stepped outside.

Dain said tonelessly, "He didn't close the door. Lady spies obtain best results in complete privacy, I understand!" He closed it, and came slowly back to her. His eyes were cruel. "I presume you want something from me? What could it be?"

"Nothing! I came to——"

"Liar!" He stood over her, and smiled. "Spying is a dangerous game. You can't always win.. This time, dear Suela—or Consuela—I think you lose! You should've known better than to come here. You should've stayed away from me, after I saw you and your father riding out to the Mexican lines!"

He dropped his hands on her shoulders. They were hard hands, dirty from working with charred timbers, and they left black smears on her cape. "Or did you gamble that your charms would still make a fool of me? Did you think that what had won so handsomely once, must win again? And what stakes are you gambling for this time?"

"I'm not a spy—I never was a spy! I came here to help you."
She did not move to pull away from him. She stood quietly
under his hands, and he thought that she was unafraid of him,
until he felt the slight trembling beneath his fingers. He knew
then that she was afraid of him and was hiding it.

She said, "Some are saying that you'll all be marched down
into Mexico, to prison. Others say Santa Anna may even order
the execution of those who weren't colonists. I think I can
save you—and Cleo."

"Cleo, too, eh?" His smile was fixed and mocking. "I doubt
if Cleo would let herself be saved by you. She's proving to be
an expert with a hammer—and I wouldn't advise you to get
too close to her! How would you go about saving us?"

"I could swear that you came to Goliad as my escort, and
that you don't belong to Fannin's army. That you were arrested by the Texians along with me and my father, and later
you were forced to accompany the Texian army's retreat."

"And what would you want from me in return?"

"Nothing."

"Then why would you do it?"

"For—for the sake of . . ." She stammered for the first
time, and caught herself. "Because I am grateful for your past
kindnesses to me."

He took one hand from her shoulder and put its palm under
her chin. "Well, well!" He raised her face and stared down
into it, and still she did not resist. She could not know that
he had to make his voice harsh and flat to keep a shakiness
from it. "I wonder—dare I hope that you would do this for
my sake?" he taunted her. "I am overwhelmed, darling Consuela!"

He raised his hand to her head, brushed back the hood of
her cape, ran his fingers through her hair, stroked it. It was
mockery, a cruel pantomime of tenderness, yet she stood and
trembled, looking up into his face. "What's the matter with
your handsome Mexican officers?" he murmured. "No women

left in town—you so young and lovely—and still you must come to me for affection!"

He drew her to him. "Let it not be said that you came to me in vain!"

He kissed her on the mouth, in that same vein of pseudo tenderness, and he felt her lean toward him. He slid his arms about her, and it was a moment before he could force his rancorous harshness to return. Then his arms tightened, and his kiss grew brutally insulting. She tried to tear away from him. He held her, crushing her against him, and at last left her mouth free.

"Why don't you scream for help?" he taunted her. "That solemn fool of a Captain is just outside. He'd be delighted to run his sword through me and rescue the fair maiden. Scream! Scream and ruin your delicate reputation—let the whole damned Mexican army know that you went too far with a Texian prisoner and got your pretty wings singed!"

He suddenly released her, and she backed away from him. "You—you——!"

" 'Beast' is the fitting term, I believe," he drawled.

She stumbled to the door and fled. After she was gone, he stood staring at the open doorway. He raised the hand that had stroked her hair, and he hit the back of it across his mouth. " 'Beast' *is* the fitting term!" he muttered, and walked back to his work.

The Captain, as he escorted Consuela out of the fort, couldn't help noticing her disordered hair and the smeared hand-prints on her cape. There was even a smear of black under her chin. He was speechless. If she sought romance, why did she have to go to that barbarian for it? Surely she could not be blind to the fact that there were a dozen ranking Mexican officers from whom she could choose at any time. He, himself, had considered them as rivals. Now he didn't know what to think, but he felt very much slighted.

So he said not a word all the way back from the fort, and

he hoped that by his stern silence he was shaming her. But Consuela didn't notice. She had nothing to say, either.

Colonel Duncaerlie stood in the quarters of the Commander of Goliad, slowly rubbing a thumb against the scabbard of his sword, and looking at the floor. He said with a false calmness, "It is hard for me to believe."

The Commander, Colonel Portilla, nodded embarrassedly. "Naturally. Yet I thought it best that you should know, so I took the liberty of friendship to tell you."

"There could be a mistake."

"My friend, I wish I could agree, but I cannot. She requested permission to see a certain prisoner. It was granted. She met him in privacy. Afterward, it was observed that she was——"

"The name of the prisoner?"

"Dain."

"Ah!" Duncaerlie swallowed. His dourly remote demeanor returned. He took a sealed dispatch from his pocket. "Here are your orders from His Excellency, regarding the prisoners."

He went to the window and stood looking out, hands clasped behind him. After a while the silence of the Commander drew his attention. He swung around. The Commander sat with the document unfolded before him. He raised his eyes to Duncaerlie and asked in a queer tone, "Are you acquainted with the nature of this order?"

"Only in that it concerns the prisoners," Duncaerlie replied. "I gained the impression that His Excellency had decided to grant them the privilege of prisoners of war."

The Commander rose from his chair. His face was a little pale. "His Excellency commands that all the prisoners be immediately executed!" he said.

They stared at each other. Duncaerlie strode to the table, and without asking leave he read the order. "It is a mistake!" He flung the order down. "His mind was on other matters, and he was not thinking of what he wrote. I cannot believe

that he would mean this! You cannot carry this out, Portilla—
you cannot! It would be murder—massacre! Send a message to
him at once, asking for a countermand!"

The Commander gnawed his lip. "His Excellency has a
short temper for those who fail to obey his commands. If you
would send him a message, also, explaining that you assured
me that it must be a mistake. . . ."

"I shall go to my quarters and write it at once!"

"Good! We will send them by the same courier."

Duncaerlie hurried into his quarters, unbuckling his sword
belt and pitching it onto a chair. "Consuela!" he called, and
she came in, surprised at his curt gruffness after being away
for several days. "Find me writing materials, please, quickly!"

She brought them to him. "Is something wrong?"

"Yes. I brought back an order from Santa Anna, and by
some mistake it condemns all the prisoners to death!"

He saw the color drain from her face. His own darkened.
"The order would include the man with whom you so shame-
lessly arranged a rendezvous!" he said icily. "I see that you
realize that. Yes, I have already heard of it. It is the scandal
of the town! Have you no shame? Have you lost all respect
for yourself and for me?"

She found her voice. "It is not a mistake," she said. She
placed her hands on the table, and her eyes blazed. "It is not
a mistake—that order—and in your heart you know it! Santa
Anna is a devil!"

"How dare you!"

"You must go back to him—tell him he can't do it! It would
be a crime that would blacken Mexico in the eyes of all the
world! Tell him—make him change it!"

"I am writing a protest to him!"

She swept paper and pen to the floor. "Go to him! Make
him see—threaten him—anything!"

He shot to his feet. "You are mad! This is what comes of
allowing you to go north to school, to live among people with
no proper conception of propriety! That—that foreign adven-

turer—that man Dain—has robbed you of your senses! Go to your room at once!"

"I shall not! You are going to Santa Anna to have that murderous order changed!"

Her flaring rebellion so astounded him that he could only stare helplessly at her. She spoke now in low, rapid tones, holding his eyes with her own. "I never expected to tell you this, father—I never expected that you would come back to Texas with the Mexican army. You remember the letter which you sent to me, asking me to come to Goliad and report to you the Texian strength here? I was not home when it arrived. When I did arrive home, our *vaqueros* and servants were gone. I think a Texian officer must have called—not looking for you, but for me! To question me! Your letter had been intercepted, and opened and read, before it was sent on to me."

"What has this to do with—" he began.

"I am going to tell you why I was not home sooner," she continued evenly. "While I was in the north, the people of Cincinnati bought two cannon for Texas. I helped to raise the subscription! I hurried their shipment! I returned by way of New Orleans. There, I gave money to arm and equip a company of penniless soldiers of fortune who wanted to come and fight for Texas! I even helped to recruit them! When I reached home I found that I was a suspected spy, because of your letter. I could not clear myself—if I had told them that I was the 'Suela Caerlie' who had been helping Texas, some day Santa Anna might have heard of it, and you would have suffered for it. I hid in the house. An opportunity finally came for me to travel to Goliad—but not to spy on the Texians! No! I hoped to warn them—somehow—without making myself known—that Santa Anna was coming with a bigger army than they knew! But after they arrested me, with you, I never had the chance. They wouldn't have listened to Consuela Duncaerlie, daughter of Colonel Baltasar Duncaerlie of Anáhuac!"

She finished, and Duncaerlie stared at her like a man

numbed by horror. "Treason!" he whispered incredulously. "My own daughter—a traitor!"

"You forget that I was born here!" she reminded him hotly. "Treason? I'm a Texian—not a Mexican! You've never liked Texas. To me it is home. You've always detested Americans—never tried to understand them—never gave them credit for their virtues—never failed to condemn them for their faults. To me, they're my people. Their ways are mine!"

She drew a long breath. "What do you suppose Santa Anna would do, if I went and told him what I have just told you? You'd be disgraced—ruined! And I—!" She shrugged. "*Now* will you go to him—or shall I?"

"You wouldn't dare!" he whispered, but he knew that she would. Her face told him that she would. He shuddered, and wandered aimlessly about the room, unable to remain still. He came to his sword on the chair, and stopped at it. He knocked the sword and belt off the chair and sat down, and looked at her.

"I should have taken you to live in Mexico, years ago," he said heavily. "I should have left you there. To think, that after two generations—! But I should have known what the Americans would do to you with their flaunting talk of liberty, independence, their swaggering assumption of superiority, their . . ."

His own bitter musings raised a solution in his mind. He caught at it, stood up, gathered his poise. "So you would force an ultimatum upon me, would you, Consuela?"

He was the iron soldier again, meeting attack with counterattack, and once more sure of himself. "I think not! Let me tell you, my daughter—rather than let you go with your boast of treason to Santa Anna, I would kill you before you left this room! But that may not be necessary. It rests with you."

He picked up his sword belt and buckled it on, carefully tugging the folds from his tunic. "I will go to Santa Anna. I will use all the influence in my power to persuade him to countermand his order of execution. That is my promise. You, in return, will start at once for Mexico—your homeland, whether you now care to call it that or not! You will live with your mother's people in Mexico City. I will join you there after this war, and I shall see to it that you never again set foot in this accursed Texas as long as I live! Well, what is your answer?"

She looked blank, and when comprehension came to her eyes, the fire was gone. She was a little girl again, obedient to the strict paternal command. "Yes, father," she said.

Days later, the garrison Commander opened another dispatch from Santa Anna. He read it through rapidly, and caught his breath. His second-in-command eyed him inquiringly. "Bad news?"

The Commander wet his lips. "Colonel Duncaerlie has been placed under arrest!" he said hushedly. "We are threatened with the same, if we do not at once obey His Excellency's order to execute the prisoners!"

The *segundo* sat for a full minute, before he exclaimed devoutly, "God save our souls!"

In their filthy, crowded quarters in the old Goliad Mission, the prisoners paid regard to the Mexican Lieutenant who came in among them. "Make ready to march!" rapped the Lieutenant.

"Where?" queried a dozen voices.

"There is brush to be cut," answered the Lieutenant.

It was morning of Palm Sunday. "Hell, can't that wait?" somebody protested.

The Lieutenant looked at none of them. "There is also to be a slaughtering of cattle," he said, and walked out swiftly.

The prisoners shrugged and got ready. Those without boots tied rags around their feet. "Maybe that means we'll be gettin' some beef to put in our gullets, boys!"

"Where d'we get the cattle?"

"In the brush! Haw!"

They were formed into three companies and marched out

of Goliad under strong guard. One of the companies was taken down the road leading to the lower ford of the river. Another went tramping along the road that led toward San Patricio. The company in which Dain, Cleo and the Indian found themselves was escorted up river; it contained well over a hundred men.

The Yucatan soldiers marched in double files on both sides of the company, and Dain estimated that there were more guards than prisoners. He felt vaguely uncomfortable about that. It occurred to him that this division of the prisoners into three companies, and marching each company off in a different direction, was an odd sort of maneuver. The company that had gone along the San Patricio road, for instance. . . . Nothing but open prairie in that direction. No brush to speak of, and no cattle visible yonder. As to that, nobody had been issued machetes or any other kind of tool with which to cut brush.

He caught the eye of the Indian. "What d'you make of this?"

The Indian shook his head moodily. "I have told you that I no longer trust my powers of prophecy. What comes, will come. It is nothing to me."

"Halt!" rang the command.

Wondering, the prisoners halted. They had come not more than half a mile up the river road from town. There wasn't any brush on this bank of the river, and certainly there were no cattle hereabouts. The soldiers on the side next to the river filed around to the other side of the captive column, although no command to do so had been heard. They did it in unusually orderly manner, too, as if they might previously have had some drilling in it.

The sound of heavy firing rolled suddenly from the south, then from the west, the directions taken by the two other companies. Somebody remarked uncertainly, "I didn't figure there was *that* much cattle round here!"

Gunlocks clicked all along the Mexican line.

"Cattle, be damned!" shouted a New Orleans man. *"Boys, they've brought us out to shoot us!"*

Cries and yells, flattened by distance, pierced through the musketry volleys and their echoes. Dain lunged at Cleo, bowled her headlong off her feet, and threw himself down beside her. As he fell, he twisted his head to look at the Mexican line, in time to see smoke burst from the levelled muskets and *escopetas*, clouding the faces and shoulders of the Yucatans, so that for the instant it had the appearance of a line of headless men.

The Goliad column melted to a few men who stood dazed and incredulous in the midst of mass murder. More than two thirds of the prisoners had been ripped down by the volley. Some crawled wildly in any direction, gasping. Others clasped their bodies and moaned. Most lay still.

The Mexican weapons were single-shots and the volley had emptied them. The soldiers came charging through their smoke, bayonets fixed. As if they were plunging in glory at an armed enemy, they howled, "Santa Anna!"—the battle cry that His Excellency himself had suggested should be adopted by his Indian troops, whose own native cries were barbarous and offensive to his cultured ears.

The surviving prisoners broke and fled. Dain and Cleo leaped up and joined the flight toward the river, the only way of escape. The Indian was ahead of them, pattering along on his bare feet, looking coolly back over his shoulder. They reached the bank and leaped in. The river was deep and swift at this point, but not wide, and they were strong swimmers. They gained the opposite bank. It was so steep, its under bank cut away by the stream, that it was impossible to climb. They swam on down river, staying under water as long as they could, and coming up only for quick gulps of air. The Yucatans were running along the lower bank, reloading their guns and firing at every struggling survivor that they could see in the water.

Dain caught hold of a dangling grapevine, hung onto it,

and caught Cleo with his other hand. The Indian swam up to them and also caught hold of it. The leaves of the vine, dragged close to the water's surface by their hands, partly shielded their heads from the sight of the hunting packs of Yucatans. They floated together, getting back their breath. The Yucatans passed by on the far bank, went on a little way down river, and came back. They went on up, scanning the river.

As soon as they were gone, the Indian went clambering hand-over-hand up the vine like a monkey, reached the leaning cottonwood from which it hung, and squatted on an overhanging limb.

Dain said to Cleo, "I'm going up, too. Hang on. We'll pull you up."

She nodded without speaking, half exhausted, and twined the vine around her hands. The water had washed most of the dirt from her face, revealing it as white and strained. She had lost her hat and the rag headband, and her hair hung wet and tumbled, glistening black against her face. Dain went up the vine. He joined the Indian on the limb, and from this vantage point they could overlook the opposite bank. Most of the Yucatans had returned to the massacre ground, stripping and robbing the bodies, killing the wounded.

The Indian called down softly, "Hold on tight, child!" He and Dain hauled up on the vine, pulling Cleo out of the water and up to them.

She was so near that Dain was reaching down a hand to catch hold of her, when the Indian hissed. Dain raised his head and uttered an ear-splitting yell. The Yucatan on the far bank, taking careful aim with his *escopeta*, started badly, but did not fire and waste his charge. He looked at the two men in the tree, and raised his sights. Changing his mind again, he reverted to his original target, and fired. After the shot, he shrieked for comrades to come quickly with their weapons, and he danced up and down like a boy unable to contain his eagerness.

Cleo dropped from the end of the vine. She floated up after she struck the water, moving her arms feebly, her hair trailing and covering her face.

Dain dove from his perch on the limb, after her. He came up under her. She had ceased her weak, automatic struggling, and he held her afloat, swimming down river with one arm. A terrible howl rang out over the water. The Indian had jumped down from the tree and was on top of the bank. He crouched there, arms bent, fingers hooked like claws, glaring and howling at the Yucatan on the other side of the river. The Yucatan uttered a frightened howl of his own, and spun around and bolted.

Dain swam on, the Indian following along the edge of the bank. He came to a spot where the bank had caved in, and the Indian slithered down and helped him ashore. Cleo, unconscious and half drowned, was a limp weight in Dain's arms. They carried her up and over the bank, and without a word they trotted eastward away from the river.

CHAPTER FIFTEEN

It was night. The two men plodded on, taking turns carrying the girl, through a strip of woods sodden by a day of drizzling rain.

They had come to another small river at sunset, and forded it, but they were keeping to the woods of the east bank and skirting a Mexican small-ranch section of country. Several times they glimpsed the light of a tiny *ranchito* shack, and heard dogs barking. There was no help or hospitality to be had in this section. Many of the Mexican ranchers, likely enough, were out helping to hunt down the few prisoners who had escaped the massacre. Few of them had any liking for the Texians, and they all feared the name of Santa Anna.

The rain had stopped before dark. Now it was cold, and the bright shine of the moon in the cleared sky made it seem colder. The two men shivered in their wet clothes, every time a light gust of wind blew through the trees. Carrying Cleo, Dain saw that her eyes were open, but her teeth were clenched and she didn't utter a sound. When she found his head bent over her, her cheeks and lips moved in a smile, and after he looked forward again her gaze remained on his face.

They knew that they were being trailed by the Yucatan killers. Twice during the late afternoon they had hidden and watched mounted searching parties riding back and forth, examining the ground. The Yucatans, it was said, loved a man hunt above all else. Dain wondered how many prisoners had escaped the massacre, and how many of those would live to get clear.

He heard the Indian's hiss, and he halted. The Indian,

walking ahead, signalled with a hand and went on, and came back after a short absence. "There is a building," he murmured. "Empty. The door is open, and some firewood is stacked outside. Do you want to take the risk?"

Dain cuddled Cleo closer to him. "Got to have a fire," he said. "She's chilled through. Lead on. We'll chance it."

The building was square, of rough planking, and stood by itself on a rise at the edge of the woods. The roof was flat, but it had a false front that rose to a point. That was all they could make out as they approached it, for some trees formed a dark background behind it.

The Indian slipped through the doorway, and Dain followed with Cleo. Dain heeled the door quietly shut behind him and waited, listening to the Indian creeping about. There were but two tiny windows, and the moonlight seeped through only one of them, but very shortly the Indian called softly, "Here is the fireplace." A pause, and then—"And here is the flintbox."

In fifteen minutes they were huddling by a fire, steam beginning to rise from their clothes. Cleo lay before the hearth, and Dain was drying her clothes, a piece at a time. When he gently removed her shirt and saw the bullet wound in her back, he bit his lip, knowing why she held her teeth so tightly clenched. The blood had clotted over it, stopping further bleeding. There was nothing that he could do for it. He dried her shirt and coat, and very carefully put them back on her.

The Indian had found some wooden benches, and with them he covered the windows to keep the glow of the fire from shining through. He squatted on his bare heels, staring into the fire, and after a long silence he murmured, "My friend, do you know that we are in a church?"

Dain had been engaging all his attentions upon Cleo. He looked around, and by the light of the fire he distinguished the outline of an altar at the far end of the room, with a cross above it. "Damned if we're not," he agreed absently.

The Indian did not remove his eyes from the fire. "A place

of worship should be spoken of with respect," he reproved gravely. "I have respect for all religions. They are paths of seeking. Some may be straighter than others, but all seek the same end."

Cleo suddenly moaned, and Dain bent quickly over her. "Pain!" she whispered. Her eyes were glazed with it. At last it had conquered her. "Make it stop, Dain! Kill me!"

Wild with helplessness, Dain instinctively turned to the Indian. "Do something for her—for God's sake do something!"

The Indian pushed him aside with a surprisingly powerful arm, and knelt by the girl. "You must sleep, child," he told her softly. It was strange to hear compassion in his voice.

"I can't! The pain. . . ."

"You must sleep," he repeated. "You *must* sleep." He lowered his wrinkled face toward hers, and she stared up into his eyes. "Sleep, child. Sleep. You are sleepy. So-o-o sleepy. . . ."

His low voice drifted into a croon, monotonous and lulling, repeating the same words over and over again. "Sleep, child. Sleep. . . ."

Cleo's dark eyes lost their glaze, grew peaceful and tired. Her eyelids drooped, fluttered lazily, and closed. Her facial muscles relaxed, and her breathing grew deep and regular.

Dain found that he was sweating from the strain of bending his own will toward that of the Indian, trying to accomplish what the Indian had done. He whispered, "She's—she's asleep! How—what did you do to her?"

The Indian sank back upon his heels, gazing into the girl's tranquil face. "You need not whisper. She will not waken for many hours. And her pain is gone—or at least she doesn't feel it any more. As I recollect, I think you call it mesmerism. It was nothing, of course, but the exercise of strong suggestion upon a subject who strongly wished to obey. She was exhausted, and her will was at its lowest ebb. She had no more resistance than a tired baby has against its mother. It was very easy."

Dain dropped a hand to his shoulder. "Thanks, friend," he said huskily. "Thanks for doing it."

The Indian smiled. "I was glad to do it. I am fond of Cleo. She is what I call an elemental. She is not complex. Her emotions and reactions are strong and simple. She knows what she wants. So few of us do."

He raised his head, still smiling gently, and it came to Dain that he was no longer the brooding, bitter little brown man. He was what he had been before the fall of the Alamo—serene, slightly mocking, remote, and endowed with a monumental self-assurance. It was good to find him like that again. Dain had not realized how the Indian's black depression had affected his own moods. Optimism flowed into him. Cleo was sleeping and out of pain. They had eluded the killers. They had a fire, and were dry and warm. Things were not too bad, after all.

As if reading his thoughts, the Indian said dryly, "The mind is a strange thing. A little nudge here, a push there, and behold! The outlook is changed. Life is changed. The world is changed. *Your* mind, my friend, certainly needs a nudge, if any mind does! It received an injury that crippled it, didn't you once tell me?"

"Yes. I was hit with a club. It left me without a memory—without a past that I can remember, that is."

The Indian cocked his shaved head quizzically in his old, irritating way. "Men have broken their legs, but lived to walk," he observed. "Not all, no. Some told themselves that they would never walk again—and so they hobbled to death on crutches. In my opinion, your mind is a lazy, malingering fake! It has probably convinced itself that it will never remember, and it resents your efforts to make it do so. Why should it try? Remembering is work, to a mind. And perhaps it doesn't particularly care to recall the kind of past that you probably led!"

"Your sympathy," said Dain, "touches me deeply!"

The Indian snorted joyfully. "Sympathy—pah! What you

need is another good clout on the head! Do you really want
to remember your past?"

"Of course I do."

"Why?"

"Well. . . ."

"There, you see? You don't even know why! It was your
past, so you think you should have it. Lost, you want it back,
but you don't know why. No reason. Just the acquisitive instinct!"

"Go to blazes!" Dain told him.

The Indian twitched his lips. "Thank you. I probably shall.
But to get back to this matter of your memory. Would you
care to try an experiment, just to prove or disprove my
theory?"

"What kind of experiment?"

The Indian laughed soundlessly. Dain had never seen him
in better humor. "There you go! That's your lazy, suspicious
mind talking. It doesn't want to get out of its invalid bed, so
it immediately begins arguing. Haven't you any better control over it? Be its master, man, not its slave!"

Dain was getting really irritated. "Damn it—" he began.

The Indian lifted an admonishing finger. "Remember where
you are, please—even if you won't remember where you
were!"

"Excuse me."

"I'll excuse you if you'll do one thing." The Indian fished a
burning stick from the fire. He whipped out its flame, leaving
one end glowing red. "Take this over to that dark corner.
Stare at it. Don't blink, and don't take your eyes off it. And
keep repeating, 'I remember everything—I remember everything.'"

"What'll that do?"

"It may only make you an even bigger fool than you already are, but that should be an accomplishment! Go on, do
it—or are you afraid to try?"

Dain felt like kicking him into the fire. The insulting, malicious, exasperating little devil! But he took the firestick, walked to the dark corner, and sat down with his back to the fireplace. Afraid? Of this ludicrously crude mumbo-jumbo?

He settled himself comfortably, leaning against the wall, and fastened a disparaging stare on the glowing tip of the stick. "I remember everything—I remember everything—I remember everything. . . ."

It was silly. That malicious little monkey was likely laughing at him.

"I remember everything—I remember everything. . . ."

It evolved into a senseless refrain.

"I remember everything. . . ."

The words lost all sense and significance. They telescoped together in a garble of sheer gibberish.

"I rememb'rev'thing—I rem'b'rev'thing. . . ."

He was infinitely weary, and wanted to stretch out on the floor. His eyes grew heavy and dry, staring drowsily at the spot of red light. He wanted to blink them, but he'd forbidden them to do that, and now he lacked even the energy to unlock his will.

"I rem'brev'thing. . . ."

Why was he doing this foolishness? Made him sleepier, was all. Damned stick was going out. Red spot was shrinking.

"I rem'ber. . . ."

He quit the mumbling. His tongue was thick. His eyes would stay open no longer. But the words continued like a repeating echo: *"Remember everything—remember everything. . . ."*

Half slumbering, completely relaxed, dreamily he was conscious of some other voice taking up the refrain and whispering it into his ear. It beat a soporific rhythm, and its effect was like that of a light rocking motion. It was pleasant. He did not resent it.

In a rising rush of sound, magnified in his ear, the whisper roared commandingly.

"Remember!"

He woke.

How long he had slept he did not know, but the firestick was cold in his hand. His left ear and side of his head hurt from pillowing against the rough planks of the wall. For a while he sat blinking, hardly knowing where he was. A slight sound caused him to look around, and he saw the Indian building up the fire.

He rose stiffly and went to the fire. The Indian finished putting on more wood, squatted, and took no notice of him. Cleo still slept soundly, and the Indian had moved her back a little from the heat. They sat in complete silence for a long time, before Dain spoke.

"My name is Galway," he said. "Dain Galway."

"Glad to meet you, Mr. Galway," murmured the Indian. His lips twitched. "You talked in your sleep. Who, may I ask, is Stephen Seymour?"

"My father's half-brother," Dain answered mechanically. He looked at Cleo's face. "He was whipping Cleo when I came home. He wanted Blake to have her. Blake was the overseer. She wouldn't go to him. Quaw held her, while Seymour used his riding whip. I took it away from him and I hit him with it, and I thrashed Quaw out of the house. I hadn't been home for years."

He could see that home-coming now. By waiting two days in St. Louis he could have caught a river boat, but he was in too burning a hurry to get home and have it out with Seymour, so he had bought a flat-bottomed rowboat and rowed down river all the way to the plantation landing. He remembered his shock at the sight of the old place. No trace left of the flower beds that his mother had planted and tended so carefully. The great green lawn, that had cost his father a small fortune, eradicated by neglect.

And then Seymour. His pale eyes and cold, chiselled face. His thin, modulated voice. "So the roving heir to the House of Galway has finally come home!"

dian commented. "I presume you were the family black sheep?"

"In a way. It began with the Morean Revolt. My father had sent me to Europe to get an education. I joined the Greek insurgents, instead. After that, some of us went to Spain and fought against the French restoration of Ferdinand the Seventh. Then to Peru and the Ayacucho defeat. That kind of life takes hold of you."

"Yes, doesn't it?" agreed the Indian. "So you're just another soldier of fortune whose wandering feet led him down the road to Texas. There are many like you—or were, until their road ended back there at Goliad. Did you ever take the trouble to inquire into the causes for which you fought?"

Dain nodded. "Yes. I'd always had a dislike for slavery in any form. After I left home I grew to hate it. The Anti-Slave Trading Act of the International Congress didn't kill the trade —it only made it dangerous, illegal, and more profitable. Blackbirders were still running slave cargoes over the Middle Passage from Africa, in fast ships and with crews armed to the teeth. It was well organized. I finally got in touch with the International Anti-Slavery Commission, and asked for information. They told me that there wasn't any doubt about the existence of a controlling slave-ring, but they hadn't been able to break it. Several of their agents had gone missing. I applied for the post of independent investigator."

"You were applying for permission to commit suicide!"

"Well, I'd seen some of the ghastly trade, and I didn't like it," Dain said. "Meantime, my father died—my mother had died while I was a boy. In his will he asked that his half-brother, Seymour, should continue as manager of the business. Seymour was the brilliant one of the family. Everybody went to him for advice in business affairs. Father was no business-man, but he had capital. Seymour had managed the business for years, and built it up from a cotton plantation to a pretty important merchant-shipping concern. I left Seymour to continue running things, and I went to the African East Coast. I

rode with slave raiders, clerked for coast traders, and shipped
with blackbirding crews. Then I came home."

He stared into the fire, like the Indian. "The center of the
slave-trading ring was the House of Galway!" he said quietly,
and he saw again Seymour's face when he had told him that.

Seymour had said, "And what are your intentions? The business is yours, you know. I've built it to what it is. Not for your
sake, I assure you! Frankly, I expected—hoped—that you'd be
killed somewhere! Would you turn in your information, wreck
the business, and send me and others to prison? No, no! Let
me advise you against that. You've seen some of my men.
Sometimes this house is full of them. They would—ah—resent
your interference!"

"Are you threatening me, Seymour?"

"I am warning you!"

Dain struck him again with the whip. "Get out! Get out of
this house and tell your blackbirding friends to take to their
holes! Tomorrow you'll all be on the wanted list!"

And then the girl, Cleo, pleading with him after Seymour
had left. "Take me with you!"

"You needn't fear now," he'd told her. "He's gone and this
is my house. I've got to hurry back to St. Louis, but I'll be
back here in a day or two. This house is going to be different.
It'll be the way it used to be—remember? Now run along and
dress those cuts on your back."

She had stood gazing after him, fear on her face, as he left
the house. . . .

The Indian said conversationally, "I think you had better
take Cleo and go, now."

"Why?"

"Some of your Yucatan friends are coming!"

Dain shot to the door and listened. He heard nothing at first
but the light gusts of wind in the trees. Another faint medley
of sounds crept in, and he analyzed them. Walking horses,
spurs and bridlebits tinkling, men talking.

Dain went and picked up Cleo. She did not waken, and he cradled her in his arms. "Come on!" he muttered to the Indian.

The Indian was piling more wood onto the fire, although it was already roaring up the chimney. He glanced aside at Dain and shook his head. "I have something to do," he said gently, "that may stop the pursuit here. Don't worry about me. I shall be perfectly all right."

Dain hesitated at the door. "If we get separated—if I don't see you again . . ."

"Then mutual good wishes, eh?" The Indian stroked Cleo's black hair. "Poor child. You knew what you wanted—but you wanted too much. I think I shall see you again soon."

He opened the door for Dain, and gave his little twitch of a smile. "Don't ever forget, my friend, that there are no real mysteries. Everything is quite simple, and well worked out. Never lose your faith."

Dain set off at a long trot, trying not to jog Cleo. He hoped that the woods would extend a good distance, but they ended before he had gone a hundred yards, and he had to take to bare, rolling ground. When he paused to rest, Cleo's breathing was deep and regular. He heard shouts behind him, and he looked back. A flicker of red light licked against the blackness of the woods. It coupled with another, and they swelled large, and suddenly there were more. They all spread and came together, and there was the wooden church ablaze. The flames burst through the tarred roof, and turned a bright blue that shed a strange radiance over the peaked false front and the cross on top.

The Indian stood balanced on an arm of the cross, high up in plain sight. Even at that distance Dain recognized easily the flame-lighted figure, round-headed, ragged, short and stocky. He saw it fling out its arms, throw back its shaved head, and its piercing cry rose above the shouts of the horsemen coming through the woods.

Muskets cracked. The little figure fell from the cross, arms outward, head up and body rigid. It struck the blazing roof, smashed a hole through it, and sparks roared up through the gap as if from a furnace funnel.

The horsemen cheered. They could be seen senselessly riding around and around the church in the glare of its fire, celebrating the end of their all-day hunt.

Dain bent low, Cleo in his arms, and hurried on over the open country. The little brown man's prediction recurred to him: *Death by violence in a holy place, my body burned, my bones never buried!*

"It happened that way!" he thought. And then—"He *made* it happen that way."

Another of the Indian's predictions cropped up in his mind, one made in the patio of the Duncaerlie house that night so long ago: *Of our party of seven, not one will escape death in Texas!*

Crockett—Boniface Eden—Thimblerig—the Pirate; dead at the Alamo. The Indian, himself, dead in a burning church. Cleo, badly wounded. . . .

"Damn! Must that come true, too?"

Morning sunlight discovered them under a cutbank of the Guadalupe River. The bank was high, and at some time the river had shifted its course, so that they were on a clay ledge of the old bank, overlooking the river bottom.

Dain had found a few wild onions growing along the lower bank, but Cleo could not eat. She wanted only water, and he got it for her by shaping a cup from a piece of his leather pocket-belt. He had made her a bed of moss and leaves, and this morning she seemed to rest comfortably and out of pain. She had wakened at dawn.

She moved her lips, and Dain had to bend over her to catch what she said. She whispered, "I like it here. It's pretty. I like rivers. Thank you, Dain—for bringing me here. Where is the Indian?"

"He died last night—the way he wanted it. He was fond of you, Cleo."

"Yes."

"And so am I."

"Yes. We're still in Texas, aren't we, Dain? I like Texas. I want to stay here—on this river. Right here. Can I?"

He nodded, not able to speak. Queer, he thought, the strong, insistent pull that liberty had for humans of all races. It must have been born in them. It was their natural right, and they sensed it, and had to have it if only for a little hour at the end.

"Dain——"

"Yes, Cléo?"

She did not go on. She swallowed, her eyes holding his. At last she whispered painfully, "My mother was—was a mulatto. A slave. I was—a slave, too."

He nodded again. Queer, he thought, that a race of men who had outlawed slave-trading should still hold slaves. That they would hunt any that escaped, setting the law after them —and stigmatizing as a pariah any white man who helped them to escape. He knew now why both the law and the secret lawless had hunted him and Cleo down the Mississippi. He knew why the Natchez Lynchers had invoked the name of justice in their attempted assassination of him. And he knew why Cleo had been so desperately anxious to reach another land and another life.

"I know, Cleo," he said.

"You—know?" Her eyes searched his face. "Oh—the Indian! He told me he thought he could do it. I asked him not to, because . . . Dain, I didn't want you to remember that I'm just a——"

"It doesn't make any difference, Cleo. No difference at all."

She smiled slowly, delightedly, like a credulous child. "Texas! They said—Colonel Crockett said—everybody got a new life—in Texas. It's true, then—isn't it? True! Pick me up, Dain—quick!"

He eased his hands under her, took her into his arms, sat with her, her head against his shoulder. She was still smiling, and he said, "Yes, Cleo, it's true." And he kissed her.

Her mouth moved almost imperceptibly against his, and he thought he heard her laugh in her throat. Then she was quiet, and when he brought his lips away her eyes were closed. He sat with her for a long time in his arms, until the feel of loneliness penetrated him and he knew that he was alone.

He dreaded what he had to do, but he remembered that she liked this river and wanted to stay here. Right here. He shifted the bed of moss well back under the cutbank, and placed her on it. He covered her face with his coat, and spread more moss over her. Then he climbed up onto the top of the overhanging bank, and dug and stamped at it with his bootheels, keeping his eyes on the river. The clay broke and fell, and he didn't look down until that part of the ledge was covered. He spent an hour gathering rocks and fitting them over the sloping mound. When he had finished he drank from the river, and walked eastward.

Houston's army would be on the Brazos, or somewhere.

"Of our party of seven, not one will escape death in Texas!"

It didn't matter any more. Nothing much mattered any more.

CHAPTER SIXTEEN

SAM HOUSTON'S TEXAS ARMY LAY WITH ITS back to Buffalo Bayou. It had the San Jacinto River on its left, Vince's Bayou on its right, and Santa Anna before it.

The Texians were worn out from long marches and short rations, and most of them sank to the ground to catch some sleep as soon as they halted, hoping that the Mexicans were just as exhausted. Santa Anna almost immediately woke them up by advancing his heavy artillery to a commanding position, but the Twin Sisters spat viciously and drove it back.

A restless band of mounted Texians dashed out in a reckless attempt to capture Santa Anna's withdrawing artillery, and got into a lively skirmish with the Mexican cavalry. Some of the Texians lost all further capacity for riding, and Dain got one of their horses by right of a chase, capture and possession. He thereupon quit the infantry unit that he had joined south of Groce's Crossing, and fell in with the mounted troops. Nobody objected. It was known that he was a Goliad survivor, and the few "Ghosts of Goliad" were known to be sharp on the edge and more than a little crazy on the coupled subject of death and Santa Anna.

Dain had found it a strange, grim, tattered army, vastly different from the happy-go-lucky crowds of the rendezvous towns, although these were the same men. They were lean and savage, their tempers rasped by retreats, dissensions, and strained faith in their leader. From them, Dain learned of that side of the campaign.

Houston had retreated farther than anyone had expected. There were those who assumed that he knew what he was doing, and kept their faith in him, but there were many others who muttered savagely of deposing him and getting another commander.

The discontent had begun at Peach Creek, first step of the retreat, where somebody claimed that the cannonading sounds in the rear came from nothing but exploding whiskey barrels in burning Gonzales. When the Colorado was reached and crossed without a fight, half the army had deserted to go and help wives and families in the Runaway Scrape from the advancing Mexicans. With the whole country west of the Colorado abandoned to the enemy, the retreat continued to San Felipe on the Brazos, and then the colonists east of the Colorado also went into wild flight. At San Felipe two company captains flatly refused to retreat any farther. The rest of the half-mutinous army reluctantly followed Houston north to Groce's Crossing, there to be shaped up and organized. Muddy roads and a driving rain did not improve tempers.

The Texian army, camped at Groce's, had time to grow. More volunteers and colonists drifted in to join it. Regiments were formed, officers nominated, and a medical staff created. It began to look like an army, small but presentable.

But dissatisfaction was general, and even the fugitive Government grew uneasy about Houston. The long retreat, and now this prolonged encampment, left morale at a low point. Texas had suffered a series of crushing defeats. Colonists were quitting Texas by the hundreds, convinced that all was lost. The whisper went around that Sam Houston was trying to dodge a fight, that he'd lost his nerve, that he intended retreating all the way to Nacogdoches, the Sabine, and Louisiana.

At last camp was broken. The Texian army was marched on to Donoho, a few miles farther east, with its few ammunition and supply wagons, and the Twin Sisters. Donoho was the crucial test. Here the road forked, one leading to Nacogdoches, route of retreat, the other south to Harrisburg and Santa Anna. The Texian army took the south road, and spirits soared. Damn the retreating and stalling—they wanted a fight!

They reached Buffalo Bayou, marched down the left bank, crossed, and pushed on across Vince's Bridge toward the San Jacinto. At midnight, on the south bank of Buffalo Bayou, the fatigued men and horses rested for a little while, but by dawn they were on the move again. Scouts brought word that Santa Anna had struck east from Harrisburg, stopped in the town of New Washington long enough to burn it, and was coming north with an army division made up of grenadiers, dragoons, sharp-shooting *cazadores,* and heavy artillery.

Houston had hard and ready fighting men around him. Colonel Burleson, tough and shabbily garbed veteran; Colonel Sid Sherman, neat and military; Deaf Smith, Karnes, Mosely Baker, Wily Martin, McNutt, Hill . . . many who had cut their teeth on Indian fights. Soldiers of fortune who had got into the war habit and couldn't live tamely any more. Colonists who had lost their homes and sought vengeance. It was a very small army, a skeleton army, but rawhide tough.

In the afternoon the two armies had come face to face.

At last Santa Anna had his enemy bottled up—"Like wild cattle in a corral," he sneered to his officers, and they laughed and nodded. He had by now conceived a royal contempt for a foe that had done nothing but keep out of his way.

The Texians had marched into the trap, and Vince's Bridge was the only possible retreat left to them—was, in fact, the only near avenue of escape for anybody on the field. Retreat to their left was barred by the San Jacinto and Galveston Bay, and their backs were to Buffalo Bayou. They were in a grove of live oaks on the low margin of the bayou bank. Before them, and extending two miles to Vince's Bridge and Vince's Bayou on their right, was an open prairie. Into this prairie Santa Anna led his army, to an eminence with a thick wood on his right, favorably overlooking the enemy.

He had them! San Patricio—the Alamo—Goliad—Refugio— those victories had merely been preliminary steps to this final culmination. Here was the crowning triumph, ripe and ready for his plucking.

To do it, he had had to move fast, dividing up his army and striking in different directions. General Cós was turning aside from a march to Velasco and hurrying here with infantry reinforcements. General Filisola was at Thompson's Crossing with another division, General Gaona was somewhere along the Brazos country with another, and it had been necessary to leave garrison troops in captured towns, fortified posts, and at various strategic positions here and there.

The sun went down on two wary, alert camps, each feeling out the other and taking the opportunity to get some rest. Next morning General Cós marched into the Mexican camp with heavy reinforcements.

The Texians cursed a little, but it didn't change their minds. They had done all the retreating they were going to do. Last night, after dark, Deaf Smith and some kindred spirits had prowled up the bayou to Vince's Bridge and wrecked it. The neck of the bottle was stoppered. No matter how the fight came out, there'd be no retreat this time for anybody. Victory or death.

Santa Anna began issuing orders to place his enlarged command in readiness for battle, but General Cós dissuaded him and urgently asked for time in which to rest and feed his men. His reinforcing brigade had been on the march for many hours, without rest or food. His supply wagons had not yet caught up with him. Why not permit his troops to rest while waiting for the supplies to come up, so that they could go freshened, fed and well armed into battle? Was not the enemy trapped? Then why hurry?

His Excellency, himself, had not slept all night, and had spent much time in the saddle. To be sure, he could pluck his triumph at his leisure. He granted the request. He stretched out under the shade of some trees, in the middle of the camp, and dozed. Even Napoleon had napped on the battlefield. Even the Tiger of Tampico was not invulnerable to fatigue.

Soon he was sleeping heavily, and dreaming of what he would do to Houston.

Gunfire and a great din woke him. He opened astonished eyes upon the disorder. An officer shouted to him, "The enemy is attacking! They have surprised our advance companies! They have taken the woods on . . ."

He was pointing to the woods on the right, and he fell. Rifles were spitting from those trees. Wild, ragged horsemen were charging the left, thundering over the plain. Lines of other men, afoot, were storming the front.

It was hardly fair, His Excellency thought dazedly and indignantly, to attack a man in his *siesta*. Anyway, *he* was supposed to be the attacker. This was against all reason. The Texian rebels must be mad. Why, they were in his camp! His legion was falling back. His invincible dragoons—his own picked bodyguards—look at them! Racing by, their flying hoofs flinging dirt over him. And his grenadiers—running for their lives.

Where were his officers? What were they doing, to allow this? Ah, there was Colonel Luelmo, lying dead. And Colonel Céspedes, groaning and wounded, staggering to the rear. And General Castrillon, trying to hold the shattered ranks, running back and forth, shouting, waving his saber. . . . And falling. Thousand devils! What hell's hurricane was this?

Then a roar. A vast, throaty, terrifying roar.

"Remember the Alamo! Remember Goliad!"

His Excellency took a horse away from an aide-de-camp, and scrambled up into the saddle. He reined it around, kicked the frightened animal, and tore out of camp. He rode through running men, knocking them out of his path, and overtook and passed dragoons in his flight.

One rider passed him—a gentleman with pale eyes and impassive face, whose cloak billowed out behind him. His guest and friend, the generous *Señor* Falconer.

"It is a rout!" shouted His Excellency, unnecessarily.

The pale eyes touched him briefly. *Señor* Falconer rode on.

Colonel Duncaerlie came loping up abreast, the lines deep in his face, his lips compressed. "Did you order this retreat, Excellency?" he called.

"Retreat? Order?" Santa Anna stared wildly at him. His ears were filled with screams, gunfire, sharp ring of steel against steel. "It is a rout!"

Colonel Duncaerlie's lips thinned tighter. "A rout, yes. A complete rout." He stared in disillusioned contempt at the fear-ridden face of his commander-in-chief, and he spoke as a soldier to something less. "Ride fast, Santa Anna—fast! *Remember Goliad!*" He too rode on.

Behind, the savage roar swept again through the broken Mexican camp: "*Remember the Alamo!*"

The sun was sinking, and the redness of it blinded the eyes. Here, along the southern extremity of Vince's Bayou, the ground was swampy, overgrown with marsh grass and high clumps of cane.

Quietness and desolation were here, miles from the battlefield of San Jacinto. This was the logical route of retreat, for Mexicans who were mounted. Those afoot had swum the bayou when they found the bridge burned out, but horses could not get across the boggy banks.

Very few had got this far. Not more than a dozen, judging from the tracks through the grass and in the yielding ground. Dain tried to shield his eyes from the sun and look westward, but the sun was too low. Somewhere not far ahead rode the pale-eyed man with a companion, a man wearing the uniform of a Mexican Colonel. Dain had seen him—first in the attack on Santa Anna's camp, and several times since during the chase, bobbing along in the distance.

"He'll make for the Brazos and on west from there, if I don't come up with him before dark," Dain thought, and heeled his stumbling horse, following the double tracks.

He had charged through the Mexican camp without halting, his eyes on that billowing grey cloak, and come straight through after it, riding past packs of stampeding Mexican soldiers. His horse, he hoped, was as good as the one ahead. At least, neither the pale-eyed man nor the Mexican Colonel had gained much ground, the last time he sighted them. He wished that he had a rifle with him, in case the two elected to make a stand. He had gone into the charge with only a single-shot pistol and a cutlass. The cutlass had bent badly when he ran it through a dragoon, and he had discarded it.

The clumps of high cane grew thicker. He rode more warily. Along here would be a perfect ground for an ambush, and it was difficult to see with the sun in his eyes. He came to the wide, shallow end of the bayou. It was marshy, but firm on the higher slopes. Here the double tracks that he was following divided. The pale-eyed man had parted from his Mexican companion. One track led around the marsh, the other into it.

He pulled up and examined the opposite slope. The circling track continued, a faint line scarred through the grass, up and over the slope. The other lost itself in the cane-brake of the marsh, and did not reappear on the other side. One of those two men was hiding and waiting in the cane-brake.

Dispassionately, Dain pondered over it. If he pushed on down into the cane-brake, mounted or afoot, the hidden man would be waiting to drop him. He probably had a rifle, or he wouldn't be trying this trick. On the other hand, if he rode around it, he'd have to pass up the man. The question was, which one had ridden around it, and which had not? There was only one way to find out. If the cane was high enough to hide one rider, it would hide another. He rode down at a walk into the cane-brake, following the track. He could tell, roughly, where the track ended in the thickest part of the cane-brake.

A shot rapped at him, not from the direction he expected. The bullet whizzed, cutting a few canes, and he heard it thump directly in front of him. He threw himself clear as his horse fell, and sprawled into the cane roots. The horse kicked once and lay still. The bullet had entered its head. It had been a close shot. Six inches higher, and it would have found its mark. It had come from a rifle.

He drew his pistol and considered. The man had evidently left that track for bait to draw him on. He had led his horse into the cane-brake, left it, and stationed himself elsewhere. That meant that his horse had played out, else he would have kept on going. And he was on some spot of ground a little higher than its surroundings, so that he had vantage for his rifle. At the same time, he was some distance off. He had failed to make allowance for the drop of his bullet. Dain nodded to himself. That was it.

Through the cane he took careful survey, picked out the direction from which the shot had come, and decided that the man was somewhere halfway up the opposite slope—had eased his way up there without leaving a track to betray him. Well and good. He crept on through the cane and came to a bald spot before he reached the bottom of the slope. He stepped out onto the bald spot, made to cross it, and took a leap aside. Halfway up the slope ahead, a little ball of smoke rose and disintegrated. He fired his pistol at a spot just below it.

Some cane-ends waved there, and others waved farther up. Dain rapidly began loading his pistol, watching. The man in the cloak ran out of the cane-brake, limping, and he called out as he went up the slope. He had left his rifle and carried a pistol in his hand. A drumming sounded. The Mexican Colonel loomed up over the slope and rode on down. He drew up, wheeled his horse, and offered a hand to help the limping man up behind him.

Dain smashed through the cane, running, spilling powder and balls, finishing his loading as he ran. That officer's worn-out horse wouldn't carry a double burden very far, but far enough to lose a pursuing man on foot.

He heard another shot, muffled, and when he got to where the cane was thinner he looked up. Both men were on the horse, the civilian up behind the officer, but there was smoke between them and the officer was slowly toppling out of the saddle. With the hand that held the discharged pistol, the civilian thrust at the officer to hasten his fall. The horse would carry one rider much faster and farther.

The officer fell and his head and shoulders struck the ground. His left foot had slipped through the stirrup and was caught in it. The man who had shot him in the back for the horse reached down and freed it. He pulled himself forward into the saddle, looked back, and slapped the horse with his smoking pistol.

The Colonel rolled over, fumbling at his belt. He elbowed the ground, holding something with both hands before his face, and there was a flash and a report. The horse went down on its haunches and pawed with its forefeet like a giant lizard while it fell over. Its rider tumbled clear and took off at a limping run the rest of the way up the slope. The Colonel lay watching him go, nodding slowly, his head sinking lower at each nod; there was no movement to him when Dain ran by, and his dour Scottish face was grey and bloodless, and bitter in its cast.

Running, Dain topped the slope. Fifty yards ahead the cloaked man had come to a halt, half sitting, half kneeling, hastily reloading his pistol. He rose awkwardly as Dain appeared, and he stood on his one good leg, but after he was upright he was no longer awkward. He stood tall and straight, his long cloak flung back, his pistol at shoulder level, like a duellist. Waiting, poised and motionless, he watched Dain come walking toward him. His waxen face was a blank mask, and his eyes were so pale that they appeared like little frosted windows.

Dain kept his eyes on that upraised pistol as he paced forward, his own weapon pointed downward. Abstractly, he conceded a respect for the pale-eyed man's chill nerve. Even now, caught in the open and forced to the bare resource of one pistol against another, he was playing that resource to its full value, carefully and with finesse. He had his thin body half turned at the waist to present a narrower mark, while his cloak flared out as a false target. Dain held his forefinger nested on his trigger, and walked steadily closer. He could do no less than match the man's nerve, even if it meant firing into each other at arm's length.

Incredibly, the man wavered, began hobbling backward step by step. He called out, "Stop! It's murder!"

Dain answered, "I'm waiting for you."

"I can't! My pistol—I didn't finish. No cap. . . ."

It was a temptation to shoot, but there was little satisfaction to be had in easy slaughter. "Put a cap in that pistol," Dain said.

He watched his enemy lower the pistol and dig his left hand into a pocket. The pistol was cocked ready to receive the cap; its barrel weaved aimlessly as its owner searched his pocket, and then became steady. On the last instant Dain grasped the meaning of it. He brought his weapon up, and fired as the pistol exploded at him. Through the thin cloud of the slowly expanding smoke he watched the man lurch and twist, his cloak swirling around him. He touched his left hand to his face, and found his cheek cut and bleeding. Seymour had always been a crack hip-shot at close quarters; given another second or two, and his aim would have been accurate.

"You're finished, Seymour. You're dying." He stood over the stricken man.

"Liar!" Stephen Seymour sat on the ground, both arms clasped about his middle. "I'll not die. I'll live, and I'll . . ." Pain racked the cold composure from his face. He rocked, lips tight.

Dain reloaded his pistol. "I'll do for you what I'd do for an animal. Do you want me to?"

"No. Curse you, no!"

"Very well."

Dain stood by. After a time the sounds of the dying man grew pitiful in his ears, and he tried to help him, and got weak struggling and whispered curses from him. So he drew his pistol and prepared himself to do the thing that he would have done for an animal, but before he brought himself to do it the need passed.

The camp on the San Jacinto reeked of death when Dain got back to it next day. Surgeons and their helpers were busy, and the burying of the dead had not yet begun. The bodies of Mexican officers and men lay where they had fallen. Others were scattered all the way to Vince's Bridge and south over the plain.

Dain joined a group of men cooking around a fire. He helped himself to coffee and speared a slice of beef. General Sam Houston, with a bandaged leg, sat under a tree with officers around him, talking to a Mexican prisoner in dirty laboring garb. A Kentucky volunteer, sitting on his heels beside Dain, ran a thumb over the edge of his knife and glowered at the Mexican prisoner.

"If 'twasn't for the Gen'ril," he rumbled, "I'd kill that varmint, wouldn't you?"

Dain was preoccupied. He hadn't looked at the Mexican. "Who is he?" he asked.

"Who?" The Kentuckian stopped munching. "Why, that's Santa Anna, hisself, that's who! Changed his clo'es last night somewheres, but some o' the boys ketched him 'smornin' other side o' the bayou and drug him in. Where you been?"

"Hunting."

"Any luck?"

"Some."

Colonel Ed Burleson, a rough and ready soldier in homespun round-jacket and blue pantaloons, came up to the group with a thick notebook and pencil. He nodded to Dain. "You just got back? Well, I'm making up the casualty list for the Gen'ral. So far it tallies six hundred and twenty-eight dead Mexicans, about two hundred wounded, and seven hundred and thirty prisoners. Not more'n forty got away. We've lost two killed and twenty-three wounded. You got anything to add?"

"Two. A man by the name of Stephen Seymour, alias Falconer—an American renegade. And Colonel Baltasar Duncaerlie, alias John Caerlie, officer in the Mexican Army."

Burleson licked his pencil. "Duncaerlie of Anáhuac, huh? He was another renegade!"

"No," Dain said. "He was a Mexican soldier."

The bearded Kentuckian nudged him. "What name was that you said? Caerlie? Mexican? Queer. There was a gal by that name in N'Orleans when I came through. *She* warn't no Mexican. She put up the cash to outfit a whole comp'ny of us, and I do hear tell it was mostly her the Gen'ril can thank for the Twin Sisters. Yeah, Caerlie was her name. Suela Caerlie. Damn' purty gal, she was, too."

"Well, how about the name 'Duncaerlie'?" put in somebody else. "That's not Mexican, either. Wonder what they'll do with all his land? He owned a hell of a big Mexican grant, up Nacogdoches way."

"Those Mexican land grants don't stand for much now," observed Burleson. "Boys, you're sitting on the Free Republic of Texas!"

The valley looked much the same—pleasant, peaceful, and deserted. But greener. Grass flourished in the fenced fields, and the wild flowers had come to the long meadows. Dain was glad to see that the peach trees were blooming in the patio. The early morning sun, just rising, tipped the blossoming tops with flaming pink crowns. As the sun rose it lighted up the paler pink of the apple trees, and made richer the green foliage.

When he had seen this place before, so long ago, it had been shabby and unkempt, the trees ragged and somber by moonlight.

He had been gone a year from Texas, back to the United States. It had taken him that long to break up and liquidate the House of Galway, a house of business that had grown foul. He had returned to Texas only a few days ago, to find it an established and recognized Free Republic.

He touched his horse and rode the descending path to the walled and double-winged ranch house, and pulled up at the patio gate. New grass hid the breaks in the stone-flagged walks, and yellow and purple irises towered triumphantly above the weeds of the neglected flower beds. The spring still tinkled in the grotto, spilling into the willow-fringed pool.

"Beautiful," he muttered, and that one word brought Boniface Eden to his mind. He remembered how young Boniface had paused here, and called softly to Cleo—his Amaryllis—to come back and look with him. And the sorry disillusionment that had come with moonlight and closer inspection. It seemed a pity that young Boniface could not see it now, in spring, in new sunshine. It would have been enough, for him, to prove true the ring of his bright idealism.

He pushed open the gate and led his horse in to drink at the pool. San Miguel still stood surrounded by minor saints on the double doors of the house, and the high Spanish windows still wore their wooden shutters. He wondered if the end window of the east wing might still prove amenable to a knife, and he went to it.

It was like going back to a gone day and reliving it, to insert his knife blade through the crack in the warped boards. The wooden bar fell with a clatter, as it had done before. He swung open the shutters. The glass pane that he had broken when he came this way before, had not been replaced. He found and released the brass bolt, opened the window, and climbed through.

Here was the low ceiling, the massive rafters, the few pieces of heavy, carved furniture; the goatskin rugs, the *santo* niche in the wall, the tall, silent clock; everything as he remembered it. He walked slowly through the house, and very slowly upstairs, stopping when he reached the upper landing. For a while he stood there, then moved on into the room that contained the glass bookcase and the rush-bottomed chairs. He walked across the floor of this room, to the closed door of the bed chamber, and he rapped on it. No answer came.

He did not rap again. He went and sat down in one of the rush-bottomed chairs, and he said, "I saw your horse in the granary shed. The door isn't closed. My apologies for calling so early in the morning. I hope you're dressed."

She was wearing a dress that he remembered, when she opened the door. He remembered it, because it was the one that she had hastily wrapped around herself after his struggle with her that night. Her eyes were much the same as they had been that night, too—stormy, the color of a cloudy sky. He half expected to see a pistol in her hand.

"The brandy," she said, "is in a chest downstairs—in the room which you broke into. Knowing that I was here, was it necessary for you to come upstairs?"

He had risen. "I wanted to see you. From past experience, I doubted that you would answer a knock on the front door." He drew a stiff paper from his inside pocket and unfolded it. The clerk of the Board of Land Commissioners had penned the document in a careful, crabbed hand.

He read gravely: " 'To Dain Galway, one third of one league of land, to which the said Dain Galway is entitled as a citizen of Texas, by award of the Land Commissioners and of the Patent from the Republic of Texas. Also, by purchase, certificate of title and ownership to forty additional leagues of land hereby passes to the said Dain Galway—the whole being situated——' "

"I came here yesterday to gather a few personal belongings to take back to Mexico," she interrupted. "I am allowed to do that, I hope?"

He saw that she was trembling, and he recalled how she had trembled like that once before, from shame and anger at him. He was bitterly sorry. "It's as well you're here. It saves me from going to Mexico to find you. I've got no use for this place. Just wanted to keep any speculators from picking it up cheap." He laid the paper on the chair. "From one Texian to another," he said, and turned quickly and left her.

Hurrying down the stairs and through the house, he closed one door of his mind and opened another. There was little for him to go back to in the United States. It was said that trouble was flaring in Algeria, with the French occupying Constantine.

Of our party of seven . . .

The Indian had gone wrong on that one. One of the party of seven—the last one left—would not die in Texas. Was leaving it and would never come back.

He caught the reins of his horse and led it out from the willows. He heard the sound of the front door opening, and he couldn't keep from looking that way. Consuela stood there. He put his toe in the stirrup to mount, and paused. A thought held him. He left the horse and walked back to her, trying to keep his face blank of feeling. With his face stiff like that, he said carefully to her, "Will you be staying here now?"

"I don't know," she answered, and he could not read her eyes. "I only came to gather a few things, when I was told at the Land Commissioners' office that the place had been sold."

"I didn't buy the title until yesterday morning," he said. "You must have ridden fast, to get here last night."

She said nothing, looking away. He saw the color rise in her face, and he bent and kissed her hair.